PRIDE AND PIÑA COLADAS

MELANIE SUMMERS

Praise For Melanie Summers

"A fun, often humorous, escapist tale that will have readers blushing, laughing and rooting for its characters." ~ *Kirkus Reviews*

A gorgeously funny, romantic and seductive modern fairy tale...

I have never laughed out loud so much in my life. I don't think that I've ever said that about a book before, and yet that doesn't even seem accurate as to just how incredibly funny, witty, romantic, swoony...and other wonderfully charming and deliriously dreamy *The Royal Treatment* was. I was so gutted when this book finished, I still haven't even processed my sadness at having to temporarily say goodbye to my latest favourite Royal couple.
~ *MammieBabbie Book Club*

The Royal Treatment is a quick and easy read with an in depth, well thought out plot. It's perfect for someone that needs a break from this world and wants to delve into a modern-day fairy tale that will keep them laughing and rooting for the main characters throughout the story. ~ *ChickLit Café*

Books by Melanie Summers

ROMANTIC COMEDIES

The Crown Jewels Series

The Royal Treatment

The Royal Wedding

The Royal Delivery

Paradise Bay Series

The Honeymooner

Whisked Away

The Suite Life

Resting Beach Face

Pride and Piña Coladas

Beach, Please (Coming Soon)

Crazy Royal Love Series

Royally Crushed

Royally Wild

Royally Tied

Stand-Alone Books

Even Better Than the Real Thing

WOMEN'S FICTION

The After Wife

Books with Whitney Dineen

The Accidentally in Love Series

Text Me on Tuesday
The Text God
Text Wars
Text in Show
Mistle Text
Text and Confused

A Gamble on Love Mom-Com Series

No Ordinary Hate
A Hate Like This
Hate, Rinse, Repeat (Coming Soon)

For Lovell Grant, a voracious reader who became a friend.
The world lost you far too soon.
Rest in peace,
Melanie

Author's Note

Dear Reader,

Welcome back to Paradise Bay, where the drinks are always cold and the men are the exact opposite! We've all been to hell and back these past three years, so I hope you're hanging in there and that life is starting to feel a whole lot better these days. If not, here's a big squeezy hug from me.

I write with the intention of providing you with a true escape – something fun, hopeful, just, and romantic. I'm a huge Jane Austen fan, so diving into a retelling of *Pride and Prejudice* has been deliciously fun—reimagining Elizabeth Bennet and Mr. Darcy in a modern-day Caribbean setting, throwing them together for work, and thinking up a juicy scandal that would rival what Lydia and Mr. Wickham did (because let's face it, going away with a guy before you're married won't exactly ruin your family these days).

Anyway, this is my homage to the great Ms. Austen. I hope I do her justice and I hope this story will make you laugh, feel good, and sigh happily.

Wishing you all the best always,
mel

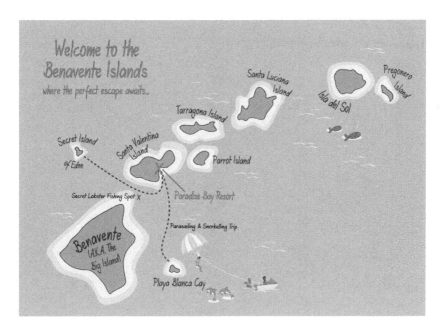

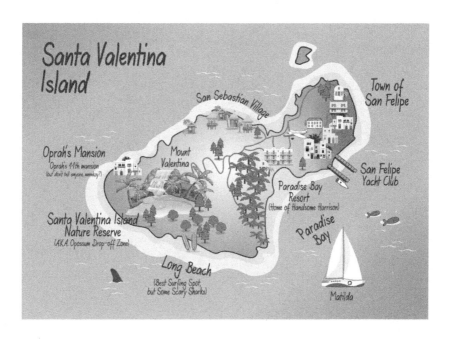

Santa Valentina Island

San Sebastian Village

Town of
San Felipe

Oprah's Mansion
*(Oprah's 11th mansion
(but don't tell anyone, mmkay?)*

Mount
Valentina

San Felipe
Yacht Club

Paradise Bay
Resort
(Home of Handsome Harrison)

Santa Valentina Island
Nature Reserve
(A.K.A. Opossum Drop-off Zone)

Paradise
Bay

Long Beach
*(Best Surfing Spot,
but Some Scary Sharks)*

Matilda

Paradise Bay
All-Inclusive Resort

Enjoy our pristine, white–sand beaches caressed by crystal-clear waters. Relax in our newly renovated luxurious rooms decorated in soft, muted tones for an elegant design. Enjoy a whole array of fun activities and excursions or just lay by one of our five pools and soak up the sun.

Paradise Bay Resort sits on a 12-acre property nestled along the calm, protected south shore of Santa Valentina so the water is always warm and inviting. Surrounded on three sides by jungle, the resort enjoys the ultimate in privacy, including our 500 ft of exclusive beach— yours to explore uninterrupted.

Our 274 rooms have spectacular views of the ocean, our lush tropical gardens, or the stunning emerald green jungle so you'll wake each morning with a smile. Immerse yourself in the relaxed pace of the Benavente Islands as you stroll through the beautiful gardens on your way to one of our seven à la carte restaurants. Treat yourself to a soothing, rejuvenating spa treatment customized to your personal needs. Spend a day snorkeling along the bay or take one of our signature catamaran trips to our private island, Playa Blanca Cay.

Dive into the culture of the Benavente Islands with salsa classes, a pottery workshop with one of our local artisans, or try the Caribbean-inspired dishes at one of our exclusive restaurants. Live the magic of the Caribbean nights with a delicious cocktail in one of our bars or enjoy an evening show, then let yourself go to the local rhythm and dance the night away at our open-air night club.

Your Authentic Caribbean Escape is Waiting for you at Paradise Bay...

Book today and get 15% off or enjoy three free spa services.

YOU'RE INVITED TO THE

2022 World Bartending Championship Mixer

An evening of music, cocktails, and mingling.

Friday, September 29, 2022 | 6 PM
Building C Poolside

HOSTED BY THE PARADISE BAY RESORT, X-STREAM
TV, AND ROJAS RUM.

Martinis and Mums with Ulterior Motives

Nora Cooper, San Felipe, Santa Valentina Island

IT IS a truth universally acknowledged that a single woman with no romantic attachments must be in want of advice.

However little known the feelings or views of such a woman may be when she first enters her auntie's house, this truth is so well fixed in the minds of her relatives that her non-existent love life is considered the rightful property of her entire family.

At least that's how it is in my family anyway. Aunt Beth is about to prove it before I can even get my sandals off. In fact, if my sister Kat had ridden over to the party with me, we'd have made a bet in the car about the first thing that would be said to me upon entering Aunt Beth and Uncle Dan's house.

Kat, who's much kinder in her opinion of human nature than me, would say that someone will tell me how nice I look in this dress. I'd go double or nothing that I'll be grilled about my dating status straight out of the gate (and that it'll be at least an hour before anyone mentions my appearance). As I've lost fifteen pounds since the last time I saw the extended family, making that bet is a testament to my lack of faith in humanity. I'm a bit of a skeptic, but years in the service industry tends to do that to a person, whereas my sister has yet to join the workforce in any capacity. She'll learn. Not tonight, when I'm immediately asked if I have a boyfriend yet, but someday…

Honestly, I hate how much focus the world puts on love and marriage. I have so many more interesting things to discuss than bagging a man (which I have no intention of doing—swiped right, got the dick pics, and am done with dating, thanks). For example, my career. There's a huge event happening at work, and when I tell them about it, maybe, if I'm really lucky, they'll be impressed enough to forget all about my relationship status for a few months. Okay, minutes, but it would be the most exquisite few minutes of my life.

When I walk into the house, the party is already in full-swing. The scent of perfumes and aftershaves fills the air, and multiple conversations compete with the sounds of Simon and Garfunkel's *Cecilia*.

"Nora, my dear," Auntie Beth says, her martini sloshing on the hardwood as she makes a beeline for me. "Are you seeing anyone lately?" She mops up the liquid with her stocking-clad foot, smiles at me, and adjusts the "Birthday Girl" tiara on her head.

I don't even bother to open my mouth, because if there's one thing Aunt Beth won't do, it's wait for an answer.

Yanking the toothpick out of her drink, she aims her olives at me, spraying me with gin and vermouth. "Because if you aren't, have I got a young man for you."

Of course she does.

"My insurance broker, Bill. Two kids, so you know he can make 'em. Recently divorced, so he's ripe for the picking," Beth says, her voice loud.

Wow. Tempting. This time I do open my mouth, only to be interrupted by her husband, Uncle Dan. "I hope you don't mean Bill Larkin," he calls across the crowded living room, which stops everyone mid-conversation.

Spinning around, Beth loses the last half of her drink to the potted palm next to her. "What's so wrong with Bill?"

"He's too old for Nora."

"Nora's not exactly a spring chicken," she whisper-yells.

I'm twenty-eight, a fact that for no good reason is causing my cheeks to run hot at the moment.

Uncle Bill counters with, "He's going bald, for Christ's sake."

Swatting her free hand in his direction, she turns back to me. "Never mind that. Bill's mum told me he's saving up for hair plugs, so you'll want to get in there now. Competition is going to be a lot stiffer after." She offers me a wink, then lifts her glass to her lips, only to appear mystified to find it empty.

"Right, well, thanks for the heads up," I tell her, turning so she can get a better look at my new physique.

Nope. She's maintaining eye contact. Sort of. She's also swaying a little at the same time.

"I'll just take my shoes off and grab a drink while I think it over." I slide out of my sandals, hand her the bouquet of pink roses I picked up on the way over, and give her a kiss on the cheek. "Happy birthday, by the way. You look lovely."

"Thanks! I always thought sixty was so old, but now that I'm here, I'm just thrilled to have all that other stuff over with."

"What stuff?" I ask, following her to the kitchen.

"You know… everything that happens before menopause."

Life?

"Finding a man, getting him to propose, having babies, raising them…"

"Oh, you mean all the stuff you've been trying to talk me into doing." We stop in front of an impressive assortment of booze on the counter.

Aunt Beth bursts into a loud laugh, clutching my arm with one hand. "Oh you! With the witty remarks all the time. I told Bill you'll be the type to keep him on his toes."

"And what did he say?"

"I can't remember, but I'm sure it was positive," she says, free-pouring gin into the steel shaker. "Martini?"

"Thank you, no," I say, recalling the one time I took her up on

3

that offer (and woke up face-down on a bench in their sunroom the next morning). "I think I'll stick with wine tonight."

"More for me," she says, dancing shoulders-only style.

"Nora, there you are!" my mum calls, making her way through the crowded room. "I hope you're not letting Beth talk you into a martini. You do remember the last time you said yes——"

"I don't remember." I give her a kiss on each cheek. "Which is why I just said no."

"Good girl."

Mum and her sister couldn't be more different. For every drink Beth has had in her life, my mother has said two prayers. She and Dad have dedicated their lives to service and are pastors at the Benavente Unity Church. Uncle Dan is a plastic surgeon, so Aunt Beth dedicated her life to having services *done*, like weekly massages and facials.

Mum points at the bright orange liquid in the punch bowl on the table. "I made a non-alcoholic drink for those of us who want to wake up feeling good tomorrow morning."

I briefly consider pouring a glass (and adding a hefty serving of vodka) but decide to go with the wine. Fewer calories for the same buzz. "I'm allowing myself one glass of Zin." I pluck a wine glass off the tray and inch my way towards the open bottles of wine, but Beth blocks me in her effort to retrieve more olives for her drink. That's fine. I'll wait. "Did Kat come with you and Dad?"

Mum's smile drops. "She said she was coming with you."

Uh-oh.

Kat is my parents' "late in life" baby. I was nine when she came along. Up until then, I was a perfectly happy only child, but after nearly a decade, Mum "prayed" her into existence. At least that's how she explained the birds and the bees to me when I was eleven. Imagine my fear the next time we went to church. Anyway, Kat has been the source of my mother's wrinkles since the moment she took her first step. She's always finding creative new ways of stirring the pot.

As much as I loathe the whole hook-up thing society's got going on these days, Kat loves it. She's swiped right on so many guys, it's a wonder she doesn't have carpal tunnel in her index finger. Not that my parents know about that, mind you. I don't dare say a word, because it would literally give my mother a heart attack. Kat's latest coup (that they know about) has been to extend her gap year into two, putting off university yet again.

Mum is beside herself, but Dad keeps insisting his little girl just needs more time to grow up, after having been coddled by us her entire life. As if he's not the biggest offender.

"I'm sure she'll be here right away," I say, even though I'm guessing she's dancing on a speaker at the Turtle's Head Pub by now.

She makes a grunting sound but says nothing else on the topic, clearly not wanting the rest of her judgy family to overhear. My second attempt at getting some wine is blocked by a neighbour of Dan and Beth's, who swoops in and plucks the bottle of Zinfandel off the counter then walks away with it. I decide to go with the red, except when I pick it up, it's only the nasty bits at the bottom that drip down into my glass.

Setting it down, I turn to Mum and Aunt Beth. "Say, I have some news."

"Really?" Mum asks.

"The resort is hosting the World Bartending Championships, and Harrison and Libby have asked me to coordinate it." I feel a swell of pride. "It's going to be televised around the globe, and it'll be incredible advertising for Paradise Bay. Well, for the Benavente Islands as a whole, actually."

Normally I wouldn't brag like this, but with family, I figure it's okay. Also, because I never seem to impress them no matter what I do, when I have the opportunity, I'm not letting it slip by.

Mum and her sister wear matching eyes-glazing-over expressions. "That's nice, dear."

"Very. What a lot of fun for you," Beth says, lifting her glass to her lips. "Oh! Bartenders have a certain *je ne sais quoi*, don't they? Maybe you'll find love… if you and Bill don't get on, that is." Wink, wink.

"A bartender?" Mum asks, her voice becoming rather shrill. "No thank you. Not for my little girl."

"What's wrong with bartenders?" Beth asks. Before Mum can answer, she adds, "If you think about it, what they do isn't all that different than what you do, Lori. You're both dedicated to serving others, and you both wind up listening to people complain about their lives."

"It is hardly the same thing, Beth," Mum tells her.

"I bet these world champion ones make good money." She turns to me. "Do they, Nora?"

"I have no idea."

"There must be a big prize," she says, then, turning in the direction of the living room, she shouts, "Dan! How much do world champion bartenders make?"

He stops demonstrating his golf swing for a group of my male relations and rolls his eyes at her. "How on earth would I know that? And in case you didn't notice, I'm in the middle of a conversation, Beth."

"Ballpark it," she orders.

"Why?"

"Because Nora here is going to be hosting the World Bartending Championships and I want to know if she should try to marry one of them!"

"Oh, really?" he asks me, looking slightly impressed.

"The resort is hosting the event, but as the events coordinator…" I shrug modestly, even though it really is massive that my bosses are letting me take the lead on this. Technically, I'm not *the* events coordinator. I'm one of the events coordinators. There are two of us: me and Oakley Knowles. No relation to the great Queen B. We pretty much can't stand each other, to be honest. On my part, it's because she's a conniving bitch who's always trying to steal the best events out from under me. I have no idea why she hates *me* though. Maybe because I'm better at the job than her, and therefore Libby and Harrison trust me most?

My dad, who was tied up with long-winded Uncle Nester this whole time, finally breaks free and walks over to me. "That sounds like a huge deal, Birdie." That's his nickname for me. Embarrassing in certain situations, but I still love it.

I beam. "If all goes well, we expect to be hosting a lot more events, which will mean hiring more coordinators and selecting one of us to be the Senior Events Manager."

"Are they considering you for that position?" Mum asks.

"I can't say for sure, but I think it's a good sign they've asked me to take the lead on this one."

"Well done, you," Dad says, grinning at me.

"I shouldn't count my chickens just yet. The film crew from the network shows up next week. Then the contestants. It'll be like coordinating several events all at once. Very complicated, logistics-wise."

"You're going to be so busy," Mum says. "Stay with us. That way, you won't have to worry about cooking for yourself."

"Thanks, Mum, but I'll be fine."

"Please, you're wasting away to nothing," Dad says, dropping a kiss on my temple.

Hint, hint, Beth! I've lost fifteen freaking pounds!

Beth narrows her eyes at me. "Film crew… Now that might be a job more to your mum's liking. Directors make good cash, don't they, Gary?"

"I'd say so," Dad answers. "But my Birdie is too busy for men. She's a career woman."

"Nonsense," Mum tells him. "It's not like she's working on the cure for cancer or something."

"Ooh! Or the cure for a hangover," Beth adds, glancing at me. "Now that would be important."

Mum purses her lips. "I'd say that's a case of an ounce of prevention—"

"Oh shush, you, it's my birthday!" Beth lifts her glass again, tipping it all the way back. When nary a drop comes out, she lowers it and makes a little grunting sound.

"So, Nora, with this big event happening, I'm guessing you'll need to bring on some new staff," Mum says.

Nope. Not doing it.

Dad's eyes light up. "Kat would be terrific for that type of thing."

"I don't think so. I really won't have time to train someone right now."

"She could be an intern," Dad suggests.

"An *unpaid* intern, Nora," Mum adds, sweetening the pot. "Please. She really needs some responsibility in her life."

Oh God, why is there no more wine? "Maybe she could, I don't know, become a dog walker or something."

Mum's eyebrows knit together. "Nora, your sister needs a hand in life. She's not like you."

"She's hardly disadvantaged," I answer.

"You know what I mean. You were born responsible. She's going to have to learn it. Besides, she could really use a boost as far as her self-esteem goes."

If there's one thing Kat doesn't need, it's an ego boost. She's the most confident nineteen-year-old in the world. "Yes, well, as far as I know, we don't have any positions open, unpaid or not."

"But check for us, will you?" Dad asks, wrapping his arm around Mum's shoulder. "Your mother needs to know Kat won't be on our couch watching reality TV the rest of her life."

She nods. "I do. I really need that."

"Well, put your foot down and tell her to find a job, then," I say.

"She's tried," Mum says, looking suddenly forlorn. "But because she's got no experience, no one will hire her, and the older she gets without experience, the more of a red flag it is for potential employers."

As it should be.

"Please, Birdie? For me?" Dad asks, pulling his sad face.

"All right, I'll ask when I get to work on Monday," I say, deciding I'll check on openings in housekeeping. "But chances are not good, so don't get your hopes up."

"We won't," Mum says, even though the look in her eyes says she has her hopes way, way up.

Uncle Dan makes his way over to pour himself a whiskey. "Say, Nora, you look like you've lost weight."

Finally. Thank you. "I have, actually."

He looks me up and down. "Well, you better stop. Your bosoms have basically disappeared."

Beth leans down so her eyes are level with my chest. "He's right, you know. You won't find a man if you don't have anything to grab onto."

"Jesus wept," Mum says. "They're not handles."

Dan wrinkles his nose as if she's just said the stupidest thing he's ever heard. "They make the most lovely handles of all. When they're there, of course."

Okay, I'm done. Time to go home for tea and *Bridgerton*.

———

Mike the Moose - Tiktok Video

A twenty-something beefy blond in a tuxedo holds up a trophy and grins at the camera. "Hey, everybody, it's your favourite Canadian bartender, Mike the MOOOOSSE, coming to you live from Montreal, where I have just beat out nine other incredible competitors in the North American Bartending Championships!" He kisses the trophy, then hollers, "Whoo! Yeah!"

Mike closes his eyes and calms his voice. "I'm so humbled to have beat such talented barkeeps. I want to thank all you guys out there for believing in me and following my journey this year."

"WHOO!!! I DID IT!" The Moose resumes yelling, then lowers his voice again. "For the third time in a row, I'll be heading to the World Bartending Championships." And... more shouting. "YEAH! I'm going to the Benaventes, baby! Watch out, because The Moose will be loose in the Caribbean!"

———

TO-DO LIST (Home Version)

Find Kat a job anywhere but at the resort

Laundry

Groceries

Clean out bathroom drawers

Water plants

Google what that white stuff is on top of the soil in fern pot

2

Scandals, Solutions, and Stubborn Men

Theo Rojas, Nassau, The Bahamas

"WELCOME TO *BUSINESS WORLD WEEKLY*. I'm your host, Barry Butler, and tonight we take a deep dive into exactly what is going on at Meta this quarter." The handsome suit-clad newscaster smiles at the camera. "But first, will a Hollywood superstar's misstep bring down liquor giant Rojas Rum? Some say yes. Here with a detailed report is Candy Higgs."

"Thank you, Barry. It's not only one of the oldest liquor companies in the Caribbean, but it's also one of the largest family-owned corporations on earth. I'm talking, of course, about Rojas Rum. The company was started in 1852 in Havana, Cuba, by Alvaro Bembe Rojas—a man with a dream of becoming one of Cuba's best names in the business. He started with one small distillery, and over the past 170 years, he and his family have turned Rojas Rum into one of the best-known, bestselling liquor brands on the planet, with over 200 premium spirits on their shelf. The company is run by Theo Bembe Rojas, the great-great-great-grandson of Alvaro Bembe Rojas, and employs over 8000 people in more than 160 countries.

"Rojas Rum made headlines last year when they partnered with James Prescott, known to most people as Matalyx from the famed *Clash of Crowns* series, for a new venture—Rojas Emerald Gin. Unfortunately, that partnership came to a swift end three months ago, when James Prescott was arrested for driving while under the influence."

The feed cuts to video footage of James Prescott attempting to walk the line on a road while giggling, stumbling, and swearing, all the while holding a bottle of Rojas Rum. The scene ends with James lying on the street, shouting, "Leave me alone, God! Leave me alone with my Rojas Rum!"

When the camera cuts back to Candy, she's wincing visibly. "The incident landed Mr. Prescott in rehab for the past twelve weeks and turned the Rojas brand into a meme that caught on like wildfire. Merchandise popped up around the globe featuring the words, "Rojas Rum. When you're done with God for good." Despite the fact that the memes and merchandise were not authorized in any way by Rojas, it sparked protests in front of Rojas Distilleries in over twenty-six countries, the largest of which were held at the headquarters in Nassau, where dozens of windows were smashed and the building was vandalized."

The feed cuts to footage of hundreds of protesters chanting, "We'll never be done with God! We'll never be done with God!"

The sound on the footage ends, but scenes of people throwing bricks at the large building continue as Candy says, "Sales all over the world plummeted, and Rojas had their worst quarter in history. Swift action on the part of Theo Rojas seemed to be righting the ship, but with James Prescott being released from the facility to start his trial for driving under the influence, it appears a resurgence of the bad press is already underway. Will the Rojas family survive this latest chapter of the biggest scandal in their history, or will James Prescott bring the rum giant to its knees?"

"Such a shame really," Barry says as the camera pulls back to include him in the shot. "I used to love their dark rum. After a long day on set, pop some ice in the glass and ahhh... But now..." He shakes his head.

Candy nods. "I know what you mean. I just can't bring myself to buy their stuff. Feels weird."

"Up next, is the world ready to go Meta?" Barry stares directly into the camera and then a commercial for Bud Light Hard Soda starts.

"*Mierda*." I shut the television off and lean back in my chair, tapping my fingers restlessly on my Lignum Vitae desk. After twelve long weeks of sleepless nights, working until well after two in the morning most days, and calling in every favour my family was owed —and there were a lot of them—we're going to end up back where we started. I've managed to avoid layoffs and closures in our distilleries and warehouses, but another massive drop in sales means I'm going to have some awful decisions to make. Come Monday, when I'm sitting at the table with the board of directors, I better have a solid plan in place, or I'm going to face a vote of no-confidence.

"Screw it. I'm going home." I'm done, for today at least. I need a long dip in the pool, followed by a cold drink and a soak in the hot tub. Tomorrow I can start over in my quest for a way to scrub the steaming turd that is James Prescott from our company's reputation.

I power down my computer and gather my things, hoping to find the office empty when I open my door. The last thing I want is to have to put on a cocky smile and pretend I'm not worried. I need to be alone, which, in my case, is not an easy feat.

I live at our family's seaside estate—a massive twenty-six-bedroom house with far too much staff for my liking. All of whom will have seen today's news. My idiot brother Markos also lives there. He's the cause of our current dilemma, having convinced me to let his "good buddy James" become the shit-faced face of our brand.

We often go weeks without seeing each other, which is odd since we live and work together. Well, *I* work. Markos has an office here on the executive floor that sits empty, as he's usually off somewhere in the world, following the roving party of trust-fund babies.

I grunt, anger searing my veins when I think of my little brother: irresponsible, reckless, a total burden on me ever since our father died and passed the reins, and responsibilities, onto my shoulders.

It's been a long six years, and even though I'm only thirty-six, today I feel like I'm ninety. I need a night off.

Before I can make my escape, there's a knock at the door.

Because it's after six, my assistant, Jaquell, has gone home. I stay silent, hoping whoever it is goes away. After a few seconds, I hear Markos's voice.

"I know you're in there, and I brought an old friend."

Mierda. "Come in."

The door swings open. Carolina Armas is with him. She glides into the room, followed by Markos, who glances at the big screen TV on the wall. "Hey, bro, how's it hanging?"

"I already saw it," I tell him, noting that it's been far too long since his black hair has seen the sharp end of a pair of scissors. He looks like a shaggy surfer dude instead of an executive of a global corporation. But I suppose it makes sense, since he spends most of his time surfing.

Carolina, on the other hand, is as polished as ever in her Chanel skirt suit. Her makeup is subtle, but I'm sure there's a lot of it, and her long dark hair is pulled back in a low bun. Our families have been friends for generations—the rich and powerful of the Caribbean. Her Uncle Luis has sat on our board of directors since I was a teenager. Her family owns Armas News Corporation, which in turn owns thirty-two television networks, five newspapers, and two movie studios. She's got that old money confidence that floats around in our circle, and she smells exactly like every other woman I know—rich.

I rise to greet her, and we give each other the customary kiss on each cheek, only she holds her second one a little too long, as she's been doing lately. "Carolina, lovely to see you."

"There's no way I would abandon you in your hour of need."

Perching on the corner of my desk, I offer her a polite smile. "That's kind of you." Turning my attention to Markos, I add, "Our family can use all the friends we can get right now."

"Told you he'd be reverting back to Angry Theo," he tells Carolina.

"You say that as if I ever stopped," I say. "What are you doing here? It's a day that ends in *Y*, which means you aren't normally found gracing the halls of corporate headquarters."

"Ha! Good one." He plants himself on an armchair that faces me. "I wanted to assure you I'm on top of this whole mess. I had a long talk with James as soon as he got out. He's not going to even utter the name Rojas ever again."

"Good, because if he does, he'll find himself on the receiving end of a cease and desist, followed by a massive lawsuit to make up for the damage he's caused."

"Oh now, Theo," Carolina says, carefully folding herself into the chair next to Markos's and crossing her long legs. "It was a mistake, but it's not a fatal one, I assure you."

"Tell that to my CFO," I say, folding my arms.

"Listen, *hermano*, I know I screwed up, but Carolina and I have a way to fix everything," Markos says.

Carolina turns to him with one eyebrow arched, which makes him hold up both hands. "Okay, okay, Carolina has a plan. She's the genius. I'm merely the man who asked the genius for help."

The last thing I want to do is accept help from this woman. It's clear what she's really after, and I'd hoped by now it would be clear to her she's not getting it. But desperate times… I smile at her and wait for the pitch.

"Uncle Luis told me you have a board meeting on Monday, and I may have a way to make them very happy," she says with a smile. "One of my pet projects is a new network, X-Stream TV—all extreme sports, competitive reality shows, that type of thing. Our demo is young, fun, and dumb. We're televising the World Bartending Championships again this year. It'll be quite the event. The best and hottest bartenders on the planet are competing for a half-million-dollar prize. Tropical resort setting, so lots of bare-chested men and bikini-clad women sipping drinks. And they could be *your* drinks. Jacardi was our major sponsor last year, but they had to pull out at the last second, and I immediately thought of you. You'd get about $7 million in ad exposure for that relatively modest prize."

I shake my head and am about to turn her down when Markos

steps in. "Theo, I spent the last two days watching previous competitions. It's exciting, cool, and, well, possibly our only chance to shift the narrative so we're the brand young people want to be associated with. We've always relied on the older crowd, but they're gone, *hermano*, never to return. We have to shift gears and find our way onto the shelves of the next generation."

No way. Nada. Not letting Markos talk me into another idea ever again. "As much as I appreciate the thought—and I do, Carolina—this sounds a little high risk. Also, too risqué for our purposes," I say, putting my diplomacy skills to use. "Thank you anyway for thinking of us. I'm sure you'll find another sponsor and the event will be a massive hit."

"I have to say, I think you're wrong about this one, Theo." Carolina lifts her chin. "Ratings for the world championships have grown exponentially over the past five years. We'll be broadcasting in forty-five different countries in both English and Spanish, including in the UK, Avonia, and the US—all problem areas for you right now."

"That may be but—"

"Sex sells, Theo," Markos says, cutting me off.

"Thanks, Captain Obvious, but I've seen ads before, so I already know that." Turning to Carolina, I say, "I'm going with my gut on this. It sounds like a situation with too many uncontrolled variables, and if anything were to go wrong, it would be the final nail in our coffin, so I'm afraid the answer is no. A conservative approach is best in this case."

"I can tell there's no changing your mind." Shrugging, she stands, crosses over to me, and takes my hands in hers. "Wonderful to see you, as always."

"You too," I say as she closes in for the cheek kiss.

Carolina leaves me in the wake of her perfume as she strides to the door. After she opens it, she glances over her shoulder at me. "You know, last year Jacardi's sales went up twelve percent in the five-week period following the competition. They made out like bandits. But I guess your sales are high enough, hmm? Adios, boys. I'm off to talk to Paulo at Havana Club."

Once she's gone, Markos gives me a meaningful look. "Twelve percent. Correct me if I'm wrong, but that's the kind of number that can save a lot of jobs, isn't it?"

"If they did so well, why are they pulling out this year?" Ha! What can he possibly say to that?

"They probably didn't need the exposure since they've been getting all our sales for the last quarter," he answers with a shrug.

Dammit, he's right. Not that I'll tell him that. "Look, I'm going to say something, and I'm not going to preface it by telling you not to take offense. Because I want you to be offended. Being offended will hopefully mean you'll remember this for the rest of your life, so we never have to have this conversation again. I am never going to take your advice again in my life. I could literally be on fire, and you could be yelling for me to stop, drop, and roll, and I will stay perfectly still and let myself burn simply because you suggested it."

Markos rolls his eyes, unimpressed by my theatrics. "Look, I screwed up. I know that. You know that. Old ladies on the street know that. I didn't know James as well as I thought I did. He's a hell of a good time to party with, but I didn't realize how out-of-control things had gotten for him. My bad. I get it. But this competition is different. It's exciting and fun and gets so much exposure, it will give people something tangible to associate Rojas with."

"Yeah, some exciting and fun new scandal that will sink the Rojas ship once and for all. One hundred and seventy years of family history wiped out under my watch." I snap my fingers to punctuate my words. "I know you're trying to fix things, but just leave it alone and go back to the beach where you belong. You've done enough."

His nostrils flare and he takes two steps towards me. "You're the most unforgiving person I've ever known, and I'm including our mother in that category," he says, setting his jaw. "I've got news for you, *hermano*. Nobody's perfect, not even you, so maybe learn how to forgive people and give them a second chance. Because if you don't, when your turn comes around, nobody will be here to forgive you."

Oh, come on. How is he possibly trying to make this about me? I'm not the one who got us into this mess. Keeping my voice calm, I say, "I'm the president of this corporation. I'm responsible for the jobs of over eight thousand people. If I make mistakes, those people can't feed their families or pay their rent. Now I know that probably means nothing to you, but it matters to me. I owe them perfection, and that is exactly what I have given them every single day for the last six years. You popped by one time with a terrible idea and fucked it all up for me and them, so please don't think I'm going to let you do it again. They don't owe a spoiled, selfish, lazy *gilipollas* a second chance."

Calling him a douchebag on top of the rest might have been one step too far. He stares, hurt in his eyes, and holds up both hands in surrender. "Okay, if that's the way you see me, I know there's no changing your mind." He leaves, closing the door softly behind him without saying goodbye.

I am rooted to the floor, torn between going after him to apologize and knowing I'm doing the right thing for the family—which is the right thing for him too. His life is paid for by my life. Guilt wiggles its way into my chest and I feel a faintly nauseating combination of righteous indignation and pity for my little brother.

There are brief moments in our lives—like this one—when I understand how hard it must be for him to be in my shadow. But the fact is he's there for a reason. He doesn't care about this business or the family name. He only cares about the next distraction. Someday he might grow up, but today is clearly not that day. Suggesting some wild bartending competition as a way to raise the profile of our brand? I cannot think of anything less likely to work.

It's up to me and me alone to find a way out of this mess, and that's exactly what I'm going to do.

If I could only think of how...

3

Monday Morning Career Hijackings

Nora

Okay, Monday morning, here I come. Today is the first day of the rest of your life. You go, girl. You got this.

These are all the things I tell myself as I feather a bit of bronzer across my face. Lately I have to talk myself up before my shift every day. Ever since the Pinder-Burrows Wedding that didn't happen, largely due to my own actions. I shudder at the memory of that fateful afternoon when the entire thing went sour, and I had to tell my bosses that the event of the season wasn't going to be an event at all after I asked the bride if she was happy. What I meant to ask was if she was happy with how we'd set everything up. What she heard was "Are you sure you want to marry this idiot?" Things quickly collapsed from there, and the father of the bride demanded his massive deposit back. Harrison and Libby had to get involved. It was a whole big, ugly thing. That was nearly four months ago, but Oakley still walks around with a smug smile over my massive misstep.

No, Nora, do not dwell on the past. Focus on today and what you can do to make it the best day possible. Be the best version of yourself you can.

Nodding firmly at my reflection, I shut off the light and scurry down the hall to the front door of my flat. When I round the corner, my arm brushes against a crunchy potted palm, and yellow leafy bits rain all over the terracotta tile floor.

"Nuts," I mutter. I really should water that. Or maybe it's beyond water at this point. I should google it when I get home, but either way, I need to do something. All the other plants are going to start believing I'm some sort of serial killer, leaving them to slowly die one by one. I mean to take good care of them, I really do. They don't all die from neglect. Some die from *over*watering.

Picking up my handbag, my vintage Scooby-Doo lunch kit that my grandma gave me, and my sunglasses off the tiny desk that serves as a credenza, I lock up, then rush down the stairs to the parking lot.

Being late today is *not* an option, but I spent so long giving myself a pep talk, I'm down to the wire to arrive on time. That alone is enough to make me sweat but add in that it's only eight-thirty a.m. and it's already as hot as a Carolina Reaper outside. I'm going to be a mess by the time I get to work.

I put on my sunglasses, toss my things on the passenger seat, then climb into my old Civic. During the drive from my building on the north side of San Felipe to the resort just south of town, I daydream about the competition. Me, in a total state of flow for the next month, managing all the moving parts with ease, impressing the socks off everyone involved, proving to Harrison, Libby, and Rosy (the general manager) that I should be the obvious choice for the senior events manager position. As I move swiftly along the free-way, with the sparkling ocean on my left, I picture Oakley's face pinched in anger as I carry my box of personal effects into my new office and swing the door shut behind me with my foot.

It'll mean a raise. A really big one, too. I'll finally be able to squirrel away some serious money to buy myself a little seaside house in a decent neighbourhood. Something small and adorable and just right for one professional independent woman who wants to listen to music (possibly even classical) while sitting on her covered veranda, staring out at the ocean, sipping wine. I'll have a greenhouse and a garden and will spend my time off tending to soil and enjoying the literal fruits (and veggies) of my labour. I'll read more. Do yoga every morning. I'll stop rushing around and take life slowly, *mindfully*.

I'll have an extra week of vacation every year—not to be used in high season, of course. I'll spend that time doing things like painting the kitchen cupboards a lovely sage green or creating an outdoor living room and hosting fabulous dinner parties for my friends.

But more than all of that, I'll never be seen as a mere service provider again. Or perhaps I should say I'll never *not* be seen as a service provider, since the wealthy people I'm helping rarely notice me at all. They want what they want when they want it, which would be the instant they think of it, and we minions are merely a conduit for their latest desire. We're not human beings with dreams and goals and people who love us.

Deep breath, Nora. Deep breath.

Anyway, the point is, as a manager of the team, I won't have direct contact with the guests unless the shit hits the fan. When it does, instead of being a subordinate, I'll be the final word, the big cheese, the head honcho. They still won't care about me, but they'll see me as a person of authority and may even treat me with the tiniest bit of respect.

Okay, so maybe they won't, but the point is, I won't have to deal with them all day, every day, for the rest of my career. There will be a lovely buffer between me and the rich, spoiled narcissists of the world. I'll oversee my team, inspiring them to do their best work, then go home to my incredible life by the sea. It's going to be glorious.

All I have to do is make sure I don't fuck anything up over the next several weeks, then a whole new life will be waiting for me. Nora Cooper: Senior Events Manager, with a small team of three people to start with. Well, likely three. Maybe more though.

That is going to be my future, I tell myself as I pull into a stall. I've visualized it, now I'm going to make it happen no matter what. This morning I'm going to hide in an empty conference room (as opposed to sitting at my desk in the bullpen), develop my SMART goals, and determine the best way possible to manage the living shit out of this competition. By the time I get back in my car this afternoon, I'll have everything sorted out, and I'll be well on my way to making all my career—and life—goals come true.

Or not.

Because when I step into the lobby, I see the last people I expected to be here on a Monday morning: my mum and Kat. They're standing in the center of the open-air lobby, chatting away with Rosy Brown, the manager.

Crap. My mum must not have believed me about trying to get Kat a job here. I wasn't actually going to do it, but still. Rude to ambush me like this.

Mum's eyes light up when she sees me. "There you are! I was just telling Rosy we thought you started at the crack of dawn, the way you go on about your long hours."

My cheeks heat up. "Were you?" I hurry over, hoping if I'm closer to them, she'll lower her voice. I absolutely don't need the front desk staff, the concierge, Kevin, the surly IT guy, who is currently fixing a computer behind the desk, and the security guys to hear any of this.

Kat, who is dressed in a baby blue onesie shorts/T-shirt combo only a teenager could get away with, looks like the very last person you'd trust with anything ever. Clearly very bored, she's staring up at the pair of doves that have built their nest on one of the cross-braces under the thatched roof. Glancing at me, she wrinkles her nose. "Don't they crap on the floor?"

"Sometimes, but the guests love them anyway. You know what? Never mind that." I smile at Rosy. "Good morning."

"Morning," Rosy answers, giving me a look I can't quite read. But I won't have to wonder long how she feels, because Rosy always lets you in on her true feelings about any topic. Especially if she's annoyed, and she must be, given the fact that my mother has shown up out of the blue on a very busy Monday morning to beg for a job for my adult sister. Actually, Rosy's straightforwardness is going to work in my favour. She's obviously going to see Kat is not suited to work here, and she'll say so, making *her* the bad guy and allowing me to be all "darn it, I was *so* hoping this would work out."

… Only she's smiling at Mum. "Your mother was just telling me your little sister is looking for work."

"Was she now?" I say, plastering a phony smile on my face.

"Uh-huh." Rosy lifts her eyebrows at me. "Apparently you need lots of help and could use your own intern."

Rage. So much rage right now that I must stuff down inside so as not to cause a scene in the lobby.

"Who could use their own intern?" That's the voice of Harrison Banks, resort owner and all-around great boss.

"Nora, apparently," Rosy says as he joins our little circle.

No, no, no, no! They're going to think I can't handle my workload. "No, I didn't—"

"Are you worried you won't be able to handle the bartending competition?" Harrison asks, screwing up his face in concern.

"Not at—"

"—Of course, she's worried," Mum says. "Not that she'd want *you* to know, of course. This one is independent to a fault."

"I'm not worried *at all*," I tell him with as much confidence as I can muster. "I have everything under control. While my mother is wrong about me being worried, she is right that I'm independent."

"To a fault?" Rosy asks.

"Not to a fault," I assure her, knowing that the more I protest the more I sound like a total liar. "I *am* independent and can easily demonstrate good leadership skills. But not to a fault though as my mum has suggested."

"See?" Mum says. "Can't admit she's in over her head."

"Because I'm not," I grind out.

She tilts her head as if to say "I don't know about that" while Kat suddenly looks interested. I'm fairly certain it's got *everything* to do with my ridiculously handsome boss, who happens to be a champion surfer, yacht captain, and general outdoorsy god. She's peering up at him from under her eyelash extensions while I try to send her "he's way too old for you, happily married, and he's my boss" vibes. Evidently, she's not picking them up, because she's twirling her hair and smiling up at him as if this is a nightclub, not a place of business.

Oh my God. Could this get any worse?

"Listen, Mum, I did say I'd ask around to see if there were any openings for Kat, and I will do that as soon as I have a chance," I tell her, hoping that she'll take the hint and leave. "But Harrison and Rosy are extremely busy. Neither of them have time for—"

"It's okay, Nora," Harrison says with that winning smile of his. "I always have time to meet a possible new recruit, especially one who's related to a trusted employee."

Kat grins up at him and blinks what must be insanely heavy eyelashes. "Maybe you could use an intern. I don't even need to be paid. I just need work experience."

Harrison nods, looking impressed. "Unpaid. That's my kind of employee," he teases. "What do you say, Rosy? Can we use some help around here?"

"It sounds like Nora certainly could," Rosy answers.

Shit, shit, shit. "No! I really don't need any help. Honestly, I've got it covered, and I'd hate for you to be accused of nepotism. It reeks of privilege, not to mention being wildly unfair and morally wrong."

Harrison's smile fades, and it's at that exact moment I remember this resort is run on nepotism. "You mean like how I made my sister Emma one of the head chefs?"

"Or how my nephew is on the pool-cleaning crew?" Rosy adds.

"That's different because you're... the... bosses. I'm just a worker bee, and both of those people are extremely talented. Emma more so than your nephew, I imagine." *Shut up. Shut up now.* "I mean, she did graduate from one of the best culinary schools in the world, so she *deserved* to have her brother give her a restaurant."

Rosy plants a hand on one hip. "Harrison didn't *give* her that restaurant. She earned it, and she had to work at Eden first. Then she had to prove she had the chops to make it as head chef."

Where's a good hurricane when you need one? "I didn't mean give, that's not what I meant," I say, with a nervous laugh. "I just don't want you two to feel obligated to hire my baby sister. You don't owe me this type of *massive favour*. Plus, she has no experience at all, and I don't have time to train her right now anyway."

I glance at Mum, whose jaw is hanging midway to her chest, and then at Kat, who has flushed cheeks and eyes filled with tears. Oh, the guilt. *Fix this now, Nora, you dum-dum!* "Not that Kat wouldn't be a great addition to the team, because she would. She's bright and friendly, and I'm sure, if given the chance, she'd do a terrific job, but since there aren't any openings at this time, she'll carry on looking, and we'll carry on working."

"Nora," Mum hisses. "I can't believe you're not willing to help your little sister in her time of need."

"I am." My underarms are soaked. I whisper, even though they can all hear me, "But I think you may have put Harrison and Rosy on the spot."

"Not at all," Harrison says, smiling at Kat. "It takes guts to put yourself out there, especially for someone your age. I respect that."

He respects my mum dragging her lazy-ass daughter here to ask us to babysit her all day?

"Thanks," Kat tells him, letting out a dainty sniff. "The truth is, I've always wanted to work here, but I haven't had a chance to apply before because I've been so busy."

Busy hooking up with randos, getting drunk, and table dancing…

"Tell you what," Harrison says. "I think this is a terrific idea. Nora is going to have her hands full with this bartending competition. Why don't we call it a trial internship, and after a few weeks, if it's working out, we make it a more permanent situation?" He says to me, "You won't mind training your sister, right, Nora?"

Yeah, I do! "Of course not. It's going to be a little difficult, on account of being so busy, but anything for family, right?"

"That's my motto," he says. "And you're all part of my family."

As cheesy as that sounds, he means it. Harrison grew up on the resort after his parents died. His uncle owned Paradise Bay at the time, and even though he was the legal guardian of the Banks children, apparently it was the staff that did much of the heavy lifting when it came to parenting Harrison and his siblings.

"Wonderful," Mum says, clapping her hands. She grins at Kat.

"See? I knew you could do it. You just have to believe in yourself a little more, sweetie."

Believe in herself? For what reason, exactly? The only thing she's accomplished since she finished high school is looking pretty on a budget.

Mum turns to me. "I should run. Let you two working girls get to it. Can you give Kat a lift home after work?"

"Sure," I say, phony smile still in place.

Harrison winks at me. "That's what I like to see. We take care of each other around here."

Kat beams at him. "That's so beautiful. I'm going to love it here. I just know it."

You know what else she's going to do? Ruin everything for me. *I* just know *that*.

———

Mike the Moose - TikTok Reel

"It's the Moose again! I'm back with a huge update on my competitors for the Worlds! The last three World semi-finals wrapped up today, so now I know who I'm up against. In the Asian semi-finals, this year's big winner is a massive upset. Her name is Binna Chu. She hails from Seoul, South Korea, and get this —she's a total newbie to the sport.

"Can you believe it? Her first competition, and she knocks it out of the park. Not only was she the only woman in the Asia-Pacific semis this year, she's also the oldest person to ever compete!" Mike claps his hands, and a photo of a lovely woman with long dark hair appears behind him. "She's a forty-two-year-old mom of four who teaches piano lessons in her spare time. Yeah, she's also a trained concert pianist. I gotta be honest, I'm a little intimidated by her."

Her photo disappears. "All right, moving on. The UK semis also ended today, and this will come as no surprise at all. You all know who I'm going to announce, don't you?"

A photo of a man with a shock of red hair appears. "The Ginger Beast himself—Ewan MacClary—has won again. Y'all will remember his controversial decision two years ago to leave Scotland and move to Avonia so he could compete for them. A lot of you out there think it was a cowardly move, based on the heavy competition in Scotland, but I happen to know he moved there for a girl, so cut him some slack, my Moose Heads, because he did it for love."

Mike breaks into an off-key rendition of "I Did it for Love" by '80s hair band Harlequin.

After a few bars, he stops and laughs. "Last but not least, we have our South American champ. From Rio de Janeiro, Brazil, Paulo Souza, who is not only talented but one hell of a great guy. We had to share a hotel room four years ago at the Worlds in Tokyo, and I can honestly say I've never had such an awesome time." Making the hang ten sign for some odd reason, Mike adds, "Paulo, I'm coming for you, dude!"

"I'll be back in two days, after Europe, the Caribbean, Oceania, Africa, and Central America have decided who they're sending to the Benaventes in two short weeks." Mike lets out a whooping sound, then claps his hands loudly. "I can't friggin' wait!"

———

TO-DO LIST (Home Version)

Laundry – definitely do whites today!

Vacuum floor

Determine which plants are beyond saving and get rid of dead ones/water survivors

4

Rocks and Hard Places

Theo

"WELCOME TO *BUSINESS WORLD WEEKLY*. I'm your host, Barry Butler. Today, more trouble for Rojas Rum, as James Prescott has a disastrous interview with Sophia Sato. I'm not sure who on his team thought an interview at this time would be a good idea, but it would seem no one on his staff had the good sense to shut it down. Candy Higgs is here with more on this breaking story. Candy?"

She smiles brightly. "Barry, good morning. It seems the strenuous effort on behalf of the team at Rojas has all been for naught. In the now infamous one-hour interview, Prescott mentioned the brand more than thirty-six times, and each time the word Rojas came out of his mouth, you could almost feel their sales falling further."

"We have a compilation," Barry says. "Should we roll the clip?"

Candy nods. "Yes, but I almost feel bad about doing it. Especially the part when he sobs as he talks about how he'll never forgive himself for letting Markos Rojas down—the best friend he's ever had."

I shut the television off and rise from my seat at the head of the boardroom table, not needing to watch that train wreck again. Staring out the tall window at the turquoise sea in the distance, I start to panic. I've been at the office all weekend—pacing, researching, allowing myself only quick naps on the couch before getting right back to work, trying desperately to come up with the perfect way to resurrect our brand.

The awful truth is I've come up with nothing. Not one viable idea that will help us climb out of this massive hole we're in. In exactly twelve minutes, I'll be facing the board of directors—seven angry, old men and two equally angry, old women, all of whom will have seen that interview and will demand that someone's head roll —likely mine.

My assistant, Jaquell Morales, hurries in. Jaquell was my father's assistant, and I was incredibly fortunate she agreed to stay on when I took over. No one knows more about this business than her. She's nearly seventy, but other than her grey hair, you'd never know it to look at her. Her skin has remained smooth over the years, which she'll tell you is because she's never in the sun because the Rojas men kept her in the office her entire adult life.

She's carrying a small mug of what I know to be espresso, as well as a plate of freshly cut fruit and a few slices of toasted French bread. She sets them on the table. "Eat up before they get here."

"Thank you, but I need to think, not eat."

"You need to eat, then you'll be able to think." She points to the chair.

Sighing, I park myself again and pick up the fork, realizing how exhausted and hungry I am. "Thank you."

She stands nearby and watches me for a second. "Do you want to know what I think you should do?"

Advice is something she rarely offers, so when she does, I jump at the chance to listen, because she's always right. I nod, popping a slice of mango into my mouth.

"Sponsor the competition."

I stop mid-chew, then swallow fruit that suddenly tastes like soap. "Too risky."

"It would be if you weren't going to be onsite the entire time to control every detail." She hands me a folder that was tucked under her arm.

"There's no way I have time for this. Not when things are in the toilet." I open the folder.

"If you oversee everything, you'll be getting the company *out* of the toilet. You're not going to let it get out of control."

"It's an uncontrollable situation."

"It's not. They've been holding these competitions for years, and nothing has come out about any type of scandal. This is the perfect opportunity to rebrand Rojas, which is what has to be done if this company is to survive. The people who drink Rojas at the moment —or I should say *used to*—are older, wealthy people. But they've all switched brands. Like it or not, they're gone. You need to tap a younger crowd. People who don't care what James Prescott did or didn't do. People who want to have a party. You think Patrón sold so well by having some old crooner do their ads? No, they got Ludacris, Juelz Santana, Rocky G and NugLife to sell their brand through their music."

I stifle a laugh at hearing NugLife come out of her mouth.

"What? You think I don't know rap music because I'm old?"

"You want me to believe you're a huge Ludacris fan these days?"

"Not really, but I know those songs because it's our business to know them."

"As much as I appreciate the effort, Jaquell, I don't see how a bunch of guys in tank tops and board shorts, flipping bottles, is going to save us."

"It's more than that. The people competing are serious about what they do. They've been training for years. They're the best of the best, and if there's one thing people love, it's to see the best in the world compete. At anything." She points at my fork, as if encouraging me to keep eating. "How else do you explain the popu-larity of all those baking shows? I bake all the time, nobody cares— not even my husband. But watching the most skilled bakers turn flour, eggs, and sugar into something special, well, that's entirely different."

I sigh and tear off a piece of the French bread and let the buttery goodness melt on my tongue.

"Trust me on this. I know I'm right." She glances at her watch. "You have exactly seven minutes to read the report and make a decision."

She pulls out a chair and sits, clearly finished with her pitch. I munch on bread while I mull over the report. Projected earnings, demographics of the competition, X-Stream TV viewers, and our customers are laid out in colourful graphs and charts. There's even a section on mitigating risks. Her numbers will be spot-on, I know.

"Why do you think Jacardi pulled out of this?" I ask. "It doesn't make sense, given these numbers."

"That's the one thing I don't like about it. The only thing I can think of is that because they've added our customers to their base, maybe they want to distance themselves from the younger crowd."

"But why not go for both?" I scratch my head.

"Good question, but we don't have time to do any digging. We need a solution in"—she glances at her watch—"three minutes."

Sighing, I sit back. These are the moments when I most miss my father. He would have known exactly what to do. I flip through the pages again, realizing how much work must have gone into the report. "Was this how you spent your weekend?"

"You weren't going to come up with anything better, so I thought I'd crunch the numbers for you," she says, adding, "You know, since you're being a stubborn ass about it."

"I could have come up with something better," I tell her, sounding exactly as defensive as I feel. "Easily."

She crosses her arms. "Well, did you?"

"No," I answer, knowing how defensive I sound.

Jaquell gives me a satisfied grin. "Look, I know you better than you know yourself, Theo. You only rejected this plan because Markos brought it to you."

"Can you blame me?"

"Yes, I can. Did he mess up? Absolutely. But that doesn't make *this* a bad idea. So pull your head out of your butt and admit that

Carolina Armas is the answer to your prayers right now." She checks her watch again. "One minute."

Hijo de puta. I hate like hell what I'm about to say. "Did you make copies of the report for all the board members?"

"Of course." She stands and starts for the door. "I'll be back with them in thirty seconds. Finish eating and wipe your mouth. You have crumbs in your stubble."

5

Is Stabby an Emotion?

Nora

SOMEHOW I MANAGE to make it through the first part of the morning without murdering Kat. Instead of getting straight to work, I had to take her to the laundry services building to scrounge up a uniform for her—polo shirt and shorts, like the rest of the resort staff. Event planners and office staff wear suits, so at least my outfit doesn't match my sister's, *à la* childhood family photo shoots.

The trip back to the office takes forever in the blistering heat, what with Kat stopping to gawk at everything along the way—especially anyone with a Y-chromosome and muscles. She somehow manages to get "snaps" from three guys by the time we return to the air-conditioned heaven I call the office, at which point I find myself sounding exactly like a parent. "You shouldn't even *be* on Snapchat. No good can come of it."

Needing to regroup, I set her up at my desk to read the employee handbook and fill out the intake forms while I gather my things and go into one of the conference rooms. Only instead of thinking clearly, I wind up stewing over this massive betrayal on the part of my mother, whom I shall *never* forgive. Then I worry about what Kat is doing so I get up to find her, only to discover she's abandoned the manual in favour of chatting up the FedEx guy with Rosy, who would definitely leave her husband of forty years if the FedEx guy gave her the nod. Or, more accurately, if his tight shorts did.

Oh God, Rosy is going to be the worst influence on her. "Hey, Kat, have you finished the employee manual already?" I ask pointedly.

She rolls her eyes. "Not yet, *boss*, but if I'm not working quickly enough for your liking, you can always dock my pay."

Rosy seems to find that hilarious, which is odd since she doesn't tolerate insubordination from anyone else.

I wait for the two of them to stop cackling and for Kat to realize I'm serious. When she finally does, she says, "I better get back to the milestone."

"Grindstone," I correct her. "You mean grindstone, and I'd hardly call reading a twenty-page manual hard labour."

"Okay, you caught me." She raises her hands in surrender. "I used the wrong word."

"Are you going to dock her pay for that too?" Rosy asks, chuckling until she starts to wheeze.

I bark out a laugh as well, then say, "Okay, back to it!"

When we arrive at my desk, Oakley (who works ten to six) has arrived and is wearing a smug look. "Oh, Nora, you're here. I thought you got replaced by a younger version of yourself."

"Ha. Good one. This is my little sister, Kat."

"We met." She smiles at me from behind her computer screen. "I hear you can't handle your workload, so your mum brought in a mini-you."

Kat blushes and offers Oakley a modest "I'll do what I can" look while I try to decide which one I'd like to slap harder. Turns out it's a tie.

"Nope, all good," I say. "In fact, if you need help with those weddings you'll be hosting while I'm handling the bartending competition, just let Kat know. She'll be happy to jump in."

"I might do that. Overseeing her work would be good management training."

Dammit, she's right. "But before she can help either of us, she needs to read the employee manual." I glance at Kat with what I hope looks like an easy (and not menacing) smile.

"Urgh, she's making you read the manual?" Oakley says to Kat, then mimes sticking her finger down her throat.

"I know, right?" Kat says. "Bossy much?"

"This is one situation where being bossy is appropriate," I say to Kat. Reaching out with my forefinger, I tap the end of her nose. "Because I am your boss."

"And she's not going to let you forget it either," Oakley mutters.

Rubbing my temples with both hands, I say, "I really need to get back to work. Try to get all those forms filled out, then we'll grab a bite of lunch with Hadley." Hadley's my recently married, very pregnant best friend, who runs a dance school out of the resort's yoga studio while the mums lie by the pool and sip cocktails or get massages.

Kat's face falls. "I have lunch plans already."

My cheeks warm with the embarrassment of being rejected by my little sister. "Really?"

"That cute guy who was cleaning the pool Snapped to see if I wanted to meet him for a burger at the beach bar."

"How nice," I say with a toothy grin. "That's... I'm glad you're settling in so fast."

"Thanks. Everyone's just so nice here. I'm not sure why you complain so much."

———

By the time I leave for lunch with Hadley, I'm a ball of ragey tension, but that's okay, because by the time lunch is over, I know I'll be feeling much better. Not only that, I'm sure I'll have a plan. Hadley will help me get back on track. That's what she and I do for each other — provide sympathy and a lot of very helpful ideas. Historically, our brainstorming sessions include copious amounts of deep-fried food, and to be honest, I would *kill* for a heaping plate of french fries right about now instead of my Jennifer Aniston *Friends* salad — but no matter. I will not harm my body just because I'm angry at my family.

When I get to the studio, I'll be greeted by the scent of orange essence and the sound of New Age music. Yes, that is exactly what I need. The view of the jungle through the wall of windows, the serenity of the quiet space, with its wide-plank hardwood floors and a tall, thatched roof, and my best friend, who is about to become super pissed off on my behalf.

Hadley has been the yoga/salsa/merengue instructor at the resort since we finished high school, but a couple of years ago, she came up with the idea to start her own dance school. When she couldn't secure a business loan to rent a space, she approached Harrison and Libby to see if they could work something out, since the studio sits empty most of the time. She was able to sell them on the idea, based on her theory that having local families drive out to the resort on a regular basis would only serve to increase business, as not only would the parents likely purchase refreshments and possibly spa services (which they do) while they wait for their children, they would also start to think of it as a go-to place for their big life events. Her idea worked out beautifully, which I'm thrilled about because it means I still get to see my best friend almost every day, even though she's happily married and has started a new career path.

I pull open the door, and walk in, but it's not orange essence I smell. Instead, it's the heavenly scent of a cheeseburger and french fries. I look across the room to see Hadley at her desk, shoving fries into her mouth. She gives me a guilty look, then swallows. "Sorry, I was hoping I'd finish eating before you got here. I couldn't stand the idea of another salad today."

I shrug and offer her an easy smile, even though the scent of all that greasy goodness is making me unreasonably agitated at the moment. "The baby needed a burger."

"And what the baby wants, the baby gets," she says with a grin.

That's all right. I'm going to enjoy my healthy salad, knowing I'm fueling my body with what it needs to get me through the rest of the afternoon.

"So? Did you get your smart goals all sorted?" she asks, dipping a fry into a dollop of ketchup.

I shake my head and flop into the office chair next to her desk. Setting my Scooby-Doo lunch kit on top of it, I say, "I got absolutely nothing done this morning."

I launch into a retelling of the morning's events — my mother and Kat ambushing me, me insulting the entire Banks family and Rosy, snide Oakley, and my horny younger sibling, who is about to ruin my life. By the time I finish, Hadley has eaten every last fry without offering me one (for which I'm glad, obviously, because the last thing I want to do is eat a delicious hot french fry), and I've only managed two bites of my—let's face it, boring—salad. My stomach growls, and I pick up my fork again, telling myself to be glad I have anything to eat for lunch at all. I stab some spinach and a sliced cherry tomato and pop them in my mouth, waiting for Hadley to make me feel all better about my predicament.

But instead of her railing at the injustice of it all, she lets out a big yawn. "Sorry. I just get so tired after lunch. I can't believe your mum did that."

"Right?" I say with my mouth full.

"But what's done is done, so I suppose rather than dwelling on how you ended up with Kat, you'll just have to make the best of it."

What? Make the best of it? That's not what she's supposed to say. "There's going to be no 'making the best of' this shit show. It's going to be an absolute disaster. Kat with hot men all over the place, feeding her drinks she doesn't need. Honestly, I do *not* have the time to babysit her right now. The next few weeks are *way* too important for me to have her waltz in here and screw it up for me."

"Maybe she won't." Hadley lets out another yawn. "I mean, who knows? Maybe she'll end up being really helpful. It's not like she's ever had a chance to prove herself, which also means she hasn't proven she *can't* do it."

Logic? I don't want logic right now. I want rage. "Come on, Hadley, we all know she's lazy. She only came today because my mum dragged her here, and now she's going to use this place as her own personal Tinder app."

"Have you laid out your expectations for her? Set some boundaries?"

"What…? No. She's only been here a few hours. Besides, she's not exactly the type to respect other people's boundaries."

"Well, she can't if you don't tell her what they are." Hadley rests her hands on her round belly. "I've been reading this book about effective parenting, and it says the most important thing to do in any relationship is to establish firm boundaries and make your expectations clear to the child—in this case, your sister. That way you're setting both of you up for success."

I blink a few times, trying to process what's happening here, but all I can think is that I'm losing my best friend to her newly developed sense of reason. "Right. That's an excellent point," I say, offering her a tight smile. "Thanks."

More yawning and apologizing, then she says, "I know that's probably not what you were hoping to hear. You were probably expecting me to get completely furious on your behalf, and I am. I mean, really deep down, I am totally annoyed, especially at your mum. But the truth is, Nora, I'm so tired right now, I don't have the energy to be upset about anything. I have to skip the part where I get all emotional about things and go straight to the bit where we solve the problem."

"Please don't apologize. You're totally right. Set the boundaries, make the expectations clear, and hope for the best."

"Exactly," she says with a smile. "I'm so glad you get it. Doesn't this feel so much better than being upset?"

No, it most certainly does not. "Mm-hmm."

"I mean, it's not like being angry about it will change the situation anyway. Kat will be working here for a while, so you just have to make the best of it, right?"

"Uh-huh." Only I don't want to make the best of it. I want her gone.

Yawning again, Hadley adds, "I guess the other way to look at it is that Kat may not even stick around until all those hot bartenders show up. Who knows? She could wind up quitting in a few days."

"Now *that's* a very good point," I say and then realize I've just implied that none of the other things she said had any merit. Hope-fully she's too tired to notice. "What am I even worried about? She's never stuck with anything for more than a couple of days in her entire life. She won't stick with this—having to get up early and actually work every day?"

"For no pay, too." She leans her elbow on the desk, props her head on her hand, and closes her eyes for a second. Managing to open them again, she adds, "And if by some chance she doesn't quit, go with the whole boundary thing. On a side note, how do *you* feel about all those hot bartenders showing up here?"

I make the same face I would if someone asked me to sniff their armpit. "No thank you. I do not need that sort of trouble in my life."

"Oh come on, what about a little fling? It could be good for you."

"Which part? The losing focus on my career just when it's finally going somewhere or the STI?"

Her eyes flutter and she says, "Pessimist."

"Realist."

"Maybe you'll meet the man of your dreams."

"I'm not even going to dignify that with an answer. Man of my dreams. *Pfft*," I scoff, stabbing at my salad with my fork, trying to make the perfect bite. "I've got bigger fish to fry, thank you very much. Promotion, little cottage by the sea, maybe a dog, but no man. Certainly not some roving man-child who pours liquids into glasses for a living. How is that even a skill? I mean, really…"

When I look back up at her, Hadley's fast asleep, sitting up, head in her hand. My heart squeezes seeing my friend so exhausted. I finish munching on my deeply unsatisfying salad while I contem-plate our conversation. She's right about one thing. I really have nothing to worry about. Kat will quit. I only hope she does it before she can tank my career.

———

Email from Carolina Armas

To: Nora Cooper
CC: Vincent St. Pierre
Subject Line: URGENT - World Bartending Championship

Dear Nora,

I am Carolina Armas, Executive Director of X-Stream TV. Our sponsor and a few of us from the network will be arriving tomorrow to get set up for the big event. We expect to find you and the rest of the Paradise Bay staff ready for us. You'll note I've copied Vincent St. Pierre. He is the showrunner/director of the World Bartending Championships TV show. What we love about Vincent is his undying passion for each project he takes on, his attention to detail, and his inability to take no for an answer when he knows there IS a way to accomplish something. You'll be working closely with him throughout the coming weeks.

Vincent, please follow up with the scheduled events for Nora, so she can begin sourcing what is required.

Regards,
Carolina

P.S. You'll note I've marked this email urgent. In the future, all emails from this address or Vincent's should be treated as such.

———

Email from Vincent St. Pierre
To: Nora Cooper
CC: Carolina Armas
Subject Line: Re: URGENT - World Bartending Championship

Hello Nora,

As Carolina mentioned, I am the showrunner and director, which means I control everything to do with filming the events. (BIG JOB. BIG.) I am employed by the network, not the International Bartenders Association which provides rules and judges for the competition. That is a separate group.

As our point person at the resort, I need you to be available to me at all times, but I also require that you stay out of our way. Anything I write/tell you is strictly confidential and is not to be shared with anyone outside of resort staff, and even then only as needed. Do NOT share the details with resort staff, only the duties they must perform. This is of the utmost importance, as we don't want any of the contestants gaining an edge over others.

We will start with the top nine competitors from around the globe (as was previously determined by the regional semi-finals held by the IBA). Two contestants will be sent home in episodes one and two, then one per episode until the final episode. We will film three episodes the first week and two the next, for a grand total of two weeks of filming at the resort, including a few days for atmosphere shots using our drones, etc.

The episodes are as follows:
1) Speed Pouring and Free Pouring Accuracy Challenges (two separate challenges, two losers going home)
2) Memory Challenge (one challenge, two losers leaving)
3) Storytelling Challenge (one challenge, one loser)
4) Flair Pouring Challenge (same)
5) Survivor Challenge Finale (featuring top three competitors, with one winner being awarded the title/prizes).

PLEASE NOTE: THIS LAST CHALLENGE IS LEVEL 5 SECRECY. Contestants will be expecting a Mystery Box Challenge, and we want something really exciting this year. We're going to create a Survivor feel to the competition, and as such, we will be dropping the contestants off on a deserted island, where they must forage for ingredients. The crew will build fun tiki-style bars on the beach of said island, and after several hours of foraging/testing, the contestants will present their drinks to the judges.

For this to work, we will require power, water, and toilets, as well as food. We will also need an expert on the local flora on hand to provide advice on which plants are poisonous, etc. We trust you will be able to make this happen.

I look forward to meeting you and getting started.

Best,
Vincent St. Pierre
Showrunner, Director, Producer, X-Stream TV

"Shit," I mutter.

Oakley peers around her computer screen. "Something wrong already?"

Oh, you'd like that, wouldn't you? "Nothing I can't sort out," I tell her with a phony smile that says "fuck off, you witch."

Picking up my massive to-do list, I add *Source deserted island*, then stare at it. How the hell am I supposed to come up with an island *and* manage to get power, water, a kitchen, and facilities to it in the next three weeks? This is some Fyre Festival-level insanity.

Next to me, Kat is flipping through the brochures I gave her so she can familiarize herself with the amenities and services the resort offers. "Huh, I didn't know you guys had a yoga studio."

"Um, yes, Hadley's been working there since high school."

"Seriously? I didn't know she was a yoga teacher."

Oh my God, she's been my best friend since before Kat was born. How does she not know this? "What did you think she did?" I ask while I search "Benavente Islands deserted islands with power and water" online.

"I don't know. I thought she worked in a doctor's office or something."

Breathe, Nora, breathe. Long, slow, deep breaths.

"Ooh! This infinity pool is *so* gorgeous. Are we allowed to swim when we're off the clock?"

"Definitely not."

Her shoulders drop. "That seems like a total waste."

"Uh-huh, but I really am busy, Kat, so if you can read quietly, that would be awesome."

"Sorry," she says but not in a sincere way, more like in a sarcastic "sooorrrrry, gawd" way.

Ha! An article on uninhabited islands in the chain of the Benaventes on a website called *Nature Review*. I click on it and scroll through what turns out to be a lengthy technical paper on the migration of the Grenadines' pink rhino iguana throughout the Eastern Caribbean.

Next!

"Wow, I didn't know that the guy who wrote *Clash of Crowns* finished his series here," Kat says, popping her gum.

"Yup, he did."

"That is sick. Like, is there a plaque outside the room he was in?"

"He actually wrote it on a private island the resort owns called Eden," I tell her. "There should be a brochure about it in the pile." My phone rings before I can remind her to be quiet again. "Nora Cooper speaking."

"Oh good. I wanted to make sure you'd pick up," a man with a North American accent says. "I *loathe* it when someone doesn't answer their phone."

"Umm… yes, can I help you with something?"

"Vincent St. Pierre. Did you get my email?"

"I just finished reading it and got straight to work on sourcing that"—glancing around, I realize I shouldn't say it out loud. Not while Mr. Secrecy is on the phone—"thing you asked for."

"The deserted island?"

"Yes, that."

"And?"

In front of me, Kat is holding the Island of Eden brochure up to her face. That's my answer. Eden is Paradise Bay's private island. It has exactly one luxury villa set atop the highest point, overlooking the sea to the south, but is otherwise surrounded by jungle. A staff of three —chef, full-time butler, and housekeeper—look after guests. They live on houseboats moored just offshore. Power, check. Water, check. Kitchen, check. It would be easy to film so it has the appearance of being deserted.

"I may already have found it, but I'll have to let you know if it'll work out."

"Hurry up and find out, please. We're running out of time."

Running out of time to do the thing you sprung on me ten minutes ago? "It's my top priority."

"If that's the case, why are you answering random phone calls?" he asks, then, just when I'm about to say something I shouldn't, he laughs. A long, drawn out, totally phony laugh. "Just kidding. Always pick up when you see my number, mmkay? Gotta run. I have twenty million things to do before I get on the plane."

He rings off, and I slouch, stunned at our conversation.

"Did whoever that was hang up on you?" Oakley asks.

"I think his phone lost connection," I mutter.

"Oh really? Because it wouldn't surprise me if those TV people are an absolute nightmare to work with." Turning to Kat, she adds, "Better her than us, am I right?"

"Oh yeah," Kat says knowingly, "but that's why she's making the big bucks and we aren't."

Oakley stiffens. "She and I are in the same pay grade."

Looking at me, Kat says, "I thought you were her boss."

"Nope," I answer, my face turning red. "She and I have the same job."

Oakley glares at me for a second, and I know she thinks I go around telling everyone she works under me. Which I don't, obviously. Kat must not have been listening when I said I'm *applying* for the management position, and there's no sense denying it, because she won't believe me anyway. Just what I needed: one more reason for Oakley to hate me.

Whatever. I've got more important things to think about, starting with figuring out if the Island of Eden is booked when we need it for the show.

———

Mike the Moose - Tiktok Video
   "Hey, everybody! Mike the Moose here, live from my office here in beautiful

Montreal, Canada." He spins the camera to show his office is actually a high-end nightclub. "The remaining semi-finals wrapped up today, and I have to say, a couple of the names have me almost leaving moose droppings on the floor." He winks. "Just kidding. Come on, it's me, The Moooooosssee! Nothing scares a moose, baby. Okay, let's get to it:

"Representing Europe is the Croatian Crusher herself, Marija Horvat! Oceania is sending the one and only Aiden Ward from New Zealand. Come on, Oceania? Ward again? I mean, I guess you can go that way if you want to lose!"

Mike laughs, then says, "From Africa, we have Junior Afumba of Johannesburg, South Africa. Central America is sending Eddy Morales of Guatemala. Yay, Eddy! And finally, the guy every man wants to be and every woman wants to be with... Paz Castillo of The Bahamas, representing the Caribbean."

Cupping his mouth on one side, as if he's about to reveal a big secret, he says, "Paz has me a little... ahem... concerned. He has mad skills, especially when it comes to flair and storytelling, but don't worry, my Moose Heads, because Mikey's been practicing non-friggin' stop for weeks. I'm heading south with a whole new level of bottle-flipping madness. YEAH!" he shouts, then lowers his voice. "I'm going to sign off and go pack because it's almost time for this moose to make tracks!"

6

Computer Crashes and
Temper Tantrums

Theo - One Week Later

WHEN I WAS at Oxford getting my master's in business, I played poker. A lot of poker. Not that I'd ever admit this to my family or employees on account of pretending I've always been the responsible man they have come to know and love. But in my early twenties, I couldn't get enough of the game. Looking back on how many classes I missed after pulling all-nighters with a cigar dangling from my lips, I can tell you, with all honesty, it was the best training ground for the business world there is. Forget Economics 512, study the World Series of Poker if you want the inside track on how to make it.

I learned how to spot my opponent's tells—a shift of his gaze, a twitch of the thumb, the bouncing of a knee. I also mastered the art of hiding my own tells. Along with those skills, I learned two valuable life lessons:

1) Everybody's bluffing most of the time.

2) If you're going in, go *all* in.

That second one is the reason why I'm currently standing in a long line of tourists in the open-air lobby of the Paradise Bay

Resort. After convincing the board that this bartending competition is "the best thing that could have happened to Rojas Rum," I spent the rest of the week getting my shit in order fast so I could hop on a plane to Santa Valentina Island, where I'll work and live for the next three weeks.

If I'm pinning all our hopes on this ridiculous spectacle, I better damn well be here to make sure it works. If it doesn't, I'm out on my *culo*. Unfortunately, Carolina and Markos have also decided to join me which, let's face it, is not ideal. Markos insisted on coming to help clean up the mess he made, which sounds noble but really isn't. He just can't stand the idea of missing the party.

Carolina was originally intending on popping over here at some point to make sure things were going well with filming, but upon hearing about my decision to sponsor the contest, she has "upped this to the top of her priority list to ensure everything goes as planned."

Fast forward to the current moment, which feels like we're a strange family—Carolina and I both in business attire and our son Markos, dressed to plunge into the pool.

He's in a cobalt blue rashguard with long-sleeves, matching board shorts, and flip-flops. I'm a little jealous, because a suit isn't exactly the most comfortable attire in this setting, but I'm not here for a vacation. I'm here as the president of a major corporation, and I've got over eight-thousand reasons to remain the pillar of professionalism.

Unfortunately, we arrived immediately after a shuttle bus filled with guests and about ten seconds before the resort's computer system crashed. If this is a sign of what's to come, my hopes that this event will resurrect our brand have shrunk considerably. I'm about at the end of my patience, and it's only ten in the morning. In precisely forty-two minutes, I have a Zoom call with one of the largest liquor store chains in the US regarding "adjustments to their order." I need to set up somewhere quiet in the next few minutes so I can prepare.

In front of us, a couple struggles with their restless son, who looks to be about six years old and happens to be wearing the same outfit as my brother, only in neon green instead of blue. The child jumps up and down on the spot and whines, "But I want to go swimming now!"

"We will, Matty, we will," his mother says, fanning her face with her passport. "Just a few more minutes and Daddy will take you to the pool."

Daddy is busy tapping away on his mobile phone, totally unaware of what's going on around him.

Markos sighs heavily, then rolls his head in my direction. "Tell me again why we couldn't stay on the yacht?"

I purse my lips. "Okay, last time. I'm here to oversee the competition, which means I need to stay in the same building as the contestants and staff. If I'm out on a yacht, I won't know what's going on here at the resort, remember?"

"It's not realistic for you to babysit all those people 24/7," he says, shaking his head. "Not that they'll need a nanny anyway."

"Theo doesn't want to leave anything to chance," Carolina tells him.

"I know, but doesn't the fact that we're standing in a line with all these tourists strongly suggest we're not exactly going to enjoy our stay? I mean, seriously. They don't even have a VIP counter."

"Which is fine, because the last thing we want to do is appear to be living large while the company is struggling," I mutter to him, hoping no one can hear me. "How would that look to our employees or the board members, for that matter?"

His shoulders drop. "I guess. I'm just so bored."

In front of us, the little boy has now moved from jumping up and down to lying on the terracotta tile floor, with his arms and legs splayed to the sides. "Mommy, I'm so bored, I think I might die!" he shouts in his ear-piercing little kid voice. "I need to go swimming! Now!"

Instead of being embarrassed (as he should), Markos points to the kid. "See? He gets it."

"Jesus," I whisper before checking my watch. Thirty-eight minutes until the big meeting.

"Why don't I take Markos for a little walk, maybe find him a drink or something?" Carolina asks, clearly noticing how close I am to snapping.

"Perfect," I tell her with a nod. Thank you."

He scowls at her. "I don't need you to mother me." Then he glances at the ceiling. "Although a drink would be nice."

You know who else could use a drink? Me. But I'm not going to have one, because I've got a mountain of work to do as soon as I get to my room.

Come on, IT guy. Let's clear the damn lobby already so little Matty can go swimming, and I can get into my air-conditioned suite and work.

I spend the next twelve minutes trying not to watch the meltdown happening in front of me, but it's hard to ignore. Matty has gone from lying on the floor to tugging on his poor mother's arm and shouting, "I want to swim! I want to swim!" to making a break for it, and, in his haste to escape, not noticing the pillar in front of him, which he slammed into face-first. This led to a screaming fit of epic proportions.

Note to self: Find out what building they're in and make sure my room is on the opposite end of the property.

The entire lobby breathes a sigh of relief the moment Matty and his parents exit, presumably to find the nearest pool. I step up to the front desk at the same time Markos and Carolina return. Smiling at the young woman across the counter, I say, "Quite the morning you're having."

She nods. "Things were running smoothly until the computers went down."

The IT guy, who is now working away on his laptop at the other end of the reception desk, says, "Hey, I'm only one man, and I'm working miracles over here."

She and I exchange a "whoops" look. "I should have a reservation under the name Theo Rojas. I have a meeting in a few minutes, so I'm in a hurry."

A look of understanding crosses her face. "Right. You're with the bartending competition. That's going to be so much fun."

"It sure will be," I say, even though for me it'll be a total nightmare.

She turns her gaze to her screen and taps on the keyboard.

"Building C has been blocked off for your group. You requested an adjoining room for you and a Markos Rojas?"

"Yes, he's my brother."

"Present and accounted for," Markos says to her with a boozy smile. "But I don't want an adjoining room with him." He points his index finger about an inch from my cheek. "He's a total bore."

She giggles and turns back to her computer. "Okaayyy… it also says you wanted a suite so you can set up an office in your room?"

"That's correct. I require a desk and chair, hopefully a meeting space of some sort, and we *do* need adjoining rooms. We're here for work."

Markos leans on the counter. "Right. Work. But I don't need an office. My work is with the people, not the spreadsheets, like this boring old guy."

Her cheeks turn red, and I glare at him, hoping that'll be enough for him to knock off the flirting. "Umm…slight problem," she says. "We don't have any adjoining rooms that are also suites with office spaces. Not in Building C, anyway. I could put you in Building A."

"I need to be in C with the rest of the crew and contestants." My phone pings. It's a text from Jaquell: *Your meeting starts in twenty minutes. Don't forget to SMILE! You're there to be charming.*

Dammit, I don't want to smile. I force one anyway. "Back to our problem. What can we do about this? Perhaps I could speak to your manager?"

"Okay, Karen," Markos says, elbowing me in the ribs.

"Could you not?" I ask him sharply.

"Right…okaayyy…so maybe I should get Nora. She's the events coordinator for your competition. She'll sort this out for you."

"Sure, if this Nora person is the one who can make things happen, let's call her," Carolina says.

Plucking the receiver off the desk phone, the young woman places a call. "Nora, hi, you're needed at the front desk. Three of your guests are checking in, and there's a bit of a problem with their room requests." There's a long pause, then she says, "I don't know.

50

His last name is Rojas so——" She hangs up and smiles. "She'll be right out."

"Thank you."

Let's just hope she's competent.

The woman behind the counter busies herself a few feet away from us while we wait. I tug at my tie, suddenly feeling like I might suffocate if I don't get the damn thing off. Markos, however, starts moving his shoulders in time with the beat of a steel drum band that started up somewhere nearby.

"You know what, *hermano*? Maybe staying at the resort will be good for you. Music, women, fun… you could let loose for once," he says. He holds his arms out to Carolina. "Come on. Let's show the old guy how it's done."

She bursts out laughing as he takes her in his arms and starts to mambo with her. Looking over his shoulder at me, he says, "See? This is called fun. It's what real humans do."

"Got it, thanks," I tell him, tapping my fingers on the counter, but not to the beat. With impatience.

"You should dance with Carolina," he says, spinning her towards me.

"Thank you, no. This is neither the time nor the place."

"Come on. Loosen up. Maybe you'll meet the woman of your dreams while we're here. You know, fall in love with some pretty *tourista* who can pop out a bunch of mini-Theos." He croons in Carolina's ear loud enough for me to hear, "Can you imagine their tiny serious faces?"

"Theo doesn't believe in love," she tells him. "Only spreadsheets."

"Spreadsheets don't leave you for being a workaholic," I say, deadpan.

A woman finally appears from the back-office area, and I assume she is Nora, based on her attire and the fact that she's hurrying towards the receptionist. Hmph, I was hoping for someone older, someone with some authority. Instead we're getting a harried-looking young woman in a cheap navy skirt suit that looks too large for her petite frame. Her curly black hair is pulled back into a bun at the nape of her neck. Or should I say was probably pulled back into a bun at some point earlier today but is now freeing itself at several strange angles.

Without bothering to look at us, she and the receptionist engage in a quick conversation before coming to the same conclusion. They can't give me what I want.

Finally, she seems to deem it appropriate to talk directly to me. "Mr. Rojas, I'm Nora Cooper, the events coordinator handling the competition. I understand you require adjoining rooms with your brother, and that you need an office space as well, but just for you, not him."

"Correct," I answer, unable to ignore the loveliness of her dark brown eyes. They're both soft and commanding at the same time, and as that is absolutely irrelevant to the situation, why I'm thinking this is a mystery.

She nods, and I'm hopeful she's going to be able to sort out this simple request until she says, "I'm afraid we don't have any suites with office spaces that also have adjoining rooms in Building C."

"Don't make them suites then. Regular rooms will do."

"No suites?" Markos asks loudly. "But we're going to be here for a month!"

"And you'll survive." I check my watch for the umpteenth time. Shit. Fourteen minutes. Turning back to Nora, I say, "I don't suppose there's any chance I'll be set up in my room in the next ten minutes, is there?"

"I'm afraid not." She offers me an apologetic look. "It's about a ten-minute ride in the golf cart to the building from here."

"Here's the thing," I say, my tone sharper than it should be. "I have a video meeting right away—an important one. I hoped when they called you, they'd be getting someone who could help. You clearly aren't the person who can provide solutions to my problems, so if you would please point me in the direction of *that* person—quickly—that would be wonderful."

Straightening her back and narrowing her eyes, Nora says, "I am the solution person. I solve *all* the problems."

"Not yet," I quip.

Shooting knives at me with her glare, she says, "I have a conference room in this building you can use. Come with me."

Carolina puts a hand on my forearm. "Listen, I'll take care of the rooms. You go to your meeting."

"Perfect, thank you." I hurry to catch up with Nora, who doesn't have to weave her way through a crowded lobby while pulling two over-sized suitcases and carrying a laptop bag.

She waves a card key in front of a set of double doors, which swing open. Pausing to look over her shoulder, she glowers again before trotting along, forcing me to run to make it through the doors before I'm locked out.

What a hag. She takes the paradise out of Paradise Bay, which, incidentally, is completely overrated. This place has nothing on The Bahamas, where I'll be returning the second this idiotic contest is over, *never* to return. And that's a promise.

7

Horrible Humans in Nice Packaging

Nora

"WHO WAS THAT?" Kat asks when I return to my desk after getting Mr. Arrogant set up in a conference room.

"Theo Rojas, president of Rojas Rum and all-around jackass," I mutter, his words about me "clearly" not being the person who can provide solutions to *his* problems rolling through my brain again. He is the perfect example of why I hate rich people so much. If he were a meal, he'd be a heaping plate of rude with a massive side order of self-importance. Theo Rojas is the embodiment of why the world's elite are the absolute worst humanity has to offer.

"Wow, he's so young and hot," she says with a wistful smile.

She's not wrong. The man is a solid twelve out of ten—tall, dark, and built, not to mention dressed in what I'm sure is a $12,000 suit. Sadly, he has the personality of a goat with a yeast infection.

"He's way too old for you," I tell her. "Also, he's off-limits, as are all the other men who are in any way connected with the competition."

Kat gives me her teenage glare and pops her bubble gum at me.

"I didn't mean for me. I just would have expected the president of a huge company to be a gross old boomer."

"Well, he's not." I retrieve a skeleton key from my desk drawer. "Come on, I'm going to need your help."

"Really?" Her eyes light up.

"Yes, really." I hurry down the hall towards the lobby. "I need to get His Highness's room set up exactly how he wants it."

When we reach the front desk, my palms go a little sweaty. Rosy is talking to the two people Mr. Rojas was with, which means they've gone over my head. Strike one for Nora. Plastering on a bright smile, I hurry over to them. "Rosy, hi, I was just getting Mr. Rojas set up for a meeting. Now that that's done, I can sort out their hotel rooms."

"You sure?" she asks. "Because according to Ms. Armas, you seem to be having trouble understanding what they need."

Of course...

My cheeks flame. "There was a bit of a mix-up, but I have everything under control now."

"Are you sure, dear?" Ms. Armas asks with a phony smile. "You seemed so flustered."

"I'm fine, believe me," I say, my voice dripping with Sucralose. Turning back to Rosy, I say, "I'm setting them up in 320 and 321. I'll have housekeeping remove the couch and armchair from 320 for Mr. Rojas and replace them with a desk and an office chair. There's already a round table there that seats four which should serve as a meeting space. Ms. Armas requested a suite, so she'll be up on the fourth floor. I was thinking of the Princess Suite for her." Looking up at Ms. Armas, I say, "It's a lovely room with a large balcony and a beautiful view of the water. You should be quite comfortable there."

"I want to stay up there with you," the other Mr. Rojas says.

Ms. Armas puts a hand on his forearm. "I know it will be a sacrifice for you, but Theo is right about this, as usual."

I spend the next couple of minutes fuming while Sandra, the front desk clerk, signs them in and gives the pair their card keys, then I get in a golf cart with Kat and zip over to building C to search for someone on the housekeeping staff to help me out.

It takes nearly an hour to remove the unneeded furniture, have the floor cleaned, source a desk and office chair suitable for his nibs, and have everything looking just so. Kat rushes in with a large bouquet of flowers to set on the table. When that final touch is in place, I take a deep breath and nod. It should do.

Just in time, too, because there's a click of the lock and in walks Theo Rojas, dragging his suitcases behind him. Without looking at me, he glances around the room, then nods.

"Will this be to your liking?" I ask, stopping just short of curtsying.

"Yes, it should be fine," he says, striding further into the room to inspect it. "But let's do away with the flowers and the tablecloth. I'll need the space."

Kat and I exchange a quick glance, then I gesture for her to remove the vase, and I make quick work of folding the offending tablecloth. Just as I finish, there's a knock at the adjoining door. Mr. Rojas strides over to it with the confidence of a rich man and swings it open.

His brother stands there, dripping all over the floor and grinning. "The rooms aren't anything special, but the pool is filled with hot chicks."

"You do realize you're soaking the floor," Theo tells him, hurrying to the bathroom and returning with a towel. He offers it to his brother. "Dry yourself off, then wipe up the floor."

Huh. That's actually sort of thoughtful toward the housekeeping staff.

Kat, who is holding the heavy vase, is grinning at Markos Rojas like she wants to be the towel he's rubbing his face with right now. I clear my throat and smile at Theo. "Will there be anything else?"

"Some fresh towels please," he says in a haughty tone.

"Of course," I tell him, making my way toward the door. Kat follows me, then breaks off towards the elevator while I go to the linen closet.

It's not exactly my job to fetch towels, but this is what separates an events manager from an events coordinator—the ability and willingness to go above and beyond. Even for the most awful of guests.

When I get back, the door to his room has been propped open, and I can hear Markos (who sounds a little tipsy). "Come on, *hermano*, she's perfect for you. She's as tightly wound as you are. Plus, she's cute."

"You're as bad as Mother, trying to find me a wife, but don't bother. In case you haven't noticed, I'm a little busy trying to save the company at the moment. And even if I *were* looking for love, I'm certainly not going to find it with some dowdy-looking hotel worker in a cheap suit that doesn't fit her."

And that's the moment when he notices me standing in the doorway, holding a stack of freshly laundered towels. The scent of the fabric softener fills my nostrils, making me slightly nauseous. Or is that from the humiliation?

Giving him a slight nod, I take the towels into the bathroom, then back out, careful to avoid seeing myself in the mirror. I already know I look like I'm about to cry. I don't need to see it. When I return to the doorway, I manage to lift my chin to look him in the eye. "Is there anything else I can help you with?"

His dark brown eyes are filled with shame, as they should be. Clearing his throat, he says, "No, thank you, Nora. Everything is… fine."

"If you have any other requests, please call the front desk." And by that I mean, *Don't bother calling me, you raging asshole.*

8

Awful Moments That Will
Haunt You Forever

Theo

"How to win friends and influence people," Markos says as soon as the door closes behind Ms. Cooper. "I had no idea you were such a fashion snob."

"Thanks a lot for that," I snap, guilt gnawing at my chest.

"Hey, you're the one who said she's plain and a terrible dresser," he says, holding up his hands.

"I didn't say she was plain."

"You said dowdy. Same thing."

Oh, for God's sake. Am I really arguing with my idiot brother about my choice of words? "Yes, well, in the future, please don't make such ridiculous suggestions. I'm supposed to be saving the reputation of the company, not creating a new one for myself as a total prick." I yank off my tie.

"It's not ridiculous. She is pretty. And very serious like you. I suspect you two would really hit it off. Or at least you would if you didn't think of yourself as so far above everyone else on the planet."

Tossing the tie on the bed, I shrug off my jacket. "I don't think

I'm better than other people. I was just trying to get you off my back."

"And hurting that poor girl's feelings in the process."

"Don't remind me," I tell him, my face heating up again with shame. "It didn't seem to bother her too much though, did it?" I ask, though I already know the answer.

He tilts his head. "I think she was holding back some tears."

My phone pings, reminding me I should be on a call with our director of distribution to give him the bad news about the Zoom meeting. "I'll try to find a way to make it up to her while we're here. In the meantime, I need you to leave so I can make some calls. It wouldn't kill you to go back to your room and spend a couple of hours reading what I'm sure is an overflowing inbox."

Scrunching up his face, he says, "Yeah, I'll have to do that another day. When I haven't started drinking already."

I let out a long sigh. "In that case, please try not to cause any type of scandal. I have enough on my plate right now."

"Like insulting women—"

"Out." I point towards his room. "And close the door behind you."

As soon as he leaves, I undo the top two buttons on my shirt and roll up the sleeves. This is going to be a very long day. Actually, it's going to be a very long year. I only hope I'll still have a company at the end of it.

9

Handsome is as Handsome Does...Unless the Guy is Insanely Handsome

Nora

"I CAN'T BELIEVE he said that." Hadley pulls me in for an awkward hug that requires me to morph my torso into a letter *C*. "What a jerk."

"He's the worst person I've ever met. Rude, arrogant, and... *rude.*"

Hadley lets me go, and instead of sitting down to eat lunch at her desk, I pace the yoga studio. "You know what? This suit wasn't cheap. It cost me over three hundred dollars, which is why I keep wearing it even though it's a bit loose."

"*Hmph.*" She stares at my outfit. "I'm not saying I agree with the creep. Obviously he's the devil incarnate, but you might want to treat yourself to a few new outfits. You know, things that don't look like they're about to slip right off."

I stop pacing. "Is it that bad?"

Nodding, Hadley says, "It's not great." Then she scrambles to add, "And you deserve great. You've worked so hard to get in terrific shape. You should definitely reward yourself."

Realizing I was about to hitch up my skirt for the thousandth time today, I pop my lower lip. "I guess it can't hurt to look more professional, but *only* for the promotion and not because Mr. Thinks-He's-King-of-the-World said anything."

"Absolutely," Hadley answers, sitting down in front of her bowl of spicy conch chowder, which smells amazing. Her husband, Heath, made it for their supper last night so she has leftovers.

I'm having a salad. Again. Yay.

I plant myself in the chair and stab at some spinach with my fork. "You know what? I *am* going shopping. Right after work. Can you come?" I ask before I remember she'll be teaching right up until the stores close for the evening.

"I wish I could," she says. "But send me pics of anything you're not sure about. I'll keep my phone on me so I can send a thumbs up or down."

"Oh, I will," I say, still sounding furious (which I am). "I'll send pics. I'll buy fabulous stuff and I'll be the queen of professionalism when I come back here tomorrow. And if I'm really lucky, Mr. Jerkface will get swallowed up by a shark in the meantime, so I never have to see him again. Can you believe he called me unprofessional?" I ask. "Me?!"

"No, I cannot. You're nothing if not professional." She slaps her desk. "He really shouldn't talk, if you ask me. Not after what's happening over at his company."

I should probably know this, shouldn't I? I mean, as someone totally professional and all. "Um, what exactly is happening?"

I'm hoping a sex scandal that leads to a future of him being canceled by polite society.

"The whole James Prescott thing? With the drunk driving charge?"

"Oh, right!" I say, snapping my fingers. "I totally forgot about that."

"Anyone who knows anything about James Prescott knows he's got a drinking problem. Rojas really should have done his homework before bringing him on board. Heath said their market share dropped big time after that happened and again last week when

Prescott gave that disastrous interview. Apparently, Rojas Rum is in major trouble."

"Talk about poor business decision-making. Hiring an alcoholic to represent your alcohol." I snort. "And here he is being all high and mighty about my suit. Someone needs to stop throwing stones from inside his glass house." I pause, hearing what I just said. "Or whatever that saying is."

"I knew what you meant," Hadley says reassuringly.

"He can kiss my ass." I shove an overly large bite of greens in my mouth.

"Mine too."

"Exactly. Yours too," I mumble. I chew quickly and swallow, my stomach tightening at the thought of spending all that money on a new wardrobe. "I mean, it's not going to be Chanel or anything. I need to be sensible. But everything will fit well."

"Who needs Chanel?" Hadley asks, wrinkling up her nose. "Nobody with any common sense."

"True that," I say, even though deep down, I'd love to have enough cash to swing a completely Chanel wardrobe. "Only idiots spend that kind of money on clothes. Even if I were rich, I wouldn't waste cash like that."

"Me neither," she says firmly. Then she screws up her face. "Well, if I were *really* rich. Like if I had enough money that even my great-grandkids would never have to worry, then I might."

"Yes, definitely in that case, because you'd have enough to make significant charitable donations."

"Exactly."

We stare at each other for a moment, then burst out laughing at ourselves. When we're done, Hadley says, "Well, good thing we sorted that out. You know, so we'll have a plan when we become wildly rich."

Swiping my fingertips across my forehead, I say, "Phew."

Hadley's eyes light up. "Oh, I just remembered seeing an ad for Apple Blossoms. It's thirty percent off everything this week."

"Perfect."

"Just try not to get stuck in a dress." That happened to her once, and she had to ask Heath to rescue her. At the time, it was completely humiliating for her, having not seen him in over a decade. But it all turned out fine, because they wound up falling in love and now they're living happily ever after.

"I don't know. It worked out pretty well for you, but with my luck, that awful Theo Rojas would be the one standing outside the dressing room door." It's a completely ridiculous thought. No way someone like him will be shopping at Apple Blossoms Women's Wear. He's probably never set foot in a store that doesn't bear the name of a designer label over the door. "I need to put him out of my mind, don't I?"

"A little bit, yeah."

Easier said than done.

———

The next two days are so busy, I barely have time to think about a certain president of a certain rum company about to go under (or so I hope in my darkest moments). I've been run off my feet preparing for the arrival of the contestants/film crew. We're holding a big mixer on Friday evening for them, so on top of room assignments, including dozens of very specific and often opposing requests, I also have to ensure the bars used for the competitions are fully stocked with certain unusual items, make sure that there will be sufficient cold storage for all the drink mixes, exotic fruits, and premium alcohols (to be supplied by Rojas Rum, of course), and I have to arrange for secured storage for all the equipment the film crews will bring. Oh, and there's that whole deserted island thing too. Turns out the Island of Eden is booked the week we'll need it, but only for two of the nights, so I had to go to Harrison to ask for permission to offer the guests an alternative date at our cost ($25,000/night). The good thing is, we'll recoup it by charging the production company for an entire week. The bad thing is, if the guests say no, I'm totally screwed.

I haven't run into Theo Rojas even once, which is sort of a shame, because my shopping trip on Monday night was a raving success. I brought home two new suits (each with a pair of slacks and a skirt), four button-up shirts, a wrap-around dress, and a silk shirtdress with cap sleeves in black that was a bit of a splurge but is so flattering, I couldn't leave it behind. All other items were very sensibly on sale, thank you very much. I even scored two pairs of shoes, including nude sandals and a pair of glossy black slingbacks.

Today I'm in dove-grey dress pants with a sunset pink, ramie, short-sleeved blouse with a stand-up collar. The blouse has beautiful details, including trocas shell buttons that do not say cheap.

Anyway, there are so many moving parts, and so many people enlisted to keep those parts moving, that my walk from the parking lot to my desk in the mornings is fraught with interruptions. As soon as the staff see me coming, they pepper me with questions, and, more often than not, excuses as to why whatever it is they're supposed to do cannot be done.

My mind has been spinning so fast, I can't seem to shut it off at bedtime, so I wind up spending the entire night in this sort of limbo between being awake and asleep, having stress-dreams about every little thing that could possibly go wrong. When the alarm goes off, I bolt out of bed, already tense and panicky.

It took me ninety minutes to get to my desk this morning. When I open my laptop, I have forty-six emails waiting for me, even though I checked before bed last night (huge mistake). Sighing, I scan them, looking for anything urgent.

My eyes land on one that makes my heart pound:

Email from Theo Rojas
To: Nora Cooper, Harrison Banks, Libby Banks, Rosy Brown
CC: Carolina Armas, Markos Rojas, Vincent St. Pierre
Subject: Request for Meeting Today

Dear Ms. Cooper,

With the arrival of the contestants and film crew quickly approaching, Carolina Armas and I would like to meet with you and the resort's administration. Our

goal is to mitigate the risk of inappropriate interactions between partici-
pants/crew/hotel staff.

We'd also like to lay out expectations around conduct so as to prevent any poten-
tial issues before they happen.

Please book a conference room for this afternoon and reply back with the location.
One o'clock would be my preferred time but if that isn't possible, I will make
myself available at another time.

Regards,
Theo Rojas
President of Rojas Rum, Inc.

———

Email from Rosy Brown:
To: Theo Rojas
CC: Nora Cooper, Harrison Banks, Libby Banks, Carolina Armas, Markos
Rojas, Vincent St. Pierre
Subject: Re: Request for Meeting Today

Dear Mr. Rojas,

Nora is tied up this morning. I have booked the Conch Conference Room located
in Building C for 1 p.m.

We look forward to partnering with you to ensure things run as smoothly as
possible for this event.

All the best,
Rosy Brown
General Manager, Paradise Bay Resort

Crap. I should have been the one to respond. And double crap, because the last thing I need today is to be held up in some stupid meeting. I have way too much on my plate as it is. I glance over at Kat, who is sitting at her desk, tapping away on her phone and grinning in response to what is presumably some sort of flirty text exchange. Oh, to be nineteen again and not have a care in the world.

She's been borrowing our mum's car to come to work every day, since she doesn't want to have to stay late to get a ride home from me. So far she hasn't quit, which I suspect is only because of the plethora of man candy available here.

I've assigned her a long list of irrelevant tasks—long, so as to discourage her from showing up (awful, I know), and irrelevant, so that if none of it gets done, it won't affect me negatively.

"Kat, how'd you make out with the name tags for the mixer?"

Not bothering to look up, she says, "I'm on it. They'll be ready by Saturday."

"Friday."

"What?" She finally does me the courtesy of some eye contact.

"Friday. The mixer is tomorrow."

"Right, they'll be done by tomorrow."

"I'd like to have them ready before you go home today, so we can check one more thing off the list."

Shrugging, she says, "Sure."

"And you'll double check the spelling from the guest register, yes?"

"Uh-huh. On it."

And I'll block off an hour to get this finished tomorrow, because there's no way she's going to do it, and if she does, she won't get it right.

I spend the rest of the morning answering emails, including a lengthy exchange with the director of housekeeping regarding various special requests. Turns out she's not all that concerned with providing extra towels for one of the judges, who sent a note from his doctor that he requires four showers per day.

As the clock counts down to one p.m., my mood shifts from bad to worse. The thought of being in a room with Theo Rojas makes my stomach churn. Add all three of my bosses to it, and I'm filled with a cold, sweaty dread. I can't even see Hadley for lunch because she's at an ultrasound appointment today. Instead of getting some Zen time, I stay at my desk, picking away at my salad, even though I'm not hungry.

At twenty to one, I remind Kat about the name tags, gather my laptop, a pad of paper, and a few pencils, and rush out to find a golf cart. I arrive in the Conch Conference Room with ten minutes to spare, which I use to remove unneeded chairs from around the large table and greet the guest services cart when it arrives with the refreshments I ordered. Platters of pastries and fruit are set out on the table, along with small plates, cutlery, and napkins. Coffee, tea, water, and juices are left on the cart, which I push up against the wall. I quickly write the names of each item on small tent cards and prop them up on the table in front of the corresponding drink. Then I rethink the water label, deciding it's pretty obvious, scrunch it up, and toss it in the bin.

At two minutes to one, all the other participants arrive together, chatting away like old friends while I stand near the table, trying not to sweat. Markos and Harrison are dressed in chinos and golf shirts, while Libby and Rosy are in light dresses. Carolina Armas, however, is in a power suit with a short skirt that shows off her long legs. Vincent St. Pierre has paired khaki shorts with a white linen shirt and a dramatic orange scarf hanging loosely down his chest. His jet-black hair is in full pompadour-mode today and the expression he's wearing makes me wonder how much coke has gone up his nose since he woke up. Theo, on the other hand, looks calm, cool, and collected in—surprise, surprise—a light grey suit and blue tie, which I cannot imagine stuffing myself into on such a hot day.

"Hi, Nora. Thanks for setting this up," Harrison says with a bright smile. "I haven't had lunch yet so this will hit the spot."

"I thought that might be the case for a few people here, so I went ahead and ordered." *See how detail-oriented I am when it comes to the comfort of others?* My gaze sweeps across the room and I announce, "Welcome, everyone. Please help yourselves to some refreshments, and we'll get started as soon as everyone is settled."

I risk a glance at Theo Rojas, who seems slightly taken aback by me playing the host when he's the one who called the meeting. *Well, get used to it, buddy, because that's my job.*

I remain standing while the group mills around for a few minutes, filling their plates and getting drinks. Vincent moves as though tethered to Carolina, not getting more than three feet from her at any given moment.

While I'm busy observing people, I can't help but notice my body heating up when Theo is nearby, but it's not because he's hot. It's because his insults tap dance their way across my brain yet again. *Ignore him, Nora. Just ignore him. He'll be gone soon, and you'll never have to see him again.*

Oh great, here he comes.

"How is your week going, Ms. Cooper?" He comes to stand in front of me with a cup of coffee on a saucer that looks comically small in his large hand. "You must be run off your feet getting everything prepared."

Huh, that was sort of nice. Or is it? Maybe that's his way of suggesting I'm in over my head. Nice try, creep. "Yes, but it's nothing I can't handle."

"I'm sure," he says with a small nod.

Rosy appears next to me. "How are the plans for the mixer coming?"

"Great, really great," I tell her with a confident smile. "I've got comprehensive to-do lists, I've been in constant contact with all the major players, and I have a schedule that will have everything set to go by the time it kicks off."

"Excellent work," she says, looking me up and down.

Please don't say anything about my new clothes. Not in front of Theo. "Are you planning to attend, Rosy?"

Her head snaps back as if I've just asked her to come over to my place and scrub the toilet with her toothbrush. "No way. It's going to be *outside*."

"I take it you're not a fan of the great outdoors?" Theo, king of the obvious, asks.

"Why would I want to be outside when I could be somewhere bug-free and climate controlled?"

Libby decides to join our little group at that moment. She's Harrison's most lovely wife. Total professional. She manages the books and has been instrumental in safeguarding the resort's future through some rough times. Tucking her curly red hair behind her shoulder, she looks me up and down like Rosy did a minute ago. "Nora, I've been meaning to compliment you on your wardrobe this week. You look so chic."

"I was thinking the same thing," Rosy tells her, then turns to me. "Did you go on a shopping spree or something? The last few days, you've shown up in such nice outfits."

Why does he have to be standing here for that? Why? Now he's going to know his jackass-y comments got to me. Which they totally did, but I seriously do not need him to be aware of that. My cheeks flame at her words. "Shopping spree?" I cry as if it's the craziest thing anyone has ever asked anyone in the history of polite conversation. "Nope, never... not really... just... clothes."

Narrowing her eyes, Libby asks, "Are you all right?"

"Yup, great. I'm just so occupied with work that what I'm wearing is completely off my radar," I say, feeling the heat of smug judgment from his gaze. Or maybe I only imagine I do. Without daring to look at him, I clear my throat and raise my voice. "Shall we get started?"

Murmurs of agreement fill the room, and everyone chooses a seat. I'm careful to sit on the same side of the table as Theo, only at the opposite end from him so it'll be much easier to avoid eye contact.

The attention of the people in the room naturally falls to him, and I'm not entirely sure if it's because he's the one who asked for the meeting, which would be logical, or if it's because they're all falling victim to the idea that he's the centre of the universe, which would be likely, given the man in question.

Theo glances around at everyone with an easy smile (i.e., lulls all the lambs into a false sense of security before the slaughter), then speaks. "First, I'd like to thank the resort staff for making us feel so welcome. I've had a few days to get settled, and I'm impressed with the high level of hospitality and amenities at the resort. Rojas is late to the party, as far as these competitions go, but we're thrilled to be here and are optimistic that Carolina's team picked the best location for the event."

I sit, pen poised over my pad of paper, awaiting instructions while he blathers on, buttering everyone up. *Well, it won't work on me, Theo Rojas. I'm onto you.*

He continues. "Having said all that, we'd be wise to put some safeguards in place to make sure we don't find ourselves embroiled in a scandal."

"You definitely don't need that," Rosy says under her breath.

"No, you do not," Vincent adds, stifling a laugh.

Theo freezes for a millisecond, then says, "Agreed. We are in a precarious position at the moment, and although our company has survived many a crisis—the biggest being the Cuban revolution that had my grandparents packing everything up and escaping at night to The Bahamas—the current situation must be managed delicately to ensure our survival. It's safe to say that Harrison and Libby will also want to avoid having Paradise Bay caught up in some sort of mess."

"Definitely," Harrison says.

"Absolutely," Libby adds. "So, what can we do to help?"

Yes, please. Get to the bloody point.

"We'd like to institute a female-only floor and ask male guests to refrain from visiting."

Carolina sits forward and pipes in, "We believe this will help to reduce off-hour interactions. As I'm on the fourth floor already, I suggest we put all of the women up there with me, and since Theo and Markos are on the third floor, let's put the men there."

"Uh-huh, uh-huh, brilliant!" Vincent says, adding literally nothing to the conversation, other than smooching his boss's behind.

"That shouldn't be a problem." Harrison turns to look at me. "Nora, can you take care of that?"

Dammit. That means I need to rework the room assignments for the entire building. "Absolutely," I say, jotting down *room assignment: women on top, men underneath.*

"Would you like me to assign someone from the front desk to handle that for you?" Libby asks.

"No, I've got it. I already have the lists of various special requests, so it's best if I stay as the point person."

"Excellent, thank you," Carolina says to me with a wide smile that's about as sincere as cheap pleather.

"Now for the tricky request," Theo says. "I don't want to tell you how to run your business, Harrison, Libby. You two are professionals, and you run a tight ship, but we are hoping you'll be willing to implement some sort of 'no fraternizing with the contestants and crew' policy."

"The thing is," Carolina adds, "These bartenders are, well, pretty much professional flirts, if I'm going to be honest. They know how to talk up a customer to get those big tips. It can be quite flattering, even when you know what they're doing." Her cheeks turn pink, and I'm suddenly curious to know who she's thinking of.

Harrison nods, looking serious. "We already have a 'no fraternizing with the guests' policy, but I don't think it could hurt for us to put out some sort of reminder."

"I'll draft something," Libby says, "and I'll make sure to point out that the people in Building C are off-limits."

"Can you include some sort of consequences?" Carolina asks her.

Libby freezes for a moment. "Like what?"

"I don't know... tell them they'll be fired on the spot?" She says this as if she's winging it when I'm sure she and awful Theo have been twirling their skinny mustaches and evil-laughing about this for days.

"That seems a bit heavy-handed," Libby says.

"Do you think so?" Carolina asks her. "I'd say it provides the clarity that would be most useful for your staff."

"Is that what you've told your staff at X-Stream TV?" I ask, even though it's definitely not my place.

"Yes, of course," she answers in a tone that suggests I'm an idiot.

"While I appreciate the way you run your business, Carolina, we're more of a family," Harrison says. "Most of our staff spend their entire careers at the resort. We find that setting expectations and trusting them to do the right thing works wonders."

"Sure, but maybe a little extra nudge this time," she says. "Theo can't afford any type of scandal."

"And *I* need to make sure my staff will want to continue on after you pack up and go home," Harrison tells her.

"Okay," Vincent mutters sarcastically. "We get it, you're a good guy boss."

"Yes, he really is," Libby says firmly.

Vincent covers his mouth with one hand, looking mock-worried about causing offense, which he clearly is not.

Rosy leans forward. "What if we move Nora into an office space in Building C? That way she can help steer things in the right direction."

Carolina nods. "That's a great idea. She should probably be there anyway, so she's more accessible for the guests she's serving." Pausing, she adds, "But I do think we should revisit the expectations and consequences for your staff."

Theo cuts in. "It's fine, Carolina. What we've come up with should suffice, thank you. My situation is not Harrison and Libby's responsibility." His tone is light, but I stupidly lean forward to look at him, and I can see he's worried. And embarrassed.

He may be human after all.

Vincent clears his throat. "While I've got you here, I'm having trouble pinning Nora down on whether we can get access to that private island or not. Any progress there?"

Harrison nods. "Yes, I managed to free up the dates this morning, so the island will be all yours on Wednesday, and if you decide to film there, you can have it Thursday and Friday the week after."

"How soon can we go on a scouting mission?" Vincent asks, stylus poised over his iPad.

"It'll be vacant Wednesday, so you can have it from noon until Thursday at three p.m., when the next guests arrive."

"Perfect!" Vincent yells.

We spend the next few minutes going over a timeline of events, during which I sound like an obnoxious teacher's pet in an effort to prove how very professional I am. I find myself saying things like "I'm on it," "already done," and my personal favourite, "all over that one, don't you worry," with a confident smile. By the time we wrap up, I pretty much hate myself.

When it's finally over, I stay behind to tidy up the room and put the chairs back, the entire time cursing myself for how I acted. After a few minutes, the door opens and Theo Rojas walks back in.

"Did you forget something?" I ask with a bright smile I don't mean.

"No, I just wanted to ask how I can help."

"What?" I ask, gawking at his stupid gorgeous face.

"You said you were busy."

"No, I didn't."

"Yes, you did," he says, looking confused. "Before the meeting, when Rosy was commenting on your new wardrobe. You mentioned you have no time to think about such things. My brother and I both have some time on our hands tomorrow. How can we help?"

"You can't, really," I tell him in a condescending tone. "Thank you for the offer though. You're off the hook."

"Seriously, put me to work. Maybe I can assist with setting up for the mixer?"

"I have staff for that."

"I see." He offers me a slight nod. "Listen, Nora, I'd like to apologize for what I said the other day."

My stomach tightens at the memory of it. "Do you mean that thing about me being dowdy in my cheap suit? Or the thing about me being unprofessional and wanting someone else who can solve problems to take over for me?" I shouldn't be this bold with someone in his position—especially someone who can have me fired —but I can't seem to help it. He was an ass, and he needs to wear it.

"Both, actually. It was unforgivably rude of me."

"Yes, it was," I tell him, my face hot for reasons I can't explain. "If you'll excuse me, I really am rather busy."

With that, I gather up my things and hurry out of the room on legs that feel like overcooked spaghetti, my heart pounding. I shouldn't have said that, but it sure felt good. Besides, he needed to hear it. He can't just waltz around insulting people and expect them to pretend he didn't. He's a very rude man. Someone has to let him know. Even if that someone is me.

———

Mike the Moose TikTok Video

"Hey, Moose Heads! It's me, Mike the MOOOSE! I have just touched down at the airport in beautiful San Felipe, on Santa Valentina Island. Check out these views!" He flips the camera around to show palm trees swaying in the breeze and the ocean in the distance. "When I lifted off in Montreal this morning, it was minus a million degrees, so arriving here feels amazing."

Mike reappears. "I'll be live-streaming tonight from the resort. There's going to be a meet and greet poolside cocktail event for the competitors and film crew, so stay tuned, because it should get pretty wild."

———

Text from Mom: Nora, I know you're swamped, but I wanted to remind you that tomorrow morning is the annual rise and shine pancake breakfast at the church. Seven a.m. start, as usual. Dad and I would love to see you there, as would the whole community. It's been a while, and you need to eat, so…

Me: Hi, Mom. I'll try. I'm not sure if Kat mentioned the meet and greet event tonight, and I suspect I'll be here quite late.

Mom: I understand. No pressure, dear. But how you spend your days is how you spend your life.

———

TO-DO LIST (Home Version)

Laundry!! Seriously – you are almost out of undies
Dishes

Clean out fridge (especially rice with suspicious looking green bits)

Water plants that are still alive

Buy vinegar and spray bottle to remove fungus from fern

Remove dead plants and clean out pots

10

Bad Fashion Choices and Even Worse Men

Theo

"What's eating you now?" Markos asks me before taking a sip of his Pina Colada.

The mixer is just getting started. We are standing off to one side, watching everyone arrive. Nora's assurances that she'd have everything pulled together in time have been backed up by her actions. Round tables with white tablecloths have been placed around the pool deck. Bright turquoise chairs are set up around them, and candles in hurricane glasses mark the centre of each table. A steel drum band creates a festive mood. Servers stroll around with trays of fruity drinks, and near the beach bar, a long table with hors d'oeuvres tempts the guests. It's all delightful, and I'm pretty sure I'm the only grump at the party.

"Nothing," I lie, my gaze falling on Ms. Nora Cooper for the tenth time in the last minute. She's standing at the reception table, greeting the newcomers. I should stop looking at her, because each glance is a punch to the *cojones*. She's dressed in a black silk shirt-dress that skims her curves. As nice as the view is, it comes with a side order of guilt, having insulted her into spending a lot of money (that she may not have).

"You're upset because you bullied that poor woman into buying a new wardrobe."

"Maybe," I tell him, jamming my hands into the front pockets of my suit pants. In hindsight, a navy suit may have been the wrong choice. It's a pool party, and the sun is still blisteringly hot, even though it's close to setting for the night. "You're charming. How would you fix this?"

"I have no idea. I've never screwed up so badly with a woman before."

"That's helpful, thanks," I say, giving him a glare. I let out a sigh, then add, "Maybe I should offer to pay for the clothes."

"Nope, terrible idea," Markos says.

"Why?"

"It'll make her feel poor."

"What'll make who feel poor?" Carolina asks, sidling up next to me with a flute of champagne in one hand.

Markos leans across me. "Theo insulted that lovely Nora Cooper person the other day. Said she was dowdy and her clothes didn't fit. Now he can't stop thinking about it and feeling bad."

Carolina blinks, her eyes growing wide. "You told her that?"

"No," I answer quickly. "I told Markos that, and she happened to overhear. Then she went out and bought what looks like a whole new wardrobe."

"What's the problem then?" Carolina asks, looking confused. "You did her a favour, if you ask me. For you to notice, she must have no fashion sense at all. So if you helped her see she needed to upgrade her look, that was a kindness."

"What if she can't afford a new wardrobe?" I ask.

"Then she shouldn't have bought one," Carolina says, sipping her drink. "Don't worry about it. She couldn't have spent much. That dress looks like it's from Zara, and I doubt those sandals are even real leather, based on the Band-Aids she's got across her ankles."

My gaze shifts to her ankles, and I notice the red skin poking out from under the bandages. Dammit. My fault.

Putting a hand over her mouth, Carolina starts to laugh. "And look, she's got sweat marks on her back. Why would someone wear silk when they're going to be rushing around in this heat?" Shaking her head, she says, "I would be embarrassed to have people see me sweating like that."

"On the contrary, I'd say the hard work has brought some colour to her cheeks. She looks very attractive." I watch Nora shake hands with a latecomer.

When I see who she's greeting, my heart stills briefly, then begins to pound. It's Paz Castillo—one of the worst human beings I've ever had the displeasure of knowing. "What is he doing here?"

"I assumed you knew Paz would be here," Carolina says. "He's one of the contestants. In fact, he's favoured to win."

"Of course he is," I mutter, my gut hardening at the sight of Nora laughing at whatever it is he just said. "Markos, did you know he'd be here?"

"I assumed he would. Did you not watch the videos of last year's competition that Carolina sent us?"

"No."

He gives me a smug smile "Well, this is a first. I'm actually more prepared than the great Theo Rojas for once."

"By all means, gloat about it," I tell him, narrowing my eyes as Paz leans into Nora and brushes something off her shoulder. I'm sure there was nothing, and it was an excuse to touch her. Her eyes light up and her cheeks redden more than they already were. "Someone needs to put a stop to that."

"To what, people talking at a mixer?" Markos asks.

"He's not talking. He's laying the groundwork to turn Ms. Cooper into one of his victims."

At that exact moment, Paz glances around and spots me staring at him. Our eyes lock, and he looks slightly taken aback (as he should) before returning his attention to Nora.

"Oh, come off it, Theo," Markos says. "Paz may have been a screw-up when he was younger, but he's worked hard to get himself together these last few years. He's really made a go of this whole bartending thing."

"It's true," Carolina adds. "He came in second last year and got a contract to come up with a cocktail menu for some big chain of restaurants in the US."

I open my mouth, ready to make my real objections to Paz known, but remind myself I've been sworn to secrecy. "I don't care what he's done lately. He's not to be trusted. In fact, if we're going to have trouble with anyone over the next few weeks, it'll come from him."

"You know, it wouldn't kill you to have a little faith in humanity, Theo. People do change," Markos says.

"I'll believe it when I see it."

Carolina and Markos exchange a look, then she sets her flute down on a nearby table. "I feel rude not going over to say hello."

"I'll come with you." Markos follows Carolina over to the other side of the pool, leaving me alone with my thoughts—none of them worth entertaining.

Snatching a margarita off a passing tray, I pull out the tiny black straw and toss it into Carolina's empty flute, then have a big swig. What was already a precarious situation has just gotten so much worse.

11

Is it Getting Hot Out Here?

Nora - Four Minutes Earlier...

"HE'S LOOKING AT YOU AGAIN," Kat says, glancing over her shoulder not-so-subtly at the Rum King.

"I really couldn't care less," I tell her, doing my best to look like I mean what I'm saying.

She gives me a knowing grin. "Sure you don't."

"Well, not for the reason you think," I say, straightening one of the few welcome bags still waiting to be picked up. She and I are at the reception table. Behind us the mixer is almost in full swing, and I have to say it is going well. Very well indeed. There's an air of excitement, the waitstaff are on top of everything, the decorations are festive and fun, with a hint of sophistication, and everyone has made a big fuss over the welcome bags—my idea.

All I have to do is make sure things run smoothly for two more hours, and when the party's over I can tell Theo Rojas to suck it because I am a professional who solves problems. I won't, but I'll have the satisfaction of knowing I could, and it would be true.

"If it's not for the reason I think, you must be blind because that man is hot with a capital hot damn. How could anyone in their right mind *not* want to go home with that?" Kat asks.

I close my eyes for a second. "Oh Kat, where did we go so wrong with you?"

"I'm not the one with something seriously wrong. You are. He cannot stop looking at you. If I had a man that fine—and that rich—giving me the eye like that, I'd be all over him like a heat rash."

"Because he's so hot?" I ask, even though I shouldn't encourage her.

"Uh, yeah."

"Okay, here's the thing. This is work. Think of all the people you work with like you would Uncle Dan."

"Ew."

"Exactly, ew. Second, he's a total jerk. He's probably staring because… I don't know… my face is too shiny for his liking or something. He's trying to decide if he should walk over to recommend a million-dollar face powder to fix my skin." Either that, or he's reveling in the fact that he's so all-powerful, he has the ability to make a woman run out and buy new clothes.

Unable to resist any longer, I glance back at him. He's dressed in another suit—jacket, tie, and all, even though it's about a thousand degrees out here. But does he look sweaty and uncomfortable, like he should? No. He looks put-together and cool as a cucumber, while I'm standing here sweating in this stupid silk dress. Why the hell did I wear silk tonight? His eyes land on mine before I can tear my gaze from him, and I feel my cheeks warm as the two of us play a game of chicken—whoever looks away first loses.

Mike the Moose, the Canadian contestant I greeted earlier, strolls over, forcing him to turn away. *Ha! I win, sucker.*

When I turn back to the table I'm greeted by a pair of green eyes and a smile that could melt a nun's resolve. The rest of him is equally impressive—muscles on muscles, thick, long chestnut hair that falls around his shoulders, but not scraggly long, like a lot of men have. This guy must use conditioner, judging by how easily he slid his hand through it and tossed it out of his face just now. He's wearing a fitted burnt orange T-shirt, distressed jeans, and a puka shell necklace. The whole look screams "totally relaxed surfer dude who understands what really matters in life."

Next to me, Kat makes a little squeaking noise, and for once in my life, I totally understand her reaction. He grins at both of us. "Hi, ladies. I'm Paz."

"Hi," Kat says, her voice nearly a whisper.

I snap out of a quick fantasy of running my hands through his luscious locks. "I'm Nora, the events coordinator for your event." *Oh, come on. Events coordinator for your event?*

"My event?" he asks, looking slightly confused.

"The competition. I work for the resort. I'm the events coordinator," I tell him. "Well, *one* of the events coordinators. And you are Paz Castillo. You came in second last year and are favoured to win this time around. You do that extra flip that sets you apart from the other competitors. Well done on that, by the way." *Stop now, Nora. Just stop.* "Anything you need, you just let me know. I'm your woman. Well, not *your* woman, obviously, just a woman who likes to help." *Seriously! Stop NOW!* "Welcome to Paradise Bay."

I can feel Kat staring at me in disbelief. *Yeah, Kat, that's how smooth your big sister is when it comes to the men folk. You better take notes.*

Paz doesn't seem put off, however. He's still smiling. "A fellow service industry pro. Nice."

He swings his lethal attention to Kat, who looks like she might melt right where she's standing. "Hi, I'm Paz."

"Kat," she manages.

"Cute name. Are you a fellow service pro?" he asks, and there's something about the way he asks that makes it sound a bit dirty. But it's probably my imagination, because my subconscious wants everything he says to be a bit dirty. *Bad, Nora, bad.*

"I'm an intern." She bats her lashes. "My big sister got me the job." She points to me.

"Sisters? Nice."

He glances at the remaining name tags, then picks up the one meant for him. Peeling the back off, he sticks it over his right pec, then flexes his chest so it dances a little. Kat and I both laugh like a couple of simpletons. "I better go size up the competition," he says with a wink.

"Don't forget your welcome bag." Kat fans her hand at them.

"Oh, cool." Looking inside, he adds, "Say, can I leave mine here and pick it up at the end? I hate walking around, carrying stuff."

"You're in the wrong job then," I say, putting on a funny voice.

It takes him a minute to get it, then his eyes light up. "Right! Because I'm a bartender. Good one."

"Thanks," I tell him, oddly proud of a joke no one laughed at.

He looks around the pool deck and his expression changes from totally relaxed to looking like he's just seen those two creepy girls from *The Shining*. I follow his gaze, only to see it's Theo Rojas he's looking at. The Rum King is staring right back with a scowl. They lock eyes for a second, then Paz lifts his chin in acknowledgment. Theo, however, does not return the gesture. Instead, he turns away, jaw set.

"Is everything okay?" I ask, hoping my question will lead him to spill the tea on what that was all about.

"Yes," he says, recovering quickly. "I better go mingle. It was lovely to meet you both, Kat, Nora."

Nuts. He didn't bite.

"See you around," Kat calls after him.

The pair of us watch Paz stride over to a group of other contestants, all of whom welcome him with loud displays of excitement.

"He's clearly the alpha," Kat tells me.

Gawking at him, I say, "Oh yeah."

"Still thinking of all the people at work like you do Uncle Dan?"

I snort out a laugh. "Okay, maybe Paz gets a pass, but *only* in our imaginations. In his case, we can look, but we cannot touch." I point a warning finger at her.

"When did you get to be so old and boring?"

"The day I paid my first month's rent."

I leave Kat at the welcome desk with strict instructions to stay put and make my way around the perimeter of the party, checking to make sure everything's running well. I probably don't have to do this. The staff knows what they're doing, and there's nothing extra difficult about what we're doing. In part I'm savoring the moment, allowing myself the smug satisfaction of knowing I set this up, and it's a raving success.

If only my bosses were here to see how smoothly everything runs under my watch. I entertain a fantasy of Libby appearing, taking in all my glorious preparation, then gushing over how amazing everything looks, and how I thought of every detail, when I hear him behind me. The man I love to hate.

"Ms. Cooper, hello."

Stopping my eyes mid-roll, I face him, phony smile in place. "Hello."

He stares at me for a moment too long before he says anything, probably taking note of clumps in my mascara or something. Jerk. Glancing around, he says, "You've created a very nice evening for everyone."

"Thanks. It's not my first rodeo so..."

Theo gets a little twinkle in his eye. "Yes, I know. You are a professional problem solver. You solve *all* the problems."

I sort of want to laugh, but I hold it in, only allowing a tiny upward curve of my lips to escape. "That's the queen problem solver to you."

He smiles down at me, and dammit, if it's not one of those "could light up the whole world" smiles. Talk about unfair. A man that rich, young, and powerful also in possession of a smile like that. Ugh. I hate him so much.

"What's your first impression of the group?" he asks. "Do you think we're going to run into any problems?"

Asking my opinion. That's slightly flattering. "Hard to say. I imagine they're all highly competitive. Hopefully that means they'll be so busy practicing they won't have time to get into any trouble."

"Let's hope so," he answers, concern written all over his face. "Anyway, Carolina and I would like to give a quick speech to welcome everyone."

"Yes, of course. When you're ready, I'll get you a microphone and ask the band to take a quick break."

"I'm ready."

Of course His Highness wants to do it now. "Perfect. I'll be right back."

12

Cock-blockers of the World Unite

Theo

CHECKING MY WATCH, I see that Ms. Cooper has been gone for nearly ten minutes, and I find myself getting increasingly irritated, because the longer we wait to make our remarks, the more out-of-control this party is getting. We probably should have done it already, based on how quickly the booze is flowing.

At least the sun has almost finished setting, so soon I won't feel like I'm being roasted alive. Carolina is nearby, chatting up one of the showrunners at X-Stream, while I scan the crowd for Ms. Cooper. My eyes land on Paz Castillo, who is cozying up to one of the young staffers—the one who brought the flowers to my room the day I got here. I'm instinctively bothered by the sight of her laughing as he leans in, and I make a mental note to tell Ms. Cooper to warn her off him.

Eleven minutes. How long can it take to find a microphone?

She finally appears, snaking her way through the crowd towards me. Her long skirt shifts with every step in a way I find hypnotic. When I manage to force my eyes up to her face, I find myself hoping she'll glance up at me and smile. But she doesn't smile. She gives me a terse nod instead. Why the hell did I say that awful thing about her being dowdy and poorly dressed? There's really no coming back from that, is there?

"Sorry that took so long. I had to go to one of the maintenance buildings to have the sound system turned on," she says when she reaches me. "Would you like to stand where the band is? It'll make it easier to keep everyone's attention."

"If that's even possible at this point," I answer, gesturing to a woman and a man who look very close to launching into some PDA.

"Oh dear," Nora says. "Let's go."

I gesture to Carolina, who nods, and I follow Ms. Cooper, itching to rest my hand on the small of her back. But of course I don't. That would be not only inappropriate, but ridiculous as well. This is a work function. I'm trying to set an example. I have no interest in dating at the moment. Oh, right, and she hates me.

When we reach the stage, we wait until the band plays the last bars of Marley's "Stir it Up," then she tells them to take a break for my speech. "Would you like to start or should I?" I ask Carolina.

"You go. I'll follow your lead," she says with a toothy grin. Hmm... if I'm not mistaken, she's had a few drinks already.

I switch on the microphone and my heart starts to pound. I hate public speaking. All those people staring at me, waiting for me to say something intelligent, or worse, hoping I screw up. I lift the mic to my mouth. "Good evening, everyone." I wait a beat for people to realize what's going on, but it's not working, so I repeat myself.

When that doesn't work, Nora sticks her fingers in her mouth and emits an ear-piercing whistle that makes anyone within twenty feet wince. It works though, because silence falls, and the crowd is now facing the right direction. I glance at Nora, holding the mic away from my mouth. "Problem solved."

She blushes and actually smiles, which gives me an unexpected lift.

Forget that, you idiot. Make your speech already. "I'm Theo Rojas, president of Rojas Rum. With me is Carolina Armas. Most of you probably know her as head of X-Stream TV. Carolina was kind enough to bring Rojas in on this year's event, and I must say we could not be more excited." We couldn't be less excited either, but... "On behalf of my brother Markos, who is here somewhere, and all the employees of Rojas, I'd like to welcome you to the thirteenth annual World Bartending Championships." Pause for applause. "I've had a chance to watch videos of previous competitions, and I must say that what you do is incredibly impressive. You have managed to turn serving drinks into a real sport. The dexterity, knowledge, and skills you possess are remarkable." More applause. "Onto business. In order to keep things running smoothly and direct the focus where it should be—on the skills of this year's competitors—Ms. Armas and I would like to set some ground rules."

Groans can be heard, so I hold up one hand and nod. "Yes, I know rules are never considered fun, but if we respect them, much fun can be found within them." Huh, it only took me thirty-six years to sound like every high school principal in every movie ever. "With the advent of social media, we need to be careful about what gets posted. Most of the competitors here are hoping to score a contract with a large restaurant chain or secure funding for your nightclub or pub. With that in mind, we want you to consider yourselves to be at work while you are here and conduct yourselves accordingly."

"Have you ever been to a bar?" a guy at the back calls. "Because that's where we work, and it's pretty much anything goes!"

This earns him a laugh. Oh great, I'm losing them. "That may be the case, but I can tell you investors are looking for people who take their careers seriously."

"I'm here to beat everyone, so I can take a year off and surf my way around the world on my winnings," a burly man with a shaved head yells.

Another voice in the crowd follows that with, "Leave me alone, God!" and snickers can be heard from every direction.

Oh perfect.

Carolina takes the microphone from me and says, "Very funny, but Mr. Rojas is trying to give you advice that could carry you through life. In the years since we started this competition, the title generally goes to the most determined, most disciplined person. My staff at X-Stream TV understands our code of conduct applies at *all times*. Even if we find ourselves in a romantic tropical setting, all the regular rules apply while we're here."

Low grumbling follows, but she's not getting heckled, so she continues. "Physical relationships will not be tolerated. As you all know, you're under strict orders not to post anything on social media or tell anyone about the results of the challenges, as the last thing we want is spoilers. You may post on social media about the resort or anything unrelated to the competition, but having said that, before you hit that submit button, ask yourself if it will elevate your image *and* that of the competition on the world stage, or will it do damage. If you're not sure, don't do it."

She continues on while I stand next to her, feeling as useless as nipples on a bull. Markos sidles up to me and whispers in my ear, "Maybe you should have left this to me."

"You think they'd listen to you?" I hiss.

Keeping his gaze straight ahead, he mutters, "Yes, because I wouldn't have come off like a dictator. That's not the way to get this group to comply."

"Thanks. That information would have been useful to me earlier."

"I didn't know you were giving a speech."

"How could you *not* have guessed that?"

He shrugs. "I don't know. I didn't think of it."

My attention returns to Carolina, who is wrapping up with, "Our competitors have the day off tomorrow, so make sure you use it wisely. My crew will meet in Conference Room A in our building at nine o'clock tomorrow morning. It'll be a full day of work, so make sure you eat some breakfast first so you're ready to roll right at nine." She glances at me and lowers the microphone. "Do you have anything to add?"

I shake my head, wishing I were back in the solitude of my room. Better yet, alone at home.

"Oh, right. Where's Nicole?" she asks into the microphone. "Nicole Cooper, the events coordinator?"

"Her name is Nora," I whisper, as Nora (who is literally standing next to Carolina) steps forward.

"Right here," she says quietly.

Carolina says, "Nora, sorry. I want everyone to look at the woman next to me. Her name is Nora, and she's the point person for the hotel. Anything you need goes through her. Problems with your rooms, special meal requests, booking a practice session at the bar... all of that goes through her. She'll be set up in Building C in, what room, Nora?"

Nora has gone bright red. "I'll have a desk set up in the lobby of Building C so it'll be easy to find me."

"That's it. Enjoy the rest of your evening," Carolina says to the audience. "But not too much! We wouldn't want to give Mr. Rojas a heart attack."

Lots of laughter and applause at that one, and Carolina switches off the mic and hands it to Nora. "Sorry, couldn't resist. But it's fine. Really. We've established you as bad cop and me as good cop."

"Great."

"Uh-oh," Markos says, clapping a hand on my back. "He's going to pout about that one."

Shrugging him off, I say, "I do not pout."

He gives me a skeptical look, then loops his arm through Carolina's. "Come on, I want you to meet Lolita, one of the resort bartenders. She's the most sarcastic woman I've ever met. Also, I want another drink."

The two of them go off together, leaving me alone with Ms. Cooper, who gives me a sympathetic look. "That couldn't have gone worse."

"Oh, I think it could have," she answers.

"How?"

She snaps her fingers. "You could have thrown up or tripped and fallen into the pool."

I smirk. "Barring those two unlikely events, it couldn't have gone worse. They hate me, and I'm not sure if you know this, but I'm here to make Rojas Rum cool with the younger crowd." I'm not sure why I'm telling her this, but I can't seem to stop. "You know, since James Prescott pretty much killed our reputation with the older generation, otherwise known as our regular customers."

Her face falls. "Oh. In that case, maybe let your brother handle the speeches from now on. And… the general face time stuff with people."

"I'm that bad, am I?" I ask, feeling utterly deflated.

"Not really. Although, you'd probably play better to a more mature audience. Like people your own age."

Wincing, I ask, "How old do you think I am?"

"I'd put you as a young-looking forty."

"Forty? Jesus, it's worse than I thought."

"You're not forty then?"

"Far from it. I'm thirty-six."

"So I was off by four years," she says, trying to hide a smirk.

"Four years is a lot, thank you very much," I answer, finding myself grinning back despite myself.

"Huge difference. Huge."

"How old are you?"

"Twenty-eight."

"Huh. I had you pegged at about twenty-four." Ha! See how she likes it.

"Thank you," she says, preening a little.

"That was supposed to bother you."

She wrinkles her nose. "Have you met women before? We like having people think we're younger than we are."

"I should have said I thought you were my age."

"Sure, if you wanted to get punched in the throat."

I burst out laughing, finding myself having fun for the first time since…well, I don't know when.

Nora laughs too, then says, "I should get the band off their bar stools so they can get back to playing."

"Of course."

"Have a nice evening." She spins on her heel and walks away.

As I watch her go, a thought pops into my head. *I just was, and it was all because of you.*

———

"What are you doing?" Markos asks, scaring the shit out of me.

I drop the small pad of paper I've been using to check off who has returned to their rooms. Scrambling, I pick it up before Markos can see what I've written on it, then resume my position at the door, one eye staring through the peephole. "Nothing."

"What is that, a logbook?" He snatches the pad from my hand. After a quick look, he says, "*Dios mío*, you're keeping watch in case one of the contestants invites a guest back to their room."

Grabbing the pad back, I say, "Not just the bartenders. The guys on the television crew seemed just as horny."

"So your plan is to stay up all night for two weeks to make sure no one gets lucky?"

I give him the stink eye. "I didn't come all this way to sleep my way through whatever scandal is about to drop."

"People can—and do—have sex during the day, you know."

"Yeah, but we've put the fear of God into them. They'll be more careful during the day." Thinking I hear something, I press my left eye up to the peephole again. "If something bad is going to happen, it'll be late at night."

"I see, and how long do you think you can keep this up?"

"Indefinitely. I figure most of the bad ideas will come before four a.m. I can get by on two hours of sleep, so I should be able to mitigate ninety-five percent of the risks and still manage my day. By the way, what are you doing up? I heard you come back to your room three hours ago."

His head snaps back. "Are you tracking me as well?"

"No, but I happen to have a good memory for these things. Why are you still up? You don't have a woman in there, do you?"

"No, I don't have a woman in there. My brother is the world's biggest cock blocker, so I can't." He yawns. "I was trying to sleep, but someone in the adjoining room keeps opening and closing his door."

"Sorry, I'll try to keep it down."

"Thanks. Look, I don't think this is the answer to your problems."

"Why not?"

"First off, you'll be crazy with paranoia by the time we leave." He stands at the peephole and squints his left eye. "Second, you can't see much through this thing. You're basically missing the far end of the hallway."

"I don't need to see down there. I can hear the elevator doors open and close from here. When that happens, I open the door and stick my head out."

"You seriously don't get how insane you sound, do you?" Markos asks.

"Do you have a better idea?"

"Yes, as a matter of fact, I do," he says, letting out a wide yawn.

"Like what? Hiring a security team to patrol the halls?"

Raising one eyebrow at me, he says, "Sure. While you're at it, give them military uniforms, including helmets with spikes on top."

"Are you calling me a Nazi?"

"Yes, except you're anti-sex instead of antisemitic. I said I had a better idea, but you didn't give me a chance to give it to you."

"Fine. Tell me."

Rubbing his face, he says, "You should get to know everyone. Hang out with them, be friendly. That way, you'll have a heads up if something is about to go down."

"That'll never work. First of all, I'm not good at making friends. Second, everyone knows I don't want them hooking up. They're not going to tell me anything."

"Good point. Your speech this evening undoubtedly left an impression," Markos says. "Why not leave this to me? I'll keep an eye on people, see what I can find out as far as scandalous activities go."

I give him a hard look. "I can't tell if you're making fun of me or not."

"Honestly, I'm not sure if I am either," he says. "It's three in the morning, Theo, and you're acting like a crazy person. On the other hand, I badly want to make up for the damage James caused to our company, so…"

"So you're willing to act as a spy?"

"It goes against all my core values, but in this case, I'm willing to be your cock-blocking wingman. I can tell you that nothing nefarious is going to happen tonight, so we might as well get some sleep."

"How do you know for sure?"

"Because I was the last one at the party, and everyone was far too loaded to be capable of hooking up." He pats me on the back. "Go to bed, Theo."

"Fine, but you better not be wrong about this."

"I'm not." He returns to his room and closes the adjoining door.

I stand at the door for another minute, glancing out at the empty hallway, then decide he's right. It is far too late at night for booty calls. I shut off my light and grope around in the dark until I get to my bed, knowing that no matter how crazy my brother thinks this is, I'm doing what must be done to save our company. That must be my singular focus for the next two weeks. Except when I climb in and lay my head on the pillow, the last thing my mind's eye sees before I drift off is Nora Cooper's lovely face.

13

And the Plot Thickens

Nora

IT'S TUESDAY AFTERNOON, and I'm seated at my new desk in the lobby of Building C, heart racing. A certain handsome, friendly, charming bartender has booked the two o'clock slot at the practice bar. This means he'll be strolling over to my desk in a few minutes, asking me to let him into the Captain Cook Ballroom, which has been set aside for the competitors to use as a practice space. I smooth my skirt for the millionth time, even though it doesn't need it. I spent way too long getting ready this morning, and all that hard work had better pay off, because, let's face it, I haven't felt butterflies in my stomach about a guy in a very long time.

Paz is everything a man should be. He's not only handsome and charming, but he's clearly ambitious, judging by how far he's come in his chosen career. There are millions of bartenders in the world, but only a few of them have risen to the top and made this into both an art form and a competitive sport. Paz is going places in life, and I know it sounds nuts, but I may or may not have entertained a fantasy of him choosing Santa Valentina Island as the perfect place to set up his flagship bar—assuming he wins the competition and all the money that comes with it. But even if he doesn't win, maybe he'll decide he fancies someone here (okay, me) enough to stay. He'd be a shoo-in to work at the resort if he wants to.

But I'm getting *way* ahead of myself. After all, he and I only had one conversation, the night we met. I wasn't here when he came to book his practice time, so Kat helped him out. Whenever we see each other in passing, which has happened exactly four times since he got here, he always makes a point of saying something deliciously flirty. Yesterday, when he walked through the lobby, he was with some of the other guys, and he pointed to me and said, "There she is, the most stunning woman on the planet." Just like that. In *front* of his friends.

Wistful sigh.

Checking the time, I see Paz should be arriving any minute. I look over at Kat, who is deeply engrossed in a text conversation. Not wanting her to tag along, I pick up a folder that's been waiting on my desk all day to be returned to Rosy. I walk the three steps over to Kat's makeshift desk, which is a small folding table and a chair from one of the ballrooms. "I need you to take this to the main lobby and leave it for Rosy, okay?"

Without looking up, she says, "Now?"

"That would be the idea, yes. Then, if you want, you can knock off early."

That got her attention. Her eyes light up and she shoots out of her chair. Grabbing her handbag, she tosses her phone in and starts towards the front door, stopping only when I call, "The folder!"

Spinning on her heel, she zips back and picks it up. "And this is going to Libby."

"Rosy."

"Got it," she says, already halfway out the door. "Have a great night!"

As soon as she leaves, I pull my compact and lipstick out of my purse, checking to make sure I'm not too shiny, then touching up my lips. I smack them together, check my teeth for errant lipstick, then throw my beauty supplies back into my purse just as the doors slide open, revealing Paz. Today he's dressed in flip-flops, board-shorts, and a fitted white tank top that affords anyone who looks his way the treat of seeing his muscly torso.

Flashing me his gorgeous smile, he says, "Hey, beautiful. Should we do this?"

Yes. Yes, we should. My entire body heats up as I open the top desk drawer and grab the master card key and head for the ballroom. I'm feeling a little self-conscious until he catches up with me, wondering if maybe he was checking me out in this form-fitting skirt (or worse—wasn't checking me out). Just as we pass the bank of elevators, one of them opens, and Theo Rojas strides out, dressed in yet another boring suit. He sees me and a smile crosses his face before he glances at who I'm walking with. Immediately the smile is replaced with a look of utter contempt, and my curiosity to know what that's all about pops back into my mind.

Nodding at me, he says, "Ms. Cooper, I trust you're having a good day."

"Very," I say a little coldly.

Without bothering to acknowledge Paz, Theo jams his hands into the front pockets of his dress slacks and makes for the exit.

Paz and I continue down the hall, and when we are safely out of Theo's earshot, he says, "Have you had the misfortune of working closely with Rojas?"

"Not too closely, but definitely too much already. I take it you know each other."

"Unfortunately, I know him very well, which is probably surprising to you, based on how he greeted me just now."

"Or didn't greet you." I give him a pointed look, as I hold up the card key. I push the door open and flick on the lights, then lead Paz over to the bar area.

"I grew up with him," he says. The look of astonishment on my face has him adding, "It's more accurate to say grew up *around* him. My father worked for his father. He was an accountant, and the two of them were good friends. Mr. Rojas Senior invited my family to their beach house on holidays and for any large family gatherings. I spent more time with their family than mine." He moves behind the bar and picks up a full rum bottle, which has been filled with water, flips it high into the air, then deftly catches it.

"Wow!" I plant myself on one of the stools at the bar.

"Wow about what I just did, or wow that I grew up with Rojas?"

"Both. I can't imagine why he would be so rude to you. After having spent time with him, I understand why anyone would want to steer clear of *him*, but seriously, who wouldn't like *you*?"

"Theo, that's who." He lines up eight shot glasses and fills them all without stopping or spilling a drop on the counter. "When I was fifteen, my dad suffered a massive heart attack. He died in Mr. Rojas's office. Mr. Rojas took me under his wing. He even offered to pay for my university education, only he passed away before I graduated high school."

"So Theo refused to honor his dad's wishes?" Anger bubbles up inside me.

"He told me I was mistaken and that his father never intended to help me out that way."

"That's just awful. What would it have been to him?" I ask.

"Nothing, whereas for me, it would've meant everything." He pauses, then gives me a level look. "You know how mechanics rarely service their own cars?"

"I've heard that before, yes," I say, finding myself leaning towards him.

"Turns out my father, the accountant, didn't bother getting life insurance. Instead of going off to school and becoming a lawyer, which is what I really wanted to do, I had to support my mother and younger sister." He picks up the bottle again, flips it into the air, spins around, then catches it.

"So, that's when you got into tending bar?"

Nodding, he says, "It hasn't been all bad."

Fury builds inside me as I digest his story. Who could be so cruel? "That's only because you've managed to turn it into something really incredible through hard work and determination."

"I always say, whatever you're going to do in life, be the best at it. Does that sound silly to you? I do know I'm only a bartender."

"That doesn't sound silly to me at all," I say, shaking my head.

"It's not like my job would be considered very important by a lot of people, but I agree. There's no sense in doing anything unless you're going to do the best you can and move up in your field. I'm actually being considered for a big promotion."

"Really?" he asks, pouring out the shots of water into the sink and creating a pyramid out of the glasses.

"Yes, the resort owners are looking to expand the scope of the events that we handle here. They're going to hire more coordinators, and they'll need someone to manage the team. I've been told that if things go well with this competition, they're looking at me for the job."

"Congratulations, Nora. That's very impressive." He stops long enough to look into my eyes.

"I wish everyone shared your opinion."

Tossing the bottle behind his back, it comes down in front of his face, and he catches it. "Let me guess, your parents had different ideas for your life?"

"They wanted me to go farther in my education than I did. I stopped after I got my business diploma, whereas they would have preferred I was still working my way towards a PhD."

"In what?"

"Theology. They're both pastors. They run the Benavente United Church in San Felipe."

"Really? So you're a preacher's kid. I would not have guessed that."

The look on his face is melting me, starting at my heart and going directly to my lady bits. "What would you have guessed?"

He glances at the ceiling as if considering his answer. "I would've guessed your father was a dentist and your mother was a swimsuit model." His eyes sweep over me, and a surge of warmth moves through me.

"Hardly. But even if that were true, I would definitely have taken after my dentist father."

"You're selling yourself short, Nora," he says, his face growing serious. "You're hot, and don't you forget it."

I watch him for the next forty-five minutes, completely forgetting about all the work piled up on my desk. What he's doing is utterly hypnotic and impressive. It's like I'm getting my own magic show, only not by some creepy magician. My heart aches when I think about him losing his father at such a young age and the deep sense of betrayal he must have felt—and probably still feels today—when Theo ripped his dreams away. When he finishes, he places the wet cups on a drying rack and wipes down the bar top with a rag. "Well, I think I'm as ready as I'm going to get for tomorrow."

A sense of disappointment comes over me because I know our time together has to end. He's going off to do whatever it is he does when he is not practicing, and I have to get back to my desk. We walk side by side across the ballroom.

"Hey, Nora, thanks so much for listening to me. I rarely talk about what happened with anyone, and it feels good to know you understand."

"I just can't believe he did that to you. I mean, obviously, I *believe* it. He's pretty much exactly what you'd expect someone who was born as rich as he was to be: demanding, critical, and unpleasant. But what he did to you, well, that's just plain evil."

"I can't help but see it that way." He pushes the door open and waits for me to exit first. "But the truth is, there's no sense in me dwelling on any of it. I can't change what happened, so I'm making the best of the life I have."

"That's very admirable of you," I tell him. "I think I'd be angry every day of my life if I were you."

"No, then he wins."

"Good point." I stare up at him for a second, then ask, "But why would he refuse to help you out? After all those years of you being part of his family?"

"I think *that* was the problem to be honest. He never really liked how close I was to his father, especially after I lost mine."

"So he needed to not only be rich and have everything handed to him on a silver platter, he also needed to have his father's undivided attention?"

"I think he did. Mr. Rojas Senior was such an open and giving man when it came to his time as well as his money. Maybe Theo never felt like he got enough of him."

"Well, regardless, you'd think as a grown man, he would set aside such pettiness and do the right thing."

"You'd think so, but apparently not everyone is capable of doing the right thing." When we reach my desk, Paz rakes a hand through his long hair. "Anyway, if you could keep all that stuff I told you between the two of us, I would appreciate it."

"Of course. I promise I won't say a word to anyone, although I *am* tempted to tweet at Rojas Rum about his awful behavior. Let the world see who he really is."

Chuckling, Paz says, "Thank you for being in my corner."

"And in your corner I shall stay. If you need anything at all while you're here, please pop by." *Please, please pop by.*

"Thanks Nora, I will." He smiles down at me, turning me completely to jelly. "I better let you get to work. I know how busy you are."

He strides out the door, leaving me with my tongue hanging out as I watch him walk away. Why is it that the good guys of the world never seem to come out ahead? Especially since nothing bad ever seems to happen to spoiled, entitled billionaires who think themselves far superior to everyone they meet. If only his dad hadn't passed away. Or if Mr. Rojas Senior, who sounds lovely, hadn't. Paz would have had a completely different life. My heart aching, I sit at my desk and turn on my laptop. As it boots up, I find myself wishing that karma would come for Theo Rojas in a big, bad way, because *that* is what he deserves.

———

TO-DO LIST (Home Version)

Laundry – rewash musty load AND DRY IT IMMEDIATELY!

Clean out bathroom drawers for real this time

Vacuum floors

Get rid of dead plants (including the fern that could have easily been saved from fungus with $0.99 worth of vinegar)

14

Just What a Guy Needs...a Lying Scoundrel Making Me Look Worse Than I Already Do

Theo

"To RECAP, I'll make sure Diana has the quarterly reports to you by tomorrow night, it's a solid no to Carlos's birthday party, with your apologies, and I'm to arrange a gift to send him," Jaquell says, leaning closer to her laptop and squinting at me. "Now, are you ready to tell me what's wrong with you yet? You've been off your game for two days."

"I'm just tired." I sit back in my chair. "I've been staying up late to keep an eye on the contestants and crew." I don't bother telling her I'm keeping a log of when people go back to their rooms for the night.

Jaquell stares for a second, then says, "That's not it. You can function on two hours of sleep without anyone noticing. Something is clearly bothering you. Do you want to talk about it today, or do you want to stew over it a little longer and tell me later?"

I stop just short of rolling my eyes and let out a sigh. "Did you know Paz Castillo is here?"

A look of understanding crosses her face. Jaquell is the only person who knows what happened. "I see."

"He's one of the competitors actually."

"Since your stepmother isn't there, I suppose he can't do the family too much harm, can he?"

Nora's face pops into my mind, as it has repeatedly since I saw them walking down the hall together. She was lit up with hope, which is the last thing anyone should have around that scoundrel. "I'm not worried about us, but there's a young woman who works here. I think he might be trying to get his claws into her."

She tilts her head and pauses for a beat before answering. "This concern of yours, could it be because you might be interested in her?"

The word yes pops into my mind, shocking the hell out of me, but I shake my head. "Of course not. It's just been jarring to see him, and as far as I can tell, she's a good person. I don't think she deserves to be put through the hell he put Alaina through."

"I'm sure she doesn't, but is she really at risk? If she works at a hotel, I doubt she's loaded with cash."

Nodding, I say, "I suppose you're right. Anyway, it's none of my business, and it shouldn't bother me to begin with."

"True. You have bigger fish to fry."

"On that note, I will let you go and get on with business."

We ring off, then I push back from my desk and cross the tile floor to the balcony. Staring out at the pool below, I see my brother standing in the water, waist-deep, sipping some pink drink while he chats up a couple of hotel guests.

"Oh, to have his life instead of mine," I mutter and return to my desk.

After an hour of answering emails, I decide to go for a stroll and find a bite of lunch. I'm also hoping to run into Nora and find some way to warn her about Paz without saying too much. After stuffing the card key in my pocket, I hurry out of the room, not bothering to put on my suit jacket or tie. When the elevator door opens on the main floor, I notice my heart rate picking up a little. A sense of disappointment comes over me when I see that Nora's not at her desk. Exiting the building, I take the path to the hamburger shack adjacent to the beach bar.

What I need is an excuse, a reason to talk to her in the first place, then hopefully I can find an in to casually bring up Paz. As I pass the pool, I give Markos a quick wave. He salutes me in return… and that will conclude the sum total of his work today.

My eyes pass over the pool bar, and suddenly I see the answer I've been seeking, lined up neatly on the shelf behind the bartender. It's the perfect excuse to talk to Nora. I just have to find her.

When I arrive at the beach bar, I see a group of three contestants standing behind it, wowing the guests with their skills. Nora is among them. I take my opportunity and walk over to her. Coming to stand next to her, I offer her a smile, and I get a scowl in return. I have a sneaking suspicion Paz has shared a wildly inaccurate account of our history.

"Mr. Rojas, did you need something?"

"Do you have a few minutes to talk?"

"Right now is good, if you'd like to come back to my desk with me."

"I'm also in search of lunch. Do you mind coming with me while I order a burger?"

"Of course not," she says.

We start off in the direction of the hamburger shack, Nora moving swiftly along the wide path in her heels, in juxtaposition to the tourists strolling along in their flip-flops and floppy hats. She's all business today. "What can I do for you?"

"I was hoping you'd act as the contact person for all stock orders from Rojas during the competition."

"We have a beverage services manager for that. I'd be happy to pass his contact information to you."

"As our point person from the resort, it'll be much smoother on my end if you do it. I'd like to give your email address to my personal assistant, Jaquell Morales. She'll be given strict instructions that any orders placed by you are to be treated as top priority and will be filled immediately."

"Certainly," she says, offering me a tight smile. "I'd be happy to take care of that for you."

We arrive at the hamburger shack, and I'm certain she's about to drop me off and leave, so I say, "Would you care to join me for lunch?"

She looks taken aback, and I'm sure she's about to say no, so I add, "There's something else I was hoping to discuss with you."

"All right," she says without inflection.

After we order—a cheeseburger with fries for me and a burger with no bun and no fries for her—we sit at a table for two overlooking the beach. A thatched roof protects us from the sun.

Nora fidgets with the napkin dispenser, then looks at me expectantly. "Is everything okay with your room?"

"Yes, it's perfectly adequate for my purposes, thank you," I tell her.

"Good. How's your week going?"

"Busy. Yours?" *I'm dying. All I can think about is how pretty she looks in this light, when what I need to do is figure out a way to bring up Paz.*

"Same. I've been spending a lot of time helping set up practice sessions for the contestants."

Ah, here we go. We're getting closer... "Is that where you were taking Paz Castillo the other day?"

"Yes." Her cheeks turn pink. "I watched him for a while. He's extremely talented. Really great personality too. I think he's got a good shot at the title."

My jaw clenches, but I do my best to look relaxed. "I'm sure he does. He's definitely capable of turning on the charm, but there's not a lot of substance to back it up."

The server stops at our table with our meals. Setting them down, she gives Nora the eye, as in "is this a date?" to which Nora replies, "Ronnie, this is Mr. Rojas, the sponsor of the bartending competition. We're having a working lunch."

Ronnie offers me a grin, then says, "Pleasure to meet you. I just love Rojas Rummies."

"Thank you. They're quite popular among the younger crowd," I answer (i.e., people too lazy to mix their own drinks).

"It's just so nice that they're premixed for you."

"Exactly."

The entire time we're chatting, I can sense Nora's outrage at what I said about Paz, and I know as soon as Ronnie leaves, I'm going to get an earful.

After Ronnie hurries off, leaving us alone, I pour ketchup on my plate, dip a fry in, and pop it in my mouth. On her side of the table, Nora is furiously cutting up the burger patty, tomato, and lettuce with a fork and knife. She selects a bite, pops it in her mouth, and chews.

A few more angry bites later, she says, "Ronnie's parents died when she was seventeen. Car accident. So sad."

"That's awful," I answer. "I'm sorry to hear that."

"It is awful, isn't it?" she asks. "Not only did she lose her parents, but she also had to give up her dream of going to university to look after her little brother."

If she thinks I don't know where she's going with this, she's dead wrong. "Are they doing all right now?"

"Yes, but only because Harrison and Libby gave her this job and gave them a place to stay in staff housing. She works flexible hours, so she's taking some classes now."

"That's wonderful. They seem like such good people."

"They are," Nora says. "They're the salt of the earth. They value people over money. Rare quality these days." She gives me a pointed look.

"I agree. That's one of the reasons why we've never taken Rojas public. We don't want shareholder profits to become the only factor that matters when we're making decisions."

"*Hmph*," is all I get back.

"Nora, is there something you'd like to say to me? I get the feeling you're upset with me, and I really can't figure out why."

"Nope, I'm not upset. I was just relaying a story I find extraordinary. I mean, it's not like Harrison or Libby had *promised* to look after Ronnie before her parents died. They just decided it was the right thing to do."

"Yes, it's a lovely story, although the thing about stories is you have to be careful that the source is reliable. Not in this case, I'm sure, but in…other situations, where someone might have a lot to lose if the truth came out."

It's then that Nora's sister Kat rushes up to us, panting. "There you are."

"What's wrong?"

"You were supposed to let that guy from Guatemala into the practice room twenty minutes ago. I can't find the key anywhere."

"It's in the top drawer of my desk," Nora tells her, looking slightly panicked.

"Nope, I checked."

Sighing, Nora stands up. "Okay, let's go." Looking down at me, she says, "Excuse me."

"Of course."

She starts to walk away, and I find myself calling to her. "Nora."

When she turns, I say, "A little advice: don't mistake charm for truth."

Her head snaps back and she says, "A little advice for you: don't mistake your millions for good morals."

With that, she disappears down the path, leaving me without a doubt that whatever Paz told her makes me look like Satan himself.

15

Oh Nothing... Just Putting Out
Fires All Day

Nora

Email from Jaquell Morales, Rojas Rum Inc.
To: Nora Cooper
Subject Line: Alcohol Orders

Dear Ms. Cooper,

Mr. Rojas has asked me to reach out to you regarding Paradise Bay's alcohol needs during the filming of the competition. Please know that I will act immediately when I hear from you so as to ensure a steady flow of product for both the resort and the production team's needs. Attached is our standard order form. It's user-friendly and allows you to easily check for errors prior to placing your order.

My direct line and mobile phone numbers are listed below should anything urgent come up. I will be available to you twenty-four hours a day.

Warmest regards,
Jaquell Morales
Rojas Rum Inc.

5603 Gladstone Road, Nassau, The Bahamas
Direct Line: 242-555-8891
Mobile Phone: 242-554-9002

———

Email from Nora Cooper
To: Jaquell Morales
Subject Line: Re: Alcohol Orders

Dear Ms. Morales,

Thank you very much for the order form and your kind offer to be of help around the clock. I'm sure I won't need to reach out after hours, but it's comforting to know you're available should an emergency pop up.

All the best,
Nora

———

Email from: Nora Cooper
To: Fidel LeCroix, Beverage Services Manager, Paradise Bay Resort

Hey, Fidel,

How are Winnie and the kiddos doing these days? I hope all is well. I have a strange request from the folks over at Rojas Rum. They want me to be the point person on all orders coming from the resort until the competition is over. Strange, I know. They've provided me with their standard order form (attached).

If you want to use it, I can add the resort's order to the one needed for the competition and will send it immediately, as you need.

Please call me if you have any questions, and don't worry—I have no designs on your job. ;)

Nora

"WHAT's this about you trying to take over Fidel's job?" Oakley asks as soon as I walk into my office. "Fidel worked really hard to make his way up from bartender to beverage services manager, you know, and he's got a family to support."

Her voice is loud, immediately causing my cheeks to heat up.

"I'm not trying to take his job." I stride past her to my desk so I can get the stapler I came for. "Far from it."

"You sure?" she sneers, following me. "I know how power-hungry you are, so I thought maybe you were gunning for any management job you could find."

Letting out a loud sigh, I turn to her, stapler in hand. "Just because I'd like to advance in my career doesn't mean I'm power hungry, Oakley. And besides, this whole stupid ordering thing was a direct request from Theo Rojas. I could hardly say no."

She shrugs. "I would have stood up to him. Told him I wasn't willing to step on the toes of my fellow coworkers just to get ahead."

"Oh, you would have?" I ask sarcastically.

"Yes," she answers, sticking her chest out.

"Are you not aware that our job is to please the guests?" I spit out.

"A truly skilled events coordinator knows how to please the guests while still doing what's best for the resort. And in case you didn't know, *employees* are part of the resort."

"You know what? Since I've been working in Building C, I'd almost forgotten how awful you are. Not quite, but almost."

I turn and start towards the door, only to run into Rosy, who, based on the look on her face, heard what I just said. She folds her arms across her ample chest and lowers her chin at me. "Everything all right here?"

My stomach flips, and my skin prickles with shame. "Yes, fine. I just needed my stapler."

"Uh-huh," Rosy says, giving me the side-eye while I slink past her.

As soon as I get outside, tears prick my eyes, but I blink them back. There's no fixing what just happened. Rosy definitely heard me tell Oakley she's awful. That is not something a person with management potential would say.

But *come on*, that witch totally had it coming. Her sneer flashes through my mind. *What's this about you trying to take over Fidel's job? I know how power-hungry you are. A truly talented events coordinator knows how to please the guests while still doing what's best for the resort.*

Urgh! Could this day get any worse?

My phone pings, and when I see the email that just landed in my inbox, I have my answer.

Yes, my day can get worse…

Email from Carolina Armas
To: Nora Cooper
CC: Vincent St. Pierre (Senior Showrunner, X-Stream TV)

Subject: URGENT LIGHTING ISSUE REQUIRING IMMEDIATE SOLUTION

Dear Ms. Cooper,

Vincent has brought a serious matter to my attention regarding lighting. We will require your immediate assistance to sort this out before we begin filming.

Please meet us at the beach bar at ten a.m. and make sure you bring the head of maintenance.

Regards,
Carolina

———

Email from Nora Cooper
To: Carolina Armas
CC: Vincent St. Pierre (Senior Showrunner, XStream TV), Sergio Sánchez (head of maintenance, Paradise Bay Resort)

Subject: Re: URGENT LIGHTING ISSUE REQUIRING IMMEDIATE SOLUTION

Dear Ms. Armas,

I'm sure we can sort this out. I've cc'd Sergio Sánchez, the head of maintenance.

All the best,
Nora

———

Well, that's just craptastic. They start filming tomorrow so whatever's wrong has to be fixed like right freaking now, and there's no way Sergio is going to see the email. He's at his desk exactly once a month to put in his timecard. Otherwise, he's busy fixing things all over the resort.

I stand and tap Kat on the shoulder to get her attention. "There's a problem at the beach bar I have to deal with. I'm not sure how long I'll be, but Paz Castillo is booked for a practice session at ten-thirty, so I'll need you to stay here at the desk and let him into the ballroom, okay?"

Her eyes light up when she hears his name, and my gut clenches. She clearly has the same response to him I do, but she's *way* too young for Paz. "I won't move until he gets here."

"Just let him in and come right back to the desk in case someone else needs anything," I say firmly.

"Yup. Got it," she says, her eyes shifting to her phone again.

"I'm serious, Kat. I need you here."

Waving me off, she says, "And I'll be here."

I stalk out the door and get into the golf cart I've commandeered for the next few weeks, then take off in search of Sergio. While I zip down the path, I use the radio to call the front desk. "It's Nora. I need to find Sergio right away. There's a problem with one of the sets for the competition."

There's a short wait before anyone answers me—just long

enough to lament my bad luck. I thought I'd have another hour of one-on-one time with Paz, where, at the very least, I'd be able to just sit and stare at him, and at the very most, I could press him for more details about him and Theo. Okay, actually, at the very most, it would end with him kissing me passionately. Well, maybe not the kissing since I *do* like my job and want to keep it, and events manager candidates don't go around snogging guests. But *after* the competition, when he has fallen head over heels in love with me, we can do all of the passionate kissing our lips can handle.

The radio clicks, then I hear, "It's Rosy. Justin said he saw Sergio heading to Building A."

Her voice lacks its usual warmth, and I know she's totally pissed about what she heard me say to Oakley. There's no way I can explain what happened. I have no excuse for speaking to a coworker the way I did. That is most likely a serious strike against me as far as the promotion goes. My stomach tightens again, but I attempt to keep my tone light. "Thank you. I'm on my way. If anyone hears from Sergio or sees him in the meantime, please tell him he's needed at the beach bar by ten, then let me know, okay?"

"Will do," Rosy says flatly. "Over and out."

It takes me over half an hour to track Sergio down, and when I find him in one of the suites, he has one foot on a toilet seat and is plunging like there's no tomorrow. There's water all over the floor, and with every plunge, Sergio makes it worse. I stand at the entrance to the bathroom, feeling awful that I have to bug him at this moment.

"What happened?"

"The little girl staying here flushed her dad's toupee," he mutters. "I see where she was going with the idea, but there defi-nitely are better ways to dispose of something this big." He reaches in and yanks out the sopping toupee, then drops it into the bin. "What can I do for you?"

"I've been asked to bring you to a meeting—hopefully a quick one—about the lighting at the beach bar. It's with the production crew."

A look of disdain crosses Sergio's face. "I can't wait until that whole thing is over. Those guys are a total pain in my ass." Letting out a long sigh, he says, "Let's go."

On the way out of the building, he stops at a nearby room that is being cleaned and tells the chambermaid about the mess. She shuts her eyes for a second, then nods, and I realize that no matter what my day brings, it's sure as hell not cleaning up toilet water.

When we reach the beach bar, Vincent and Carolina are already there, along with a few crew members. Vincent is wearing a yellow fitted button-down and what looks like culottes in a funky lime green colour. They're staring at the bar as though hoping the answers to the mysteries of the universe are going to unfold before them.

Sergio gets out of his maintenance cart and goes over to them, the front of his pants still wet. I hurry to introduce him. "Hi, Vincent, Carolina. This is Sergio, our head of maintenance."

They look him up and down with pinched faces, then Vincent launches into all the problems the sun is creating for them in getting a "clean shot."

Sergio listens with his arms crossed and says nothing while Vincent rants, finally coming to the point. "So if we can just pick up the bar and flip it ninety degrees by tomorrow morning, that would be perfect."

"Can't be done," Sergio says. "Is there anything else? Because I'm busy."

You can actually see the colour rising in Vincent's face as he starts making odd puffing sounds. "Can't be done? That is *not* an answer."

"Yes, it is," Sergio says calmly. "We can't just turn the bar ninety degrees."

Vincent's head snaps back, causing his pompadour to come undone in front. It flaps wildly over his forehead as he shouts, "Why not?! It's not like it has *walls*."

"The plumbing and electrical are already in place. Do you know how long it would take to have everything rerouted?"

"Look, you, if we start now, I'm certain it can be done by morning," Vincent snaps, lifting his chin.

Sergio puffs out his chest and takes a couple of rather menacing steps forward. "It would take *weeks* to even get the permits for that. If you have a lighting problem, come up with a workaround."

"How?" Vincent yells, stamping his foot. "By magically blocking out the sun?"

Carolina stands next to me calmly, watching the scene play out as curious resort guests start to look over. I start to feel a bit panicky. I'm supposed to be the solution person, and I don't have the first clue how to solve this, but what I do know is we need to shut this show down before someone gets out their mobile phone and records what is brewing to be a very strange and likely comical physical altercation.

"Okay, okay," I say, raising my voice as I get between the two men. "Thank you, Serge. I'll take it from here."

He gives Vincent a long glare, then storms off while I do my best to look as though I know exactly what to do. "All right, Vincent, let's take a step back. Tell me what the ideal lighting conditions are for filming outside."

"How is that going to help? Are you a weather goddess or something?"

"No, but I'm a person who believes every problem has a solution. There has to be some way to create the conditions you need. What if we film only during certain hours of the day?"

"That would mean we'd be here for several months, and no offense, but I need to get the hell out of this place as soon as possible."

I don't like Vincent very much. I offer him an easy smile anyway. "Gotcha. So, let's go back to your suggestion of blocking out the sun. Maybe we can figure something out."

Pointing straight above his head, he yells, "The sun is way up there, and in case you hadn't noticed, it *moves!*"

"So we need something tall that we can move." I tap my chin with one finger, do a slow spin while I think, and when I'm facing the ocean, a sailboat in the distance catches my eye. "Like a sail from a yacht perhaps?"

"What are you going to do? Park a yacht on the pool deck?" Vincent scoffs. "Okay, genius."

"No, but what if we just use the sail? Maybe on wheels?"

Looking slightly deflated, Vincent says, "And where are you going to get a sail on such short notice?"

Harrison.

———

Four hours later, the main sail has been removed from the *Waltzing Matilda*, the Banks' family yacht. Sergio, Harrison, and a few of the crew members managed to rig up a makeshift rolling cart for it. Vincent, who went to lie down, and Carolina, who returned to her room to work, are just arriving back at the beach bar.

I know it's not time to take my victory lap yet, but this has got to help balance what happened this morning with Awful Oakley. Harrison, whom I doubt has talked to Rosy based on how friendly he's been to me today, told me he's very impressed by my ingenuity. *So there, Oakley! Suck on that.*

I can almost smell the salty air at my cottage... probably because I can actually smell the sea air, being only steps away from the beach, but still...

When Vincent gets out of the golf cart, his jaw drops. I smile. "Tall enough to block the sun and portable so it'll move where you need it to."

He rushes over to it, looking like he's going to kiss the sail. "You did it! I can't believe you did it."

Pointing to the people who did the work, I say, "They did it. I just thought of it."

He rushes over and gives me a big hug, then proceeds to shake hands with the rest of the group. I stand back and watch, feeling like I should be wearing a cape, because I feel a lot like Wonder Woman at the moment.

Carolina approaches me. "Well done. This is very good."

"Thanks. I'm glad I could help."

"I appreciate it. Vincent is wonderful at his job—extremely passionate—which is what makes him so brilliant. It also makes him challenging at times, but that's what it is to work with a genius."

I don't want to agree with her, so I say nothing.

After a moment, she says, "Listen, I know it's none of my business, but I understand you've been spending some time with Paz Castillo."

My cheeks flame, and I am instantly defensive. "No more than the other contestants, although Paz and I did have a lengthy conversation about how he ended up in his current profession."

"Oh yes, the whole attorney thing."

Of course she'd think being an attorney is low class. Everything must seem to be beneath you when you're born stinking rich. "A noble calling," I tell her. "If he hadn't had to support his family straight out of school."

"I'd caution you to take what Paz says with a grain of salt."

"Why?" I ask, sounding downright hostile.

"I don't know the exact details, but I do know that Theo had a serious run-in with him a few years ago. He's too much of a gentleman to gossip, but I've known Theo all my life, and I know him to be a man of honour. He cut ties with Paz for a very good reason."

What a shock. All the rich people sticking together to push the poor guy out of their inner circle. "I'm sure in Mr. Rojas's mind, it was justified. However, I have my doubts that those born in the top one percent are actually able to develop a true sense of justice, not when the entire world bends around them wherever they go."

Carolina looks taken aback, then makes a *tsk*ing sound. "Well, if that's your opinion of us, I'm not going to bother trying to change your mind. I only wanted to help."

She walks away before I can say anything, not that I would even know what to say. I stay rooted to the spot for a moment, too furious to go back to my desk. How dare these terrible rich people go around screwing people over, then gaslighting them everywhere they go? Someone should do it to them and see how much they like it.

I fume all the way back to Building C. When I get there, I expect to see a note from Kat, saying she left, but she's hurrying down the hall towards me with a goofy grin on her face. "What's so funny?" I ask.

"Just thinking of a thing I saw on TikTok. Did you manage to fix whatever crisis was happening?"

"I did," I tell her, my irritation replaced by a flash of pride. "Anything happen here while I was away?"

"No." She busies herself with her backpack. "I opened the ballroom for the contestants who came by. Other than that, nothing."

"Okay, thanks," I say dropping into my chair.

"I'm taking off. Have a good night."

"You too." I watch as she hurries out the door. A sense of foreboding comes over me. I know Kat, and she's definitely hiding something. The question is, do I really want to know what?

———

The Next Day

Email from Vincent St. Pierre
To: Nora Cooper
Subject: TOP SECRET!!! Today's Results

Nora,

I wanted to do you the courtesy of letting you know which competitors were struck from the competition today, in case they need some extra TLC in the coming weeks. As you know, we've asked all contestants to remain here until the competition ends so as to not tip off the media about who wins.
Aiden Ward of New Zealand and Paulo Souza of Brazil will no longer be participating, therefore they do not require—nor should they be allowed—access to practice spaces.

Best,
Vincent

———

Mike the Moose TikTok Reel

"Hey, all! It's Mike the Moose, coming to you poolside at the incredible *Paradise Bay Resort* on Santa Valentina Island." *Mike flips the camera around and scans the area before returning it to his smiling face.* "For those of you who have been in a coma or something, I'm here for the World Bartending Championships. Today was the first big day in our competition—they held the Speed Pouring and Free Pouring Accuracy Challenges, meaning we've lost two contestants already."

Pointing to his mouth, Mike says, "I'm not allowed to talk about who won and who went home, so I won't. I just wanted to check in with my Moose Heads and say that Mikey's thinking about you!

"I also have two competitors with me. They wanted to say hi to you."

Two more faces join Mike on screen. "You all know Ewan MacClary, or the *Ginger Beast,* as he's known around the globe. Say hi, Ginger."

"That's Ginger Beast, ya wee bawbag," *Ewan shouts.*

"What's a bawbag?" *the woman next to him asks in a Slavic accent.*

"You don't want to know, Marija," *Mike says with a laugh.*

"It's a scrotum," *Ewan tells her.*

Marija shakes her head in disgust.

"Anyhoo… gang, I'd like you to officially meet Marija Horvat from Croatia. Marija is one tough lady and a hell of a barkeep."

The camera pans to show the pool and the deck surrounding it. "Let's see who else we can find. Oooh! There he is, Paz Castillo of The Bahamas, and if I'm not mistaken, he's got himself a very lovely tourista at the resort."

Mike zooms in to show Paz on the opposite side of the pool, sharing a chaise longue with a woman in a tiny bikini. He's nuzzling her nose, brushing one hand down her outer thigh. Mike shouts at him, "Hey, Paz, is she the most stunning woman in the world?"

Paz laughs and nods. "Just look at her."

Ewan's voice cuts in. "On the planet, Mikey. He tells every woman she's the most stunning woman on the planet."

The girl wraps an arm around Paz's neck, and he goes in for the kiss, which prompts Mike to flip the camera back to himself. "Whoops! We better cut that off before my buddy Paz causes a scandal.

"That's it for me. My workday is over, and it's officially party time! Good night, my Moose Calves!"

Huh. Turns out Paz is a bit of a player. I toss my phone on the bed, wishing I hadn't followed Mike the Moose on TikTok. Deep down I knew Paz was one of the biggest flirts to ever come to Santa Valentina, but finding out he uses the same line on every girl he meets stings a little. It was kind of nice to believe a guy as hot as Paz could find a dowdy girl like me attractive.

I go in search of a glass of water, only to come face-to-face with that crunchy spider plant I should have dealt with already. But the thought of emptying the pot and washing it out at this late hour feels like too much. It'll have to wait for tomorrow. Or maybe until after the competition is over. It's not like that plant is getting any deader. Kind of like my love life.

Oh screw it, I really should tackle my to-do list. The fern looks to be beyond hope at this point. Also, like my love life...

16

The Delicate Genius

Theo

"SHE SAID THAT?" I ask Carolina, who has just relayed her conversation with Nora to me.

"Um-hmm," she answers, looking bored. "But who cares what *she* thinks, anyway? She's nothing to us."

"I don't care, but it's a little aggravating to have someone assume we don't understand the concept of justice simply because of our upbringing."

"Yes, I suppose there is a certain irony to it all." Carolina opens the mini-bar fridge and pulls out a bottle of Pellegrino. "Anyway, enough about what's-her-name."

"Nora."

"Whatever. Two months from now we'll both have forgotten all about her. More importantly, what are you doing this afternoon? I'm in videoconferences until two o'clock, but I thought I would book us each massages after that. I'd say we've earned it."

"I'm going to Eden today with Vincent, so maybe Markos can go with you."

Wrinkling up her nose, Carolina says, "Why on earth would you do that? It's not like you know anything about the wilderness."

"I resent that," I say. "I've had lots of experience in the wild— the Amazon, the Nile, Antarctica."

Flopping down onto my bed, she leans an elbow on it. This is something she's been doing more in the last few days, and I'm not entirely comfortable with it. "I forgot you love to pretend you're a caveman in your time off. But this thing today, you could skip it. Vincent knows what he's looking for."

"Vincent is going to be looking for the best shots and lighting. *I'm* going to be looking for danger."

"And I'm sure it will be found at every turn." She laughs. "Theo, it's a luxury private island. Do you really think there are wild animals poised to eat the guests paying that kind of money to spend the night?"

"I'm sure you're right about the animals, but I didn't come here to sit in my room. I came to mitigate any risks to Rojas that this competition might produce. Therefore, I am going."

She makes a little huffing sound. "What time will you be back? Because I'm sure I could book later massages."

"It won't work. I have a call with my COO at five."

"Another time then?" She sips her water.

"I don't think so. I'm not a big fan of letting strangers touch me."

"Okay, but you don't know what you're missing."

"I assure you I do."

———

Markos answers his door only after I knock on it for a solid minute. Based on the state of his hair and breath, it's safe to say I woke him. "I have to go to that private island today with Vincent to take a look at it. I thought you might want to join me."

"Why would you think that?"

"I don't know … maybe to spend some time with your big brother, pretend you're actually working?"

"Nah, I think I'll skip it. I'll stay here and hold down the fort."

"And by that I assume you mean you'll spend the day at the swim-up bar."

"Yes, but it's a very valuable reconnaissance mission, *hermano*. I'm getting to know everyone really well and soon I'll be able to tell who's trouble and who's not."

"Any front runners yet?"

"So far, everyone seems pretty terrific."

"Of course they do, but that's because you're incapable of seeing the negative in anyone until it's too late."

"And you, my dear brother, are incapable of seeing the good in your fellow man." He retreats to his bed, bare feet slapping the tile floor. "Now, I need at least two more hours of beauty sleep, but you have fun with Vincent today." He laughs, and I know it's at the thought that anyone would have fun with Vincent.

"As always, thank you."

"No problem." Yawning, he climbs into bed. "I'm happy to provide advice whenever needed."

I close the adjoining door, then change into a pair of cargo shorts, a T-shirt, and my hiking shoes, realizing that part of me is looking forward to spending the afternoon away from my hotel room. Although I could do without Vincent, the drama queen, it will be good for me to stretch my legs and get some sunshine. I pocket my room key and am about to do the same with my mobile phone when I remember what it says on the brochure: *No cellular or Wi-Fi access for the ultimate escape.* I send Jaquell a text to let her know I'll be unavailable for the next few hours but will return in time for the meeting at five o'clock.

By the time I arrive at the dock, I see that Vincent is already on the speedboat we'll be taking—the Rogue Fun. He's wearing a life jacket that looks too big for him, and his face is set in a grimace.

A young man in the Paradise Bay uniform of a golf shirt and shorts waves to me. He has the look of the quintessential surfer—shoulder-length blond hair and dark tan. I bet he cleans up as far as hookups with lonely tourists go. "I'm Justin. I'll be giving you a ride over to Eden."

"Nice to meet you. I'm Theo." Stepping onto the boat, I take a seat next to Vincent, leaving the one next to Justin open. "Should we get going?"

"We're just waiting for Nora," Vincent says.

"Nora's coming?" I ask before I can stop myself.

"Yes, of course. That girl is becoming my right arm. She's on top of everything," he tells me. Then, leaning towards me a little, he adds, "Why? Do you have a problem with her?"

Only that she hates me. "No, of course not," I say casually. Glancing at my watch, I say, "I'm just in a hurry is all."

A few seconds later, Nora appears on the dock, rushing towards us and apologizing. She's got her hair in two braids that flap with each step and is dressed much like me, only on her it doesn't look out of place. She's got that cute, outdoorsy girl-next-door thing going on. It takes me about thirty full seconds of appreciating how she looks to remember what she said about people bending over backwards for people like me (who also don't know the first thing about true justice). "Sorry I'm late. Kat called to say that she won't be in until noon so I had to find a replacement to man the desk for me."

Justin holds his hand out and helps her into the boat, and for some stupid reason, the sight of it scratches at my chest a little.

"Good morning, Vincent," she says with a bright smile. After giving me a quick nod, she adds a terse, "Hello. I didn't know you were coming."

"Likewise," I say, matching her tone.

"Good morning, Nora. You're looking gorgeous," Vincent tells her.

Blushing, she waves off his compliment, then seats herself next to Justin, who starts the engine and hits the gas, causing the boat to tip back so far, it feels like we're going to get dumped. Nora lets out a little squeal of laughter, and Vincent reaches out and grips my arm, digging his nails into it. Well, this is awkward. I hope he doesn't hold onto me the entire ride.

"Jesus Christ," he mutters.

"I take it you're not a boat guy?" I ask.

Instead of answering, he closes his eyes tightly.

"So, Nora, word on the street is you're up for a big promotion," Justin shouts over the engine.

"I hope so," she tells him. "There's a lot riding on the bartending competition. If I can manage everything without a hitch, I think I have a good shot at it."

"How's it going so far?" he asks, steering right as we leave the bay and head into open water.

The boat skips along the surface, and Vincent grips my arm harder.

"Really well," she shouts. "It's a lot of moving parts, but so far, so good."

"If anyone can do it, it's you," he says. "You're so smart."

Oh barf. Keep your eyes on the ocean, Studly.

"Aww, thanks, Justin."

Not wanting to watch them flirt any longer, I turn my gaze to the shoreline and take in the sight of white sand beaches, villas, and the jungle beyond.

"Have you been working out?" Justin asks.

"A little," Nora says.

"It shows. You're a total smoke show lately," he yells.

Gross. A total smoke show. Who says stuff like that to a woman?

She laughs, her cheeks turning pink with what I can only assume is embarrassment at his clumsy attempt to woo her.

Vincent finally lets go of my arm, and when I glance over at him, I see his face has gone green. His eyes are closed, and his head is bouncing around as though trying to escape from his neck.

"You all right, Vincent?"

"No," he groans.

Uh-oh. "How long until we reach Eden?" I ask Justin.

"Another thirty minutes," he shouts. His face screws up into a wince when he notices Vincent. "Oh, bud, you gonna make it?"

"Yes," Vincent answers with a complete lack of conviction.

Justin points to a bucket at the back of the boat. "Grab that for him, okay?"

Nodding, I stand, wobble, fall back into my seat, then get back up again. Well, that was emasculating.

"You need me to get it?" Justin asks. "Nora, you take the wheel!"

"I got it!" I shout, getting up again, but this time keeping my center of gravity low, crouching and gripping the seats as I make my way to the bucket. Perfect, I must look like an absolute moron.

I reach Vincent just in time for him to get sick.

Gross. This is not what I signed up for. I sit next to him, unsure of what to do. What I *want* to do is go sit somewhere else, but I pat his back instead. "You'll be okay. Just get it out."

Nora gives me a look that is both sympathetic and disgusted at the same time. Seems about right for the situation.

The next twenty minutes are the slowest of my life, although I'm sure for Vincent they're far worse. Nora and Justin continue to flirt while I'm periodically handed the bucket to empty over the side—which is pretty much the last thing I thought I'd be doing today. By the time we reach the island, every inch of Vincent's visible skin has taken on a sickly green pallor. Justin cuts the engine, and the boat glides up to the wooden dock that juts out from a beach with sand so white, it looks like icing sugar. He jumps out and ties the rope to the dock, then holds his hand out to help us off.

Vincent doesn't move a muscle. He just moans.

"Come on," I tell him. "You'll feel one hundred percent better when you get off the boat."

"I can't," he groans, shaking his head.

"We have to," I say.

"I'm too weak. I need to go lie down."

"You can lie down here for a few minutes," I say, desperate not to spend the entire day alone with someone who hates everything about me.

Abandoning proper grammar, Vincent says, "I go back now." He reaches for Nora's hand. "I trust you. Take as much video as you can, okay?"

Nora's eyes grow wide. "I...I don't know your criteria for whether or not Eden will work."

"Jungle, fruit, edible plants, must look uninhabited."

We exchange a look, and I can tell she's about as excited about doing this with me as I am her.

"Justin, take me back now. I must get to my room so I can lie down in the dark for the rest of the day," Vincent tells him.

Justin looks at Nora. "I can take him back. You guys'll need a couple of hours here anyway, right?"

She nods, even though she's chewing on her bottom lip. "Go ahead. We'll go do what we need to and meet you back here at, say, two o'clock?"

"No later than that though, okay?" he says. "We're supposed to get a wicked storm around dinnertime, and I'd like to make sure we're all safely back home long before that happens."

Vincent groans loudly, which prompts Justin to untie the rope. He tosses it in the boat and gives Nora a flirty wink. "I better get going. Good luck, you two."

He hops in the boat and it rocks, causing Vincent to lurch forward dramatically and retch. Justin fires up the motor and salutes me. "Thanks for being on bucket duty! See you in a while!"

And then he's gone, leaving Nora and me alone together on a deserted island.

Wonderful. This day is turning out exactly how I hoped it would.

17

When It Rains, It Pours

Nora

"Should we set off, then?" I ask, stunned this is happening.

He nods once, and we start along the beach toward the path that will take us into the jungle and up the mountain. Neither of us says a word, which suits me fine. I have nothing to say to a man who would treat someone the way he treated Paz. Especially not after he tried to get that awful Carolina Armas to plead his case for him.

You can own what you did, you big jerk. I am not going to let you off the hook, as I'm sure everyone else in your disgustingly privileged life has done.

Even though Paz didn't turn out to be who I hoped he was, my heart still goes out to him. As disappointed as I am that he uses that stunning line on every woman he sees, I can't blame him for trying to seek happiness wherever he goes. After all, the poor guy has been through so much.

Anyway, the point is I'm too annoyed to enjoy the gentle waves lapping against the shore or the way the sun warms my skin. I don't care that I've always wanted to see the Island of Eden, and I'm getting a chance to explore it. And I *certainly* won't revel in the fact that I'm not spending the day following a demanding showrunner around, because if said person were here, he'd provide the perfect buffer between Mr. High and Mighty and myself, even if Vincent is one of the most irritating people I've met.

I'm going to get this over with so I can get the hell back to the resort and away from him, hopefully forever, but more realistically, for the rest of the day. In a few short hours, I'll be back at my flat doing laundry and watching *Bridgerton* with the windows open so I can smell the rain. It'll be a perfect Theo Rojas-free evening. I may even get rid of those crunchy plants.

I shoot a video of the beach with my phone, slowly turning a full circle to get all angles while I narrate. "This is the beach on the south side of the island. You can see the path that leads to the villa over here. I'm guessing you'll want to avoid filming the dock, but otherwise, this would probably be a good place to drop the contestants."

I shut it off and carry on walking, my feet sinking into the soft sand, making each step an effort. I turn back to make sure Theo is with me only to discover he's directly behind me. I catch a whiff of his aftershave, which is probably made from baby dolphins or something equally evil and expensive. Whatever it is, it smells sinfully delicious. Like so good, I'm tempted to knock him out so I can sniff his neck for a couple of hours.

His outfit looks like something straight out of a J.Crew catalog. It's a little too put together, and I entertain a vision of him in a high-end department store, telling a clerk he wants something that says "active and outdoorsy but also rich." That's so him. Blech.

The beach curves right, and when we get around to the other side, two houseboats gently bob side by side offshore.

"Whose are those?" Theo asks.

"The resort's," I answer with absolutely no enthusiasm. "The bigger one is for the housekeeper and butler, who are married to each other. The other one is for the island's chef. I understand it's basically a kitchen with a bed."

Lifting my phone, I make a quick video of the boats, explaining that all food prep can be done on the houseboat.

"Should we go meet the staff? To see if they have any questions about the challenge?"

Shaking my head, I say, "They're not here. They go back to Santa Valentina when there are no guests."

"Oh."

I can't help but wonder if he's working out the fact that we're alone here. "Let's keep going. We have a lot of ground to cover in a short amount of time."

We hike through the jungle for the next hour in silence, other than the odd comment made by one or the other of us. Things like "is that a mango tree?" and "I'd say yes, based on the mangoes hanging from it."

When I spot something that could possibly be used to make a cocktail, I take photos, video, and note the location. Other than the mangoes, I've found wild basil, peppermint, and jackass bitters. When I'm finished documenting the jackass bitters, I point to them. "Do you use these in any of your liquors?"

"Why? Because you think I'm a jackass?"

Don't say yes. He's the most VIP of all the VIP guests you've had to handle. "Because they might add a new flavour. You'd have to use the tiniest bit and blend them with a few things that would offset the level of bitterness, but they'd also be fun to market."

"Huh, that's actually not a bad idea."

"I have them occasionally," I say, continuing on.

I'm taking a couple shots of a tall fruit tree when he says, "What's that one called?"

"Soursop. The contestants are in luck that the fruit is in season. It could make for a very interesting cocktail actually," I say, forgetting all about how much I hate him. "It smells sort of like a strawberry but tastes like a combination of a coconut, mango, citrus fruit, and banana all blended together."

We gaze at each other a moment too long before I remember I can't stand him, and if I had to guess, I'd say he remembered he hates me right back, based on his change of expression. I clear my throat. "We should get back to the beach. Justin should be back soon."

"Right, yes."

We start down the mountain in silence. The air has grown heavy and still in the way it does before a big storm. Through the thick veil of trees, I can't see enough of the sky to know if the clouds are growing near, but I assume they are. By the time we reach the beach, I'm so hot, I want to run straight into the water, clothes and all.

A swell of black clouds pushes into the sky above us. I jog, legs exhausted from the last couple of hours and hoping Justin's at the dock waiting for us.

We round the curve, only to see an empty dock. No Rogue Fun. No nice Justin to rescue us from each other. We are very much still alone.

A deafening crack of thunder makes me cringe, charging the air and causing the hair on the back of my neck to stand straight up. A couple of miles offshore, lightning flashes, hitting the ocean in several places at once. Seconds later, sheets of rain pour down, drenching us in cold, needle-sharp drops.

"What do we do?" he asks.

"We need to get to the villa!" I shout over the rain. "So we can call for help."

Turning back the way we came, I run to get under cover of the forest.

"We're going to have to haul ass before that lightning gets here," Theo yells, and we pick up our pace to a quick jog.

After about thirty seconds, I'm sucking serious wind. We're not only going uphill, but the path is covered with soft debris from the trees and shrubs, making it thick and spongy, and within minutes, it's so slippery it makes each step harder and more dangerous. My lungs burn, and I'm tempted to stop and flop onto the ground to catch my breath, but another clap of thunder has me speeding up instead.

By the time we reach the villa, I'm certain my legs are going to give out and my lungs are literally going to explode. Theo, on the other hand, looks fine. It's as if we are out for a light stroll. God, I hate him. I dig into the pocket of my shorts for the master key while

I climb the wide wooden steps that lead to an expansive deck that wraps around the house.

I push the oversized wooden door open and step inside the luxurious living room, dripping all over the terracotta tile. Theo follows me in and shuts the door, which muffles the sound of the driving rain.

We stare at each other while I pant and he runs his hands through his dark hair. Bastard, looking ridiculously sexy at a time like this. I'm sure my face is blotchy and my makeup is running. Glancing down, I see that my T-shirt is stuck to my chest, and my beige bra is most definitely visible. Then I remember today is laundry day, and I'm wearing my super sexy beige granny panties. Perfect. Just perfect.

I attempt to recover from all that running while I glance around the room. It's decorated with light woods, cream-coloured fabrics, and has floor-to-ceiling windows on nearly every wall. On the far side of the space is a kitchen that looks fit for a gourmet chef. A hallway on the left leads to what I'm sure are the bathroom and bedroom.

Something about being alone with him in a place like this—a villa literally designed and built for romance—is oddly electrifying. Nothing is going to happen, other than me calling the resort to make plans to be picked up when the storm passes, but my mind is going to all kinds of places it shouldn't about a man I shouldn't be thinking about.

I hurry over to the radio, which is on a console table, and pick up the receiver. Before I push the button, I say, "The fridge should be fully stocked. Help yourself."

Instead of doing that, Theo strides towards the hallway. "I'll get us some towels."

I call the resort. "Eden Villa to Front Desk. Front Desk, do you read me?" I immediately feel silly using walkie-talkie speak in front of Theo, but at the same time, I hope I sound like I know what I'm doing.

A sharp blast of static fills the room, then I hear Rosy's voice. "Front Desk, Rosy here."

"Hi Rosy, it's Nora. I'm at the villa with Mr. Rojas."

Her tone changes when she hears it's me. She goes from chipper to cold, which tells me she hasn't forgotten what I said to Oakley. "We've been waiting for you to call. Is it pouring there too?"

"Yup."

"This storm was supposed to blow in this evening, but it got here a lot faster than the forecasters expected. It's also a lot worse than they said it would be. The Coast Guard has issued a tropical storm warning with a potential storm surge."

My heart drops at her words. Theo, who has returned with a couple of towels, screws up his face in confusion.

"How long until it passes?" I ask, taking a towel and pressing it to my face.

"The Benaventes will be under the warning for twelve hours minimum."

"Twelve hours?" Theo asks, rubbing his hair with his towel. "I have an important meeting at five."

Okay, Mr. Big. We'll stop the storm for you. I press the button again. "That's not going to work for Mr. Rojas. He has a meeting at five." I add, "An important one," just to be extra assy.

There's a pause, then Rosy says, "He's joking, right?"

"No, I'm not—" he starts, then gestures for me to push the button. "I'm not joking. There must be some way to get back. You can't just leave us stranded out here."

"We're not going to risk your life or the lives of our employees because you have a meeting, but I'm happy to make some calls for you to cancel it on your behalf."

"*Mierda,*" he mutters. "Thank you, yes. Could you please call my brother's room, explain what's happening, and tell him to get ahold of Jaquell immediately?"

"Of course."

While he talks, I calculate what time it'll be when the storm is supposed to end. At a break in their conversation, I say, "Umm, Rosy, twelve hours from now, it'll be the middle of the night."

"That's correct."

Theo's eyes grow wide, so clearly he knows what my next question is.

"So, no one's coming until tomorrow morning then," I say, shutting my eyes (because that's what one does when one doesn't want to hear an answer).

"That's right. You two will be fine. There's no chef, but there should be food you can cook for dinner."

Theo sighs and rakes his hand through his wet hair. "Rosy, I need you to pass another message to Markos for me. Please tell him to keep watch tonight. He'll know what that means."

I wonder what the hell he's talking about but know he's not going to tell me, judging by the whole "he'll know what that means" thing.

"Okay." Rosy sounds as confused as I am. "Nora, is there anyone you want me to call for you?"

My cheeks heat up at the fact that there isn't anyone at home to worry about me. "Um…if you can let Hadley know, she can tell my parents. Oh, and I was supposed to place the alcohol order this afternoon when I got back." Shit. "It's completed, but I ran out of time to write a quick email to go with it."

"Why don't I tell Kat to do it?" Rosy asks.

I consider telling her it's far too important but realize it's going to sound as if I don't trust Kat to do something as simple as pressing send on an email. This is my chance to prove I can be a good manager. Trusting your employees is part of that, isn't it? Besides, I can check it tomorrow when I get back. "Yes, sure. If you can have her log onto my computer, then open the email for Jaquell Morales —it should be on top of my drafts and the attachment is already there—have her type in a quick note to Jaquell, thanking her for her help and signing my name to it. Hit send, and that's it."

"Consider it done. Just give us a holler if you need anything else."

"Except actual help," Theo mutters.

"Thanks so much, Rosy. Over and out."

"Over and out."

I place the receiver back in its cradle. "I guess we're stuck here."

The question is, what are we going to do about it?

18

Superheroes of Sarcasm

Theo

"THE FIRST THING we should do is get out of these wet clothes," I say before I realize how it sounds.

Nora narrows her eyes. "I know you've had a lifetime of getting your own way, but believe me when I say I'm not going to give it to you." Her eyes pop open, and she quickly adds, "Give you what you want, that is. Because... no."

Smirking at her, I say, "What exactly do you think I want, Nora?"

She's completely flustered, and I have to say I'm enjoying this more than I should. But hey, she's accused me of some pretty rotten things, so I'd say it's only fair.

"Nothing... I don't know. But now that we're stranded here, I'm off the clock, so for the next however many hours we're stuck here together, I'm not an events coordinator, and you're not a guest who...*needs things*. We're just two people who happen to be stranded in the same villa. So, don't think you can tell me to get out of my wet clothes, because *I'll* decide if and when I'm going to take my clothes off!"

"Someone clearly thinks highly of herself if she's suggesting I want to get her naked," I say before pursing my lips.

Nora gasps. "She does not!"

I shrug. "If you say so, but it really did seem like it when you said that whole thing about not 'giving it to me,' when the only reason I suggested getting out of our wet clothes is because you're shivering and I came across a couple of plush bathrobes in the closet when I went to find the towels."

"Oh," she says, dropping her shoulders a little.

"There's also a washing machine and a dryer, so I'm planning to launder my things, but if you want to stay—" I point to her—"as you are, suit yourself. I am going to have a hot shower."

Her teeth start to chatter, but she still has that stubborn look on her face. "I can see how that would be a reasonable idea."

"Is that your way of apologizing?"

"I don't owe you an apology," she snaps.

"Don't you? Where I come from, when we make false accusations, we apologize and then commit to not doing it again," I tell her. And before I can stop myself, I add, "But perhaps that's only common courtesy among the top one percent of the world."

Her cheeks turn bright red and she sputters, "You know what? I *am* going to have a shower. A nice, long one, but not because you told me to. Because I want to."

"Have fun, Captain Justice," I murmur when she turns to leave the room.

That did it. She does a U-turn. "Captain Justice?" she hisses.

"I'd say that suits someone who thinks she's the paragon of all things just in this world, listening to only one side of a story and casting judgment on who's right and who's the devil." Okay, so now I'm just being a jerk, but at this point, I don't care. "Or should I call you Captain Jumps to Conclusions, based on you accusing me of trying to get you into bed just now?"

"Captain Jumps to Conclusions? Do you even hear yourself? That's quite possibly *the most* ridiculous thing anyone has ever said in the history of speaking!"

"Captain Accusations, then?" I ask calmly.

"You are the most rude, most arrogant, entitled man I've ever met!" she shouts, moving towards me until she's so close she has to tilt her head back to look up at me. "You should be called Captain Thinks His Shit Doesn't Stink!"

I scoff, leaning closer to her. "It's not so easy, is it? Coming up with sarcastic super-hero names when you're angry."

"No, it's not!" she yells.

"Exactly! So don't make fun of my attempt," I yell back, too angry to laugh at the level of insanity we've reached.

I stare down at her face, only inches from mine. She's still shivering, and even though I'm furious, I want to wrap my arms around her and warm her up. Or kiss her hard on the mouth. Or both.

There's a shift in the energy between us, and her eyes flick to my lips. Then she shakes her head. "I hate you! I really, really hate you."

"Not as much as I hate you," I say, even though I only sort of hate her.

"Oh, really? Because if the only two men left on earth were you and Hitler, I'd sleep with Hitler!"

"News flash! Nobody's asking to sleep with you."

"Good!" She glares at me, then barks, "I'm going to take a shower now!"

"Don't worry about locking the door. I promise I won't sneak in and try to seduce you."

"I'm sure you won't, since I'm so dowdy and all."

"Oh, that's not why. It's because you're a total harpy."

Tears of rage spring to her eyes. She spins on her heel and rushes off, slips a little on the wet floor, catches herself just before she falls, then swears under her breath. A moment later, the door to the bedroom slams shut, and she lets out a loud growl.

I stay rooted to the spot, cold, soaking wet, and wishing I'd grabbed a robe before engaging in this stupid fight. Stalking to the bar, I pour myself a generous serving of whiskey, then down it fast so it burns my throat and warms me from head to toe. I spend the next twenty minutes going over what just happened, muttering to myself about how awful she is, imitating her voice and the things she said, imagining myself coming up with the perfect comeback instead of the garbage I actually said.

If this were a romance movie instead of real life, we would have kissed, possibly right after she called me rude, arrogant, and entitled. It would have been one hell of a kiss too, and likely would have led to me picking her up by her bottom and carrying her over to the couch, where we'd tear each other's clothes off and have wild sex with some sexy song playing in the background. Then it would cut to a shower scene, where we'd still be at it. I'd be nice and warm, instead of chilled to the bone, and the satisfaction of releasing all this pent-up tension I have when I'm around her would be incredible.

I'd explain what really happened with Paz—how, upon my father's death, he came to me for money, and I offered to pay his tuition and boarding for any university he wanted, but he said he just wanted the cash. When I didn't give it to him, hoping he'd grow up a little and change his mind, he made a sex tape of himself with my stepmother without her knowledge. Nora would listen as I'd tell her how Paz blackmailed her with it, forcing her to come to me for help since my father's bank accounts had been automatically frozen for sixty days after he died. I'd tell her how I paid him off, had my best IT guy scrub all of Paz's devices of any versions of the video, and told him to stay away from us forever. Nora would apologize for assuming the worst and tell me she's never known a more honourable man and, well, who knows what would happen after that? Probably more sex. A lot more rigorous, incredible, mind-blowing sex that would leave us both panting and grinning like fools.

But it's not a movie. This is reality. I can't tell her what happened. She hates me. She does not lust after me. None of that stuff is *ever* going to happen, even though the very thought of it is enough to do me in. And if it did happen, it would make me the biggest hypocrite in all of the Caribbean, because I'm the guy who made a big speech about keeping things professional (i.e., no sex with anyone involved with the competition/resort).

I'm going to have to make it through the next eighteen or so hours until we're rescued without letting things veer off into Hollywood film territory. Not that it'll be hard, as she's definitely not going to be making any moves in that direction. I'll have to accept that she's always going to believe the worst of me, and that's that.

As much as it sucks.

I think I'll have another drink.

19

Pasta, Wine, and Understanding

Nora

OH, that... that... asshole! I have never in my entire life hated someone like I hate him. He's the absolute worst human being on the planet except for Hitler and a bunch of other dictators and serial killers whose names I'm too angry to think of. How dare he call me Captain Justice? And Captain Jumps to Conclusions? And a *harpy*? Wow. Just wow.

How about Captain Knows the Truth and Doesn't Approve? That's more like it.

Ouch. I've been angry-scrubbing my scalp for quite a while now. I should calm down.

Taking a deep breath, I tell myself to let all my tension out on my exhale as the hot water rushes over me. I do this a few times, but each time, I find myself focusing on my rage instead of letting it go. I'm suddenly desperate to get back to San Felipe so I can find Hadley and tell her everything. But I can't. I'm stranded here for the rest of the day and night with *him*.

And although it was gentlemanly for Theo to let me have the first shower and notice I was shivering and want to fix it, I still hate him. He treats everyone like they're below him. Although he was rather sweet with Vincent when he was getting sick. But still, he *is* entitled and rude and arrogant. That's true too.

I suppose if I was that good-looking, I might be arrogant too. His body under those wet, clingy clothes? The sight of it did something to me akin to breaking a million synapses in my brain that I require for higher level thinking, because when we were fighting, it was all I could do to stop my hands from running all over that manly goodness.

What is wrong with me? How can I have *those* feelings for *that* man? I hate him. I shouldn't want to tear off his clothes and have my way with him. Oh God, does this mean I secretly have some sort of masochistic tendencies I don't know about? Is my self-worth so low I want to be with a terrible man?

No, that can't be it. He's just stupidly hot, and he's got me all bothered, so I'm mixing up loathing with lust.

I shut off the water and stand in the shower, for the first time noticing how incredible this en suite is. The shower is massive. The water rains down from the ceiling, which is a huge departure from my apartment shower, with the weak spray that forces you to run around to get wet under it. And I didn't even enjoy it.

That bastard.

I towel off and pull on a plush white robe that hangs off me and feels like a cozy cocoon when I tie the sash. Sliding my feet into slippers, I finally feel myself calming down a bit, until guilt nudges me to hurry up so Theo can have his turn. He may not deserve my kindness, but choosing to be selfish isn't exactly taking the high road. Gathering my clothes, I hurry out of the bedroom and stop at the laundry closet in the hall to drop them into the washer.

When I enter the living area, I smell something divine. Theo is in front of the stove. He glances over at me, and we both quickly look away. Suddenly the things we said feel all too real.

"The shower's all yours," I tell him in my most business-like tone. "And I put my clothes in the machine, but I didn't turn it on. I thought we'd wash them all together."

He turns down the heat on the stove top. "I found spaghetti, so I made a tomato sauce. If you don't mind keeping an eye on it while I shower, I'll make the pasta when I get out."

"I can make the pasta."

"Only if you want to. I know you're off the clock." He rests the lid on the pot, leaving it slightly tilted, then strides out of the room, leaving me feeling restless and stupid.

———

By the time the noodles are cooked, Theo has rejoined me in the kitchen after turning on the washing machine. I'm tempted to make a crack about how I wasn't sure he knew how to work those things, but I hold my tongue. I'm hungry and tired from all the hiking and emotional upheaval. I also can't help noticing how the same robe I'm drowning in pulls tautly across his muscular chest and back. That thought leads me to the realization that underneath that robe is nothing but body. And what a body it is.

Nope! Erase that image from your brain, both immediately and permanently.

We work together silently—Theo opening a bottle of red wine while I plate the spaghetti and sauce. When we sit at the table, I stare down at the meal for a second, realizing how utterly surreal it is that we both had a hand in cooking it, and that we're sitting here in nothing but our robes, about to eat together. Me, a lowly hotel events coordinator, with one of the richest men in the world.

"Thank you for the spaghetti," he says, twirling some onto his fork.

"Thank you for the sauce," I tell him, doing the same.

The first bite is amazing. Hot but not too hot, and the sauce—wow. It's the perfect blend of tangy, salty, garlic, and oregano. Unable to contain myself, I let out a moan of delight.

Of course he smirks at the sound.

Outside, dark clouds swirl above the ocean in the distance, and the rain pelts the windows, creating a moody backdrop that suits the situation.

Theo lifts his glass and takes a sip. "The pasta is cooked to perfection."

"Thanks. Your sauce is surprisingly good."

"You assumed I wouldn't know how to cook."

"I may have, yes," I answer, twirling more noodles onto my fork.

"I got sick of eating ramen during my first year of university, so I made it a point to learn how to make a few dishes when I went home for the summer. And yes, it was our family's chef who taught me, not my mother."

The way he says mother lacks any hint of warmth, and I wonder what his childhood was like. Knowing that's off-limits, I say, "Where'd you go to school?"

"Cambridge for my undergrad degree, then Oxford for my master's in business. You?"

"San Felipe Community College for my business diploma," I say, a hot flash of shame hitting me. I pick up my wine and have a big sip to douse the feeling.

"Did you always know you wanted to be an events coordinator?" he asks, and I can't tell if he's being an ass or not. The look on his face says not, so I answer him honestly.

"It's not exactly the kind of job you dream of doing when you're a kid."

Tilting his head, he says, "What did you want to be?"

"Jennifer Lopez."

"Of course."

"You?"

"Same, yeah. Jenny from the block."

I can't help but laugh, and after fighting it for a few seconds, Theo joins in. When we're done, he grows serious. "Listen, Nora, I owe you an apology. I didn't mean any of those awful things I said to you earlier. It was wrong of me to speak to you that way, and I am sorry."

I stiffen slightly, but the wall I've been constructing since I met him crumbles a little. "I'm sorry too. I don't know what came over me. I'm normally not a total harpy."

He cringes, then shakes his head. "You are not a harpy. This is a very unusual situation we find ourselves in. I think we were both thrown off by it—not that it's an excuse for how I acted."

"Or how I acted." I sigh. "Could we wipe the slate clean? In the name of making the best of a bad situation?"

"I'd like that very much."

"Good. Me too."

We go back to eating, but this time the silence isn't marred by tension. It feels reflective and calm.

After a few minutes, Theo finishes and sits back. "I've been wondering how you know so much about plants."

"My grandmother. We used to go for long walks in the forest to find herbs and mushrooms."

"That sounds nice."

"It was," I tell him. "She isn't able to go that far anymore though, so it's been a few years since we've done it."

"Does she have mobility issues?" he asks.

"Dementia," I tell him. "It's too easy to lose her now."

"I'm sorry to hear that."

"Yeah, me too. It's the worst, losing her in tiny increments." Then, for no reason at all, I start talking about her. "She lives on the big island. The last several years, when I visit, she sends me home with the funniest things. One time, she sneaked a jar of pickled eggs into my suitcase."

Theo chuckles. "That must have smelled nice."

"Yeah, especially when the jar broke on the drive to the airport." I laugh at the memory. "Liquid everywhere. Then there was the time she bought me a necklace with a marijuana leaf on it and insisted I wear it on the flight. Security triple-checked my bags and did an extremely thorough search of my person." His smile is so encouraging, I keep talking. "Last year she gave me a Scooby-Doo lunch kit."

"The Mystery Machine?" he asks.

"You're familiar with it?"

"I may have had one when I was a child."

I squint at him. "You were once a child?"

"Shocking, I know," he says with a smirk.

"I'm getting an image of an eight-year-old you in a suit and tie, ordering all the other kids around."

"That's a surprisingly accurate portrait of a younger me," he says, and I can't tell if he's joking or not. "I knew from a very early age what my future held and what I had to do to live up to the Rojas name."

"Heavy is the head that wears the crown," I say lightly.

"It can be. Take these last weeks, for example." He stops and gives me a speculative look. "Everything we're telling each other is off the record, yes?"

Giving him a half-grin, I say, "Don't worry. I'm not trying to uphold my oath to journalistic integrity."

"Good, because I'm about to tell you an embarrassing secret, and I can only do it if you've sworn yourself to secrecy."

I hold up one hand, my curiosity piqued. "I swear. Whatever your deliciously juicy secret is will be safe with me."

The look on his face suggests this may not be a laughing matter. "I've been staying awake until after three a.m. every night to make sure there's no funny business going on."

Funny business? Is he an old timey boarding school headmaster? "What do you mean? You sit in the hallway on a chair or something?"

"I watch through my peephole. I don't want people to think I'm crazy." His cheeks turn red, and he quickly adds, "And before you say it, I do know it's possible for people to make bad choices during the day, but I figure there's less chance then because everybody's busy working or practicing. As illogical as I know it is, I have to do whatever possible to keep our brand out of the news."

"So that's what you meant when you said that thing about keeping watch."

He nods, and I'm suddenly overcome by the desire to give him a hug. I won't, obviously, but I can't help feeling bad for the guy. "You must be exhausted."

"I'm a little tired," he admits. "But more than that, I'm worried. Agreeing to sponsor the competition was a risk. A calculated one, of course, but a risk nonetheless. If anything goes wrong, it could be the last nail in the coffin for our company."

"But it won't be your responsibility if a couple of employees of the network or the contestants get into a little trouble."

"I know that, but it doesn't matter. Public perception is everything in my business, just like it is in yours. It literally translates to money. This hole my company is in is deep, and if I can't pull us up out of it soon, I'm going to have to start shutting down distilleries. The last thing I want is to have to lay people off, especially over something as stupid as a marketing campaign gone wrong."

I chew on my bottom lip while I consider his words. "That must be a lot of pressure on you."

"Yes, sometimes. Lately especially. Not that I'd dare complain openly. I do know how fortunate I am." He tops off our glasses. "My father made sure I understood how lucky we were. He also taught me to take my position very seriously. Over eight thousand employees count on me to show up every day and make the right decisions, not just the easy ones. I owe them perfection."

I take in his features while he talks—the way the skin around his eyes crinkles a little, and the worry lines that stretch across his forehead. He really does feel the weight of his responsibility. It's etched on his face. "Do you want to be the president of the company?"

He has a sip of wine before answering. "I was born to do what I'm doing and trained from a very early age to lead the company into the future."

Picking up my glass, I say, "That's not what I asked. I asked if you want to do it."

"It's not a question of want. It's a case of obligation. Rojas Rum has been in my family for over 170 years. It's a legacy. I can't just walk away from that because I'm not hashtag *living my best life*."

"You could turn it over to your brother, couldn't you?"

He scoffs. "Markos wasn't raised to be a leader. He was raised to be the comic relief."

My head snaps back. "Ouch. That's a little harsh, isn't it?"

"He'd say the same thing if he were here."

"So, what will you do? Have a son and pass it all onto him, burdens and all?"

Theo shrugs. "I haven't thought that far ahead, but... probably." He gazes out the window, then sighs. "Although I'd hate myself for it."

I'm tempted to tell him not to do it then and to find a way to get out of it if he's miserable, but I don't. I don't know Theo Rojas well enough to say such a thing to him.

He snaps out of whatever thoughts he was entertaining. "Don't worry about me. I'm fine."

"What makes you think I was worrying?"

"The little crease between your eyebrows."

Blushing, I rub that spot on my forehead. "I have every faith that you're going to be okay."

"I will, and I'll do whatever it takes to get things back on track. After that, it'll be business as usual." His tone is light but there's something disingenuous about it, and if I had to guess, I'd say he's trying to convince himself he wants to go back to the way things have always been.

"And *I'm* going to do whatever it takes to make sure things go smoothly," I tell him.

"I know you will. Despite our difficulties, I trust you, Nora. You're intelligent, you work hard, and more than that, you care about what you do. That's a rare combination these days. Harrison and Libby are lucky to have you."

I shrug, feeling awkward accepting his praise. "Just doing my job."

"Don't sell yourself short. You're a remarkable person."

We gaze at each other longer than we should, then we both seem to realize we shouldn't be doing that at all. Theo stands and picks up dishes while I hurry to finish my pasta, my mind swirling with confusion.

Hearing him compliment me feels like the heat of a thousand suns on my skin.

Okay, dingus, don't think like that. Because getting all poetic and gooey will very likely lead to a desperate and possibly pathetic attempt to act on those feelings. And that will most certainly lead to a total disaster.

20

Candlelight Poker and Wishing I Could Poke Her

Theo

WE'RE JUST FINISHING the dishes when the washing machine buzzes, indicating it's finished. Nora all but runs to put the clothes in the dryer, and when I offer to do it, she says, "I've got it. In fact, I'll take the clothes out of the dryer too, okay?"

I can tell by her strained voice she's worried about me seeing something in there, and if I had to guess, I'd say it's her underwear.

Hm… what kind of panties does she wear? Something really sexy, I bet. Lacy and small. Maybe French cut with a matching bra. Possibly in hot pink. Although now that I think about it, I would have seen anything that bright through her wet clothes earlier. Annnddd…I should not be thinking about any of this.

Stop. Stop now. That way lies madness.

I finish drying the pasta pot and put it away, then fold the dish towel and hang it over the oven door handle. For the first time, I realize there's no television, which makes sense, since they're going for that total escape from civilization thing.

I cross to the credenza in the living room and open the doors, hoping to find a board game or a book—anything to take my mind off what I really want to do right now. A deck of cards sits neatly next to a wooden box containing dominoes. I take them both over to the table.

When Nora appears, I say, "Game night?"

A smile crosses her face. "Sure."

"Do you know how to play dominoes?"

She shakes her head. "Me neither. I was hoping you'd teach me."

"You have Cuban roots, and you don't play dominoes?"

"We're not those kind of Cubans," I tell her wryly. "Besides, my people left there long ago. How about poker? We don't have chips, but we can find something to use."

"Okay, but we need to make it interesting."

I raise an eyebrow. "Interesting how?"

"Not like *that*," she says, going to the kitchen and randomly opening cupboards.

"I suppose it would be a very short game, as you only have one item to take off."

"Who says *I'd* be the one stripping?" She stops her search long enough to give me a confident grin.

"I'm pretty sure I'm going to win."

"Wow, talk about cocky." She holds up a large bag of trail mix. "Let's separate it. We use all the yicky healthy bits as poker chips, and the M&Ms are the prize."

"You're on."

A few minutes later, we're seated at the table, each with piles of squirrel food and bottles of Corona. I show off a little while I shuffle the deck. "The game is Texas hold 'em. The ante is one raisin. No wild cards, just straight up poker."

Sliding a raisin to the centre of the table, she says, "Those M&Ms are going to taste so good."

"Yes, they will. I might even give you one if I feel sorry for you." I toss two cards out for each of us, set the deck down, and check my cards. A four of clubs and a seven of diamonds. Crap.

Nora checks her cards and bets two walnuts.

"Ooh, pricey." I slide my walnuts in. "Wait. Walnuts are worth more than raisins, yes?"

"Uh-huh. It's by size. Sunflower seeds are worth one, raisins are two, cashews are five, and walnuts are ten."

"Ten?" I emit a low whistle and deal the flop—jack of clubs, queen of diamonds, and four of spades. *Mierda*, all I've got is a pair of fours, and based on Nora's gleeful expression, I'd say she has at least another jack in her hand. "Do you want to call or raise?"

"I'm raising." She pushes two raisins and three walnuts into the pile.

"*Phew!* You must have something nice. Maybe a pair of jacks?"

"You're going to have to pay to find out."

I do, then turn the fourth card. A queen of hearts.

"This is too good," she says, going all in.

"What? You can't go all in this early in the game."

"Oh, I can. And I just did," she says, giving me the crazy eyes.

"I have to fold," I say, shaking my head. "It's always the queen of hearts that'll get you."

She scoops up her winnings while I rake up the cards and shuffle.

She holds out her hand. "My turn to deal."

Our fingertips brush while I hand her the cards, and I can literally feel my level of concentration dropping. "What'd you have in your hand?"

"Nice try, but I'm not about to tell you."

"Come on, it's just a friendly game."

"If you wanted to see it, you should have paid."

It takes her an hour to clean me out, then she begins slowly eating her M&Ms one at a time, smiling smugly. "Mm, so good."

"I bet."

"You did bet, and you lost." She laughs, and I can't help but find her adorable.

The dryer stops, and she jumps up, suddenly panicked. "I'll get that."

"Why do I get the feeling you're hiding something from me?"

Her cheeks turn pink. "I'm not hiding anything. Just trying to be helpful."

She scurries off and returns with my clothes, which have been neatly folded. She's still in her robe, but I suspect she's now wearing her top-secret panties and bra. She sets the pile down on the credenza. "Here you go. All clean and dry."

"Thanks," I tell her with a smirk, then I say, "You know all this secrecy is making me extremely curious."

"Well, you're going to have to stay that way. A lady never tells." We grin at each other. "There's a bag of Doritos in the cupboard. Should we play again?"

"Yes. I have a reputation to repair."

It's at that moment when the power goes out, leaving us in complete darkness.

"Whoa, it is pitch black here," Nora says. "I literally can't see my hand."

"There must be some candles around here somewhere," I tell her, getting up and groping my way to the living room. She does the same, and the two of us spend the next few minutes bumping into various pieces of furniture while we search.

Nora finally finds a box of candles and a lighter in the hall closet, likely stored there for just such an emergency. We set them around the kitchen and on the table, then get back to our game while the storm continues.

There's a cozy warmth to sitting together, dry and safe while the wind howls outside and rain batters the roof and windows. The evening wears on, and I realize I don't want it to end. I want to stay here with her for a very long time, making her laugh and asking about her life. I want to know everything about her—what she eats for breakfast, what keeps her up at night, what she loves, what she hates, what she wants out of life. I want to pull her onto my lap and feel her body against mine and taste her. I want to know what her skin feels like and discover the sounds she makes when something I do satisfies her.

Then I remember who she is and who I am and who we are to each other. I must set all those thoughts aside, because they're only going to confuse things. The last thing I need is more confusion.

"It must be late," she says, yawning.

"We should get some sleep." I feel an acute pang of disappointment that this time together must come to an end, but suddenly it occurs to me how exhausted I am. I haven't had more than three hours of sleep a night for weeks. "I'll take the couch."

"You sure?"

"Yes."

We clean up the table, and I put the cards away. When we're finished, we are standing in front of each other next to the sink. I watch, mesmerized, as she licks her lips. She's beautiful like this. In the candlelit room, her hair down, no makeup. All the things I want come flooding back into my brain and course through my veins.

"Nora, why do you hate rich people so much?" I ask before I can rethink the question. "I mean, I know we're generally not the most lovable demographic, but with you, it feels personal."

She looks taken aback. "I don't hate rich people."

"I think you do," I say gently. "I'm not going to try to change your opinion. I only want to understand."

"I... well, I've worked in the service industry my entire life. I started as a hostess at a restaurant in town when I was fourteen. Most people you come across are nice, but there's a certain class of people who don't seem to realize that servers have feelings. They're demanding and rude, and they need you to know how rich they are. They don't see you as a human being with feelings and dreams and ambitions, just a means to an end. After enough years of it, I put up a wall, you know?"

Nodding, I say, "I know people like that, and you're right to feel the way you do about them. I know I would."

"I am sorry I painted you with the same brush. You're not like that."

"I can come off that way sometimes, when I'm so focused on what I'm doing that I don't bother to see what's going on around me."

"Maybe a little."

"I'm sorry, Nora." I want so badly to pull her into my arms. "This will sound strange, but even though I've only known you for a short time, it's going to make me a better man."

"Really?" she asks, her voice almost a whisper.

"Really. You've changed me. This day and this night have changed me, and I'm grateful for that. I'm grateful for you."

She swallows hard, and I can tell by the look on her face that if I kissed her right now, she would kiss me back with everything in her. And one thing would most certainly lead to another. And it would be incredible. And I cannot allow that to happen.

So instead of lowering my face and brushing my lips ever so softly against hers, I say, "We should get some sleep."

Disappointment fills her eyes, but she nods and smiles. "Definitely. I'm wiped."

She turns towards the bedroom, then calls over her shoulder, "Good night, Theo."

"Good night."

Only it won't be a good night, will it? It'll be one of tossing and turning and listening for the sound of her footsteps on the floor and trying to ignore the longing. There will be so much longing.

21

Gelato and Girl Talk

Nora

HE'S GRATEFUL FOR ME. Knowing me is going to make him a better man. I changed him. I—Nora Cooper, lowly hotel employee— changed Theo Rojas, heir to and president of the Rojas Rum fortune.

My eyes popped open the second the sun came up, and I've been lying in this sinfully comfortable fluffy white bed, wide awake and thinking about him ever since. The crazy part is I'm not even tired, even though it took forever to fall asleep, my brain opting instead to waste half the night willing him to knock on my door to see if I was awake so he could pledge his undying devotion, then make sweet, sweet, spicy love to me all night.

But that's just silliness. He doesn't think of me *that way*, despite a whole lot of deliciously flirty banter yesterday (once we got over ourselves and decided that getting along would be more fun than bickering).

Could he maybe be attracted to me? It's possible. I'm not hideous after all.

No, no he's not. I'm sure of it. He's looking for someone altogether different than me as far as a long-term relationship goes. Or is he? Because if it turned out I was the girl for him, I could make peace with that idea quickly. I know that a mere eighteen hours ago, I was certain I hated him and everything he stands for, but now I feel like I've gotten past his hard outer-shell, and it's nothing but gooey, yummy chocolate inside.

I can imagine us cooking meals together, playing cards, snuggling up on the couch watching movies, going out dancing. I bet he's an amazing dancer. He probably had to take classes at whatever highbrow boarding school he went to, which left him light on his feet with a keen knowledge of how to lead, a commanding sense of rhythm, and a firm grip around his partner's waist.

Gah! This is killing me.

I've been lying here for nearly two hours, listening for some sign of him being awake. So far, nothing. But as soon as I hear one sound, I'm going to jump out of bed. Because the thing is, I can't wait to have more time alone with him. Like, maybe the next week or so. That would be enough time to find out if maybe a little something might happen between us.

Okay, Nora, you need a plan. As soon as he moves, go out there and be bright, chipper, and generally fabulous. Oh, and sexy. Be sexy too, but without seeming like you're trying. Be bright, chipper, fabulous, and effortlessly sexy, like Mila Kunis or a woman in an ad for hair dye. With any luck, Justin won't be back until the end of the day, which will give us plenty of time to be together in the world's most romantic villa on a private island.

A knock at the door interrupts my scheming. "Yes?" I do my best to sound sleepy. Like a sleepy, cozy, sexy kitten. All right, so a sexy kitten isn't a thing.

"Nora? Our ride is here."

Shit. Fuck. Son of a bitch. "Great! I'll be out in a minute," I call back in a smooth voice.

I throw my T-shirt and shorts back on, then hurry out of the room only to see Harrison Banks standing in the living room, chatting with Theo. Theo is also dressed and looks as though he probably slept like the dead last night, unlike me. If that's not a sure sign he's not into me, I don't know what would be.

As soon as he sees me, Harrison says, "Nora, are you okay? I've been worried sick about the two of you."

"I'm great," I tell him with a smile. "I'm surprised you came to pick us up."

"I wanted to get here as fast as possible, and Justin doesn't start work for another hour," Harrison says. "I was just telling Theo that this kind of thing has never happened before. We're always so careful about the weather reports, but this storm blew in hours before it was supposed to. I'm so sorry this happened."

"No need to apologize, we're fine," I answer. "Mr. Rojas missed an important meeting, but otherwise, all is well."

"You sure? I know the last thing you thought you'd be doing last night was winding up stuck here."

With a little shrug, I say, "It was okay, Harrison. It was no one's fault, and we made out just fine." *Made out? FIX THAT NOW!* "We *did* just fine. Not made out. That makes it sound like there was… and there wasn't." I let out a laugh, my skin prickling at the sight of the two men cringing as I ramble. "There was plenty of food, and we were safe the whole time. We even had some fun, didn't we?"

Theo nods. "We played cards to pass the time."

"Poker. Just the regular kind," I add.

"Okay, well, good," Harrison says, looking puzzled (as he should, since apparently, I'm a bumbling idiot this morning). "Should we get going? Get you two back to civilization?"

"Absolutely," I answer with a firm nod. "I have so much to do when we get back to the resort."

"I was thinking you may want the day off, since you were basically on the clock for the last twenty-four hours," Harrison says, holding the door open for us.

"Nope, not this lady," I announce as I step outside into the already-hot day. "I have far too much to do. Plus, I'm really well-rested so I'm ready to work."

Ha! See? I slept well too, so there, Theo.

The trek down to the beach is filled with small talk, mostly between the two men. I stroll along behind them, replaying my ridiculous behavior earlier. If Harrison doesn't suspect something, I'd be shocked. But what's to suspect? Nothing happened. Although with the way I'm acting, he very well might think something did.

When we reach the dock, Harrison helps me aboard the Rogue Fun, and I secretly wish it were Theo. As soon as we're off, Harrison points to a cooler on the floor. "I brought breakfast for you, in case you're starving."

I flip the lid and take out two plastic containers of yogurt with berries and granola. "Brilliant, thank you." I hand one to Theo and keep one for myself. I dig around and find two spoons. Holding one out to him, I ask, "How'd you sleep?"

"Very well, thanks." He takes the spoon without touching his fingertips to mine.

Damn. He slept really well and no gentle finger brushing? That seals it. He doesn't like me. Even though I am going to make him a better man. "I was worried you might not have been able to sleep on the couch."

"It was surprisingly comfortable," he says, lifting the lid off the yogurt.

"Good." I give him a smile that quite likely looks like I'm the top sales rep for Amway. *Do you use soap?* "I'm glad. Sleep is important."

Narrowing his eyes, Theo says, "Are you all right, Nora? You seem a little keyed up this morning."

"Fine. Totally fine." I pronounce each syllable of totally as if it's its own word. "If I am keyed up, it's only because I have so many great ideas—all work-related, of course."

Shut up. Just. Shut. Up.

Harrison glances over his shoulder. "That's what I like to hear." Glancing at Theo, he adds, "Nora is a consummate professional. We're lucky to have her."

"I believe it," Theo says vaguely, and the look on his face indicates he could not be less interested.

My stomach suddenly feels like a lead balloon. Whatever I thought we were both feeling last night was clearly a one-way thing. *Stupid, Nora. So stupid to let your hopes soar like that. Of course he doesn't have feelings for you.* Turning my attention to the yogurt, I dip my spoon in and take tiny bites, careful not to look up again for a long time.

Harrison strikes up a conversation with Theo about football, which continues for the rest of the ride. I do my best not to look upset, bored, or as though I'm feeling like the world's most awkward woman, which I most definitely am.

By the time the resort is in sight, I've disabused myself of any notion that Theo Rojas will ever be anything other than a VIP guest at the hotel. He's going to stay only until the filming is over, then he'll disappear forever, and I'll never see him again. Eventually I'll forget all about him and our night at Eden. It might take a few years to completely wipe him from my mind, but by God, I will do it.

Unless I don't.

————

Text from Hadley: *Um, what the hell is going on? You're stranded overnight with Mr. Rude?*

Hadley: *Are you back yet? Text me the second you see this. I must know what's happening.*

Me: *Just got back, thank God.*

Hadley: *And…??*

Me: *And… I've never been this confused in my life.*

Hadley: *Lunch?*

Me: *I'm going to be run off my feet catching up today.*

Hadley: *It's Thursday. I have the evening off. Want to come shopping for baby stuff after work?*

Me: *I'm in. :)*

159

———

Babyland is located in the seaside market district of San Felipe, along the main boardwalk. It's an enormous store that used to be a boat repair shop, but you'd never know it by looking at it now. It has cream-coloured walls, hardwood floors, and soft lighting. The cribs are at the front of the store, with a beautiful, round one directly in the centre of the display, with a price tag of $3300. Behind it is the bedding, mostly made of bamboo but all organic, then comes chemical-free wooden learning toys and BPA-free soothers and teething rings, and so on.

I find Hadley and Heath in the Bath Time for Baby section, gazing intently at a bathtub for newborns. My initial reaction is to feel a little miffed that Heath is here, since what I really need is some good old-fashioned girl talk. But then I remember Heath is fully capable of girl talk. In fact he's pretty damn good at it, having been raised by his wild, larger-than-life single mum, Minerva. When Hadley was going through a horrible breakup with he-who-shall-not-be-named, Heath showed up at her place one night and got right in on the man-bashing.

"That looks comfy. Does it come in my size?" I ask them.

Turning to me, Hadley grins. "I wish, right?"

"You know what else would be nice?" Heath asks. "Having a giant put you in the bath and do all the work for you."

Hadley and I wrinkle our noses at the idea, and Heath shakes his head. "On second thought, maybe not. What happened between you and his nibs?"

Hadley gives me an apologetic look. "I hope you don't mind, but I brought Heath up-to-speed on how much we hate Theo Rojas."

My gut tightens at the word "hate," but I smile. "Typical rich guy who gets whatever he wants when he wants it."

"Nightmare," Heath says. "Did he try anything when you were out there?"

"Heath's all ready to 'go have a talk with him, man-to-man' if needed," Hadley says, pointing to a white and lime green bath. "That one."

Heath points a price gun at it and pushes the trigger. "Good choice. Added to the registry."

"Nothing happened. He was a perfect gentleman," I tell them before commencing with the long, not-at-all sordid details of our time at Eden. The story is broken up by various baby-related item decisions, but by the time Heath has handed the gun over to the saleslady, and we're walking out into the warm night air, they've both been fully filled in.

"Gelato?" Hadley asks.

Deciding that I've easily burned off one scoop today, between hiking down the mountain and all the running around I had to do at the resort, I nod. "Let's do it."

We stroll the boardwalk until we reach Gina's Gelato and place our order. Hadley and I go for Nutella, and Heath orders rum raisin. With our ice creams in hand, we find a bistro table and sit.

"Rum raisin?" Hadley asks him. "You know we're going to have to tease you mercilessly for that, right?"

"I do, but I don't care. I'm a rum raisin guy through and through." He dips his spoon into the cup and scoops. "It's probably because I was raised by an older mum."

"You can't blame Minerva for your bad taste," I tell him with a grin before enjoying the first melt-on-my-tongue bit of creamy hazelnut and chocolatey goodness. "Mm, that is... I forgot how good ice cream was."

"Ours, anyway," Hadley says, giving Heath's treat the side eye. After we laugh at him some more, she gives me a serious look. "I couldn't help but notice that when you were talking about your night of being stranded with Theo, you didn't sound nearly as distraught as I thought you would."

My cheeks burn, and I turn my attention to the gelato. "There wasn't any need to be distraught. We had shelter and food to eat."

"It sounds like you had quite a lot of fun," Heath says, his mouth full.

"I wouldn't call it *fun*," I answer. "It wasn't awful, if that's what you mean, and I did enjoy beating him at poker." When neither of them says anything, I continue. "He did say something rather sweet. He said that knowing me was making him a better man."

Hadley's eyes grow wide. "He said that?"

"Mm-hmm. It was right after I told him why I can't stand rich people."

"You told him that?" Heath asks, his jaw dropping.

"He asked so I told him the truth," I say, my mind taking me back to that moment in the kitchen when both of us were in our robes in the candlelight. "After I explained my experience with the upper class has been generally as a servant, something sort of shifted for him." *And for me.* "That's when he told me that thing about being a better man."

"Huh, that's either very sweet or the best pickup line ever," she says.

"If it was a pickup line, he certainly didn't follow up to see if it worked." My heart feels all floppy and happy at the thought that he might actually be sweet. Then I remember he's not interested in me. "But he probably had some ulterior motive."

"Maybe not," Heath says. "Maybe he meant what he said. Generally speaking, if a man is in that kind of situation, and he's giving a woman a line meant to get her in bed, he'd try to get her in bed."

"But he can't act on his feelings," Hadley tells him. "Not after making a big show of telling everyone else they can't fraternize."

Shaking my head, I say, "I'm sure he doesn't have any feelings for me. He thinks I'm dowdy, remember?"

"But he only said that to get his brother off his back," Hadley says. "He didn't really mean it."

"If the thought popped into his head, he must have meant it," I tell her, doing my best to send that same message to my mixed-up heart.

"But you *did* look dowdy in that suit. It was literally hanging off you," she says firmly, then seeing the look on my face, she adds, "I'm sorry, but you did. You don't anymore though. Tell her Heath. Nora doesn't look dowdy now, does she?"

162

"Not at all. She looks…what's the opposite of dowdy?" His face turns pink at having to compliment his wife's best friend.

"Well dressed, and thank you, Heath. Hadley, never make your poor husband compliment me again. He's clearly uncomfortable." My mind goes directly back to Theo, and I realize that even after careful friend-assisted analysis, I'm still as clueless as I was before regarding Theo's intentions. That's probably because he doesn't have any, other than the ones I've dreamed up. "Anyway, none of it matters in the end, does it? He's only here for another week, then he'll be gone forever. If he were going to make his move, he should have done it last night. But he didn't, so it's over. Not that it ever got started, but you know what I mean." They both stare at me. "It means he doesn't like me *that* way, which is a good thing, because I can't stand him anyway."

"Uh-huh." Hadley nods.

Heath screws his face up in confusion. "Then why have we spent all evening talking about him?"

"It's a woman thing," she tells him.

"To try to sort out the exact thoughts and feelings of a guy you have no intention of ever dating?" he asks.

She and I nod. "Yes."

"But… why?"

"It's a form of entertainment," Hadley says, scraping her nearly-empty cup with her tiny spoon.

"Oh yes, quite fun," I say.

"No offense, but I am so glad I'm a man. Things are much simpler for us."

"That's because you're simple creatures," she tells him with an evil grin.

I eat another spoonful of ice cream, the phrase "simple creatures" bouncing around in my head. If there's anything Theo Rojas is not, it's simple. Sadly, neither are my feelings for him.

———

TO-DO LIST (Home Version)

Laundry – whites and darks (fold and put away for once to prevent digging around in dryer before work)

Clean out one bathroom drawer. Just one. You can do it.

Vacuum and wash floors

Look into cost of purchasing fake plants that actually look real

22

The Not-So-Great Pretender

Theo

AFTER RETURNING FROM EDEN, my day was so packed with meetings and emails, I've barely had time to process what happened, or more accurately, try to discern the origin of Nora's odd behavior this morning. Gone was the flirty, confident woman I spent the evening with, having been replaced by someone whose spirit animal is a flightless bird in a cat café. If I had to guess, I'd say she was worried that Harrison would think something happened between us last night. But the fact that she seemed worried (or possibly even a little guilty) leads me to wonder if our time together last night softened her opinion of me more than I could've hoped.

Not that I'm hoping for anything. Obviously, we don't have a future together, and more to the point, I'm not looking for a future with anyone, but somehow I have a strange niggling hope in my chest as I rush along the path from Building C to the Carib Asian fusion restaurant, where I am meeting my brother and Carolina for a late supper. I'm running fifteen minutes behind schedule, which *never* happens. I can count on one hand the number of times I've been late for anything since I took over the company. But because I stood up Robin, my COO, yesterday, I could hardly rush through our meeting today. I hate being late with a passion.

Although having a few moments to think isn't the worst thing, since I know as soon as I arrive at the table, Markos and Carolina are going to pepper me with questions about last night. Markos will want to find out if something unprofessional happened out there with the woman he believes to be my perfect match. He's going to tease me mercilessly, especially after he discovers I did not take advantage of an opportunity he most certainly would have. Carolina, on the other hand, is likely to be relieved by that very same information.

Oh, this is a lot longer walk than I thought. Between the suit I'm wearing (without a tie, I might add), the sweltering night air, and the pace at which I'm moving, I'm going to be a mess by the time I get there. I glance around for a golf cart ferrying guests around the grounds, but no such luck. The ones I have spotted so far have all been filled with people dressed up for dinner.

I finally see my destination—a large open-air restaurant with a thatched roof. A young woman greets me when I arrive at the reception desk. "Good evening, do you have a reservation?"

Making sure I look her directly in the eye, instead of what I would usually do, which is glance around for Markos and Carolina, I say, "Yes. I'm meeting my brother and a friend, who are here already."

"I believe I know who you're referring to." She takes a menu off the pile and leads me to the other side of the restaurant, where Markos and Carolina are waiting.

"There they are," I say as we near their table.

I sit down on one of the two empty sides of the table and when she hands me the menu, I thank her.

As soon as she walks away, Carolina picks up the bottle of wine and pours some into my glass. "You must need a drink after what happened. Was it dreadful? An entire night alone with that woman!"

I stiffen slightly at her words, then do my best to look totally breezy. "Actually, it was surprisingly fun."

"Really?" Markos says with a mischievous grin. "Just how fun are we talking?"

"Not like that, you *tonto del culo*." I pick up my glass of water instead of the wine.

"If you weren't doing that, what did you do?"

"We made dinner, then played poker most of the evening." My mind flashes to her sitting in her robe in the candlelight, laughing as she rakes all the trail mix towards herself.

The gleam returns to Markos's eyes, and he opens his mouth, but I anticipate what he's going to say. "No, not strip poker. The regular kind."

In my head, I hear Nora telling Harrison that, and it makes me want to laugh. But smiling or laughing at this particular moment would be a disaster. This is one of those situations where one must keep his cards close to his vest. I certainly can't have my dinner companions suspecting that there's a possibility of anything happening between Nora and me, especially as it would force me to admit three things I have no intention of doing: 1) my brother was right about Nora, 2) I'm not immune from being bitten by the romance bug, and, 3) I'm the world's biggest hypocrite, who is pulling a "do what I say and not what I do" thing on everyone participating in the competition.

Our server arrives at the table. He's a short man dressed in a white button-up shirt and black pants. "I'm Zak. I'm your server this evening," he says to me. "Your dinner companions have already ordered, but I can get the kitchen to rush yours so your food will all be ready at the same time."

"Only if it's not too much trouble. If it is, waiting while they start their meals seems like a just consequence for being late."

"Have you had a chance to look at the menu?"

"I haven't. What do you recommend?"

"Let me start by saying everything on the menu is terrific, of course. Our world-famous head chef, Emma Banks, personally created each item and, in fact, is credited around the globe as the inventor of the Caribbean Asian food craze," Zak says. "My personal favorite appetizer is the roti stuffed with stir-fried sweet potato and pineapple chutney. For a main, I suggest the spicy citrus tuna tiradito with sliced red onion, pickled jalapeños, truffled shishito glaze, and crunchy ramen noodles."

Picking up my menu, I hand it to him. "You sold me, Zak. Thank you." As soon as he leaves, I notice Markos and Carolina are both wearing matching dumbfounded expressions. "What?"

"Did something happen to you on that island?" Markos asks.

"Like what?"

"Like a lobotomy?" Carolina says with a nasty laugh.

"What makes you say that?" I ask, even though I know exactly why they're reacting this way.

"First off, you're not wearing a tie, which is very un-Theo of you," she says. "And second, rather than spending twenty minutes analyzing the menu, you decide to trust the waiter's word?"

"I believe the proper term now is server, and why not trust him?" I answer with a shrug. "He knows the menu far better than I ever will."

Needing to steer the subject away from the new and improved Theo, I pick up the small beverage and dessert menu propped up beside the candle holder, flip through it, and land on a picture of an attractive young woman in a chef's jacket. Next to it is a brief biography, including her awards. It also mentions her husband. "This is interesting. The chef is married to the author of the *Clash of Crowns* series, Pierce Davenport."

"Really?" Markos says. "That's my all-time favorite TV series."

"Did you never read the books?"

"I started with the TV series and heard the books were basically the same, so I never felt the need."

"That's a shame. They're so much better than the show," I say. Turning to Carolina, I say, "How about you? Are you a crown head at all?"

"No. I can't stand all that fantasy stuff."

Nodding, I say, "Well, hopefully his wife's work will be more to your taste."

"Strange that she still works, don't you think?" Carolina says.

"You're rich, and you still work," Markos says.

"That's family money. I have to work to get it. If I'd married into that *Clash of Crowns* money, there's no way I'd work another day in my life, and I certainly wouldn't be caught dead cooking for other people."

Oh my God. She really is awful. "I admire her for not quitting. If a person has something they're truly passionate about, it's much better to pursue it than succumbing to the boredom of retirement."

"'Only boring people get bored,'" Markos says, quoting our father.

Zak appears with our appetizers, sets them down in front of us, and leaves again. I pop a bite of the roti into my mouth. The bread is crispy on the outside and slightly chewy on the inside, giving it the perfect texture. There's just the right balance of saltiness to counterbalance the sauce that is both sweet and tart.

After a few minutes of companionable silence, Carolina takes a sip of her wine. "Theo, back to your evening with Nora. I'm just too curious to let it go."

"What do you want to know?" I ask, keeping my expression and tone neutral.

"I just can't imagine having a pleasant time with her, given the way she feels about people like us."

The phrase "people like us" irritates me. "Have you ever considered that she might have a good reason for the way she feels?"

"Of course not," Carolina says, looking taken aback. "How dare she lump us all together, as though we're all exactly the same or something."

"Ironic, since *you* just lumped us together," I say. "Let me ask you a question, Carolina. What colour is Zak's hair?"

"Who's Zak?"

"The waiter," Markos says, quickly adding, "*Server*, sorry."

"I don't know. Brown?" Carolina says, looking perplexed.

"*Hermano*, do you want to take a guess?" I ask Markos.

"I don't know either. I'm going with blond, to cover the odds."

"The fact that you both have to guess says something, don't you think?"

She shakes her head. "What could it possibly say? That I don't memorize every detail about the person bringing us food? And what does this have to do with how much Nora hates us?"

"First of all, she doesn't hate *all* of us. And secondly, after spending some time with her, I'd say she has good reason for her disdain. Nora has spent a lifetime being ignored and ordered around by 'people like us,'" I say, doing air quotes. "That would turn even the softest of hearts hard."

"I can't believe you're defending her," Carolina says, pushing her plate away. "We've been nothing but nice to her and yet she acts like we're the root of all evil in the world."

"*I* certainly wasn't nice to her when we first met. I was demanding and rude, and even worse, I didn't even realize it."

With a smug grin, Markos says, "You like her."

"Of course I like her," I answer, my face heating up. "But not in the way you mean."

"Obviously he doesn't have feelings for her," she tells him, stiffening visibly.

"You're wrong," Markos tells her. "He likes her. I can see it in his eyes." He laughs, then shakes his finger at me. "I told you! The first day we were here, I said you two would be perfect together. Looks like I was right."

"You were not right," I say, rolling my eyes. "I respect her as a professional and as a person. She's intelligent, has a good work ethic, and happens to be very insightful." *And is also sexy and beautiful and fun…*

He smirks. "The more you try to convince me you don't like her, the more I know you do."

"I don't—" I stop myself, realizing he wants me to continue trying to prove my lack of feelings. "You know what? Think what you want, *hermano*. Your opinion is of no consequence."

Looking at Carolina, he says, "He likes her."

Ignoring him, I scoop up more of the sauce with the roti, my cheeks flaming with embarrassment. Apparently my poker face isn't quite what it used to be.

Later, after we've gotten off the elevator on the third floor of Building C, with Carolina continuing up, I turn to Markos and ask the question that's been burning in my mind. "Did you keep watch last night?"

"I did, except not the way you do it." He strolls casually down the hall. "Your way is too boring, so I held a party at one of the bars so I could watch everyone without the peephole impeding my vision."

"You had a party?" I ask, stopping mid-stride.

Without stopping, he says, "I thought it best if everyone let off a little steam in a controlled environment. Don't worry, I cut myself off at three drinks so I could play nanny. They're a good group of people, Theo. Seriously. Very professional. The party broke up before midnight, because everyone had to be up early for filming this morning. You'll be happy to know there were no signs of anyone trying to hook up."

"Not even Paz?" I hurry to catch up with him.

"Not even him, and if I were you, I'd let go of whatever vendetta you've got as far as he's concerned. Trust me, he's a changed man. He didn't make a move on anyone the entire evening."

Deciding I'd rather not have to defend myself again concerning my hatred for Paz, I steer the conversation back to where we started. "How can you be so sure no one is hooking up?"

"This ain't my first rodeo," he says, putting on a Southern drawl.

Using my card key, I unlock the door and push it open, expecting Markos to do the same so he can go through his own door.

Instead, he follows me in. "I forgot my key."

Of course, he did.

"So? Have I convinced you or are you planning to stay up half the night watching everyone?" he asks, opening the door to his room.

"I'm staying up."

He turns back to me. "Can I ask you something?"

"Sure."

"Would it really be so bad if some people had sex while they were here? Ninety-five percent of the time, nobody gets hurt and there's no scandal. It's not like we've got a bunch of A-list celebs and paparazzi camped outside the hotel."

"Did you know the three most common causes for murder are revenge, money, and sex?" I ask him, opening the mini-bar and grabbing a bottle of water.

"Nobody's getting murdered, Theo. I know things are bad for the company, and I know you're worried. If you want to drive yourself crazy staying up all night, believing you can stop something bad from happening, that's up to you. But the truth is, if anyone here wants to hook up, they'll find a way."

"Well that's not exactly comforting."

"Sometimes life is messy, and all you can do is hope for the best. If shit happens, you clean up the mess, but spending all your time trying to prevent it will only stop you from having a life."

"Thanks, sensei," I say sarcastically.

Markos shakes his head. "Make fun of me if you like, but I'm trying to save you from yourself. You denied your feelings for that lovely events planner at dinner, which was smart with Carolina around, but if you're not careful, you're going to get to the end of your life having done nothing but worry about things you can't control. You gotta live a little before it's too late."

23

Lemur Stink Fights
Masquerading as Civilized
Meetings

Nora

THE NEXT MORNING I'm up with the sun. Vincent, who is finally
starting to bounce back from his violent illness, set up a meeting at
seven a.m. to go over everything Theo and I learned during our
reconnaissance mission. Unfortunately, Carolina Armas will be
there as well, so it's pretty much the worst way to start a day that I
can think of. Well, I'm sure there are worse ways… say, waking up
to find your house has flooded with raw sewage and everything you
love is ruined or stepping outside to find it's raining sewage. Pretty
much anything with sewage would be worse than an hour with
Carolina Armas, but not by much.

I arrive at the resort just after six and go straight to my desk in
the lobby, where I'll have access to a colour printer. First, I call
catering services and request coffee, water, and a continental breakfast for six (in case any of the assistant directors show up). Next, I
prepare a few packages of the various flora that can be found on the
island, complete with photos and location maps. By the time I finish,
I have to rush to make it to the meeting but I'm ready.

Food and drinks are waiting when I arrive. I smile to myself. I've got this shit down. I'm a total events-coordinating boss bitch who shall impress everyone in the vicinity with her kick-ass organizational abilities.

At ten after seven, Vincent and Carolina stroll in. "You poor, dear man," Carolina is saying. "Imagine being sea-sick for two days after you've gotten back to land?"

"My digestive system is just so delicate. The slightest thing can totally disrupt it," he says, scanning the room. When he sees the pastries, he lets out a squeal. "Ooh, are those bear claws?"

"They are," I answer, digging my nails into my palm to stop from laughing.

He moans with delight. "I'm absolutely famished." Piling two bear claws, a croissant drizzled in chocolate, and strawberries on his plate, he saunters over to the table while Carolina picks at the fruit with a set of tongs, joining him with a single slice of cantaloupe.

"Are we expecting anyone else or can we get started?" I ask, seating myself kitty-corner to them.

Narrowing her eyes, Carolina asks, "Who else do you think should be here?"

Uh-oh, I do not like that look she's giving me. "No one," I answer with what I hope is a pleasant smile and not my "fuck you" face. According to Hadley, they're shockingly similar. "I wasn't sure if anyone else on the production team needed to be here."

Vincent shakes his head, his words coming out muffled by the massive bite of bear claw in his mouth. "Just us. I'll convey anything necessary to the team."

"Perfect." I slide a package to each of them. "Theo and I were able to find a surprising number of herbs and fruits that should work for the challenge. We're in luck because a couple of them are ripe right now."

"Brilliant," Vincent says, jamming more pastry in his mouth. He flicks through the package, leaving gooey thumb prints on each page. "Ha! Jackass bitters! *Perfect.*"

Carolina seems unimpressed, however. She flips the pages while making a little *hmph* sound. I'm pretty sure she's busy thinking of a way to insult me, based on her sour expression.

The door opens and Theo comes in, no jacket or tie today. Just grey slacks and a sexy white dress shirt with the sleeves rolled up to reveal those muscular forearms he takes with him everywhere he goes. "Sorry I'm late. I had an urgent call I couldn't ignore."

"Theo! I'm surprised to see you. Last night at dinner you said you wouldn't have time to make it," Carolina purrs. Like seriously, she's purring. I'm half-expecting her to stand up and start rubbing her butt on him like a lemur marking a tree.

Oh, Nora. That wasn't very nice.

Accurate though.

Theo forgoes the refreshments and strides over to the table. "I thought it would be helpful if I was here, since I was fifty percent of the recon team."

He gives me a little wink, and my heart does a happy dance while he settles himself on the side opposite Carolina and Vincent, perpendicular to me. I slide him a package, and he immediately starts examining it. "Look at this. Very thorough, Nora. You've got maps and everything."

I beam at him for a second before my brains screams at me that I'm being *way too obvious!* Quickly wiping the smile off my face, I clear my throat, and say in an oddly low voice, "I thought maps would prove useful. I was also thinking maybe we give cards to each competitor with photos, names, and a brief description of the herb or fruit as well. No sense in having them wander around lost and confused all day. We could even set it up like a scavenger hunt with clues and such if you like."

"Who's we?" Carolina asks, scrunching her nose. She laughs. "I don't remember hiring you to be part of the production team."

Humiliation floods through me, starting at my gut and working its way out to my extremities. "Right, no. I didn't mean we, I meant you."

Theo gives her a glare, and she wilts a little in her chair. *Ha! Suck on that, be-otch.*

Meanwhile Vincent is so involved in his pastry eating that he's bobbing his head up and down to a beat no one else can hear. "I like her idea. Sounds fun."

"I don't think so," Carolina says, her face pinched. "That would make it far too easy."

Theo shakes his head. "Sorry, Carolina, I have to disagree with you. It's a surprisingly big island. Even with a map and pictures, it will still take them *hours* to find everything they need."

"The other thing to consider is that without instructions, there's a possibility they might try something toxic," I add.

"How likely is that?" Carolina asks me.

"I'm sorry?"

Maintaining direct eye contact, she says, "If you take into account all the non-toxic plants versus toxic plants, what would the ratio be? Since apparently you're an expert and all." She laughs to soften her words, but no one joins her.

I stare back until her smile fades. *Yeah, Miss Fancy Pants, it's on. I'll go all lemur stink fight if I have to. God, what is with me and lemurs this morning?* "I'm not an expert. In fact, I am still sourcing a botanist to be onsite during the challenge."

"If you're not an expert, how about you let us sort this out?" she says.

"We should listen to her, Carolina." Theo gives her a hard look. "Nora knows a lot about this stuff. She's the one that found everything and identified it. If you don't trust her opinion, maybe you should go out to Eden yourself and hike around for a few hours. See what you come up with."

She scoffs at the thought. "I don't do those things. I delegate them."

"And the person you delegated this to had a tummy ache, so Nora stepped up and got the job done. The least you can do is listen to her," Theo says firmly.

Vincent chokes a little on whatever he's jammed into his mouth during his last bite, then says, "I was violently ill."

"Oh, I know. I held the bucket for you."

I love him so much right now. I'm tempted to crawl into his lap and rub my butt on him while evil-grinning at Carolina. Instead, I decide to get out while I still look like the level-headed professional I'm pretending to be. I check my watch, even though I don't actually have anything pressing after this, and say, "I don't really have anything else to add, so if there's nothing else, I'll leave so you can discuss everything."

I stand, and Theo smiles up at me. "Thanks so much, Nora. Great work on this."

"You're welcome," I tell him, before striding out of the room.

I smile all the way to my desk. Theo stuck up for me against his hoity-toity childhood friend, who clearly wants to marry him so they can have lots of uppity babies.

Sorry, Carolina, I don't think he wants to make new humans with you. Not that he wants to make them with me either, but this morning I'd say I have a better shot at it than she does. Not that it's a contest.

But if it were…

———

Email From Vincent St. Pierre
To: Nora Cooper
Subject: TOP SECRET!! TODAY'S RESULTS

Nora,

As you know, we had to postpone filming of the Memory Challenge due to that big storm, so we filmed both the Memory and the Storytelling Challenges today (and culled three losers).
Their names are Eddy Morales, Marija Horvat, and Junior Afumba.

Five down, four to go!

V

P.S. Great work on the survivor challenge stuff. I've managed to convince Carolina that your suggestions are the way to go. Not sure why she was such a Grumpy Gus this morning, but don't take it personally. ;)

Mike the Moose TikTok Reel

Mike walks along a resort path in the early evening. "Hey Moose Heads! I'm coming to you live from the beautiful Paradise Bay Resort where we're still filming the World Championships! As you know, everything is hush hush as far as who's moving onto the next round. I wish I could tell you, but it'll mean automatically being disqualified."

Mike widens his eyes and mimes chewing on his nails like he's scared. "Anyway, I wanted to ask you what your favourite unconventional cocktail is. Comment below for your chance to win this T-shirt I'm wearing right now." He pans down to show a black shirt with the words: I MAKE BEER DISAPPEAR. WHAT'S YOUR SUPERPOWER? written on it.

"Okay, gang, I'm heading to a party with Markos Rojas, the fun Rojas brother. Peace out!"

TO-DO LIST (Home Version)

Laundry — whites and darks (fold and put away for once to prevent digging around in dryer before work) YAY!!!

Clean out one bathroom drawer. Just one. You can do it.
Vacuum and wash floors

Look into cost of purchasing fake plants that actually look real Ridiculously expensive – Google indestructible plants instead

24

You Know When You Know

Theo

I THINK I'm having an early midlife crisis, and there are two people to blame for it—Nora Cooper and my brother. I'm unsettled in a way I have never been in my life. I can't stop thinking about Nora, no matter what I do. Not even work is enough to keep her off my mind. Her face pops into my brain a thousand times a day, causing a pang in my chest each time. The truth is, I know I'm falling for her. We may have gotten off to a rocky start, but if we can get past that—and I think we're well on our way—we really would be perfect for each other.

Unfortunately, that makes Markos right about something, and I can just imagine all the gloating that would undoubtedly go on for the rest of my life if I end up with her— especially after I told him I'd never take his advice again for the rest of my life, even if I were on fire and he told me to stop, drop, and roll. But all the teasing in the world would be worth it, and maybe it wouldn't be the worst thing for him to be right about something. He has shown the odd moment of wisdom.

Case in point, his comment the other night about how if I'm

not careful, I'll get to the end of my life having done nothing but worry about things I can't control. He's right about that. Since I took over the company, I've done very little other than worry. I certainly haven't lived. Deep down, I'm terrified I'm going to live and die exactly like my father—my entire life spent at the office, tending to the company. At least he had a family. I only have my work.

It's not only what Markos said to me. It's the questions Nora asked when we were on Eden, about whether I plan to have a son and pass on all my burdens to him. She started me thinking about what I want out of life, which is not something I've allowed myself the luxury of considering. I was born into my role in life, and I took it on because that's what was expected and what I believed I wanted. My destiny, corny as that sounds. But now I'm not so sure that's true, and what's worse is that I'm not sure it ever was. Deep, deep, deep down in a place I don't ever allow myself to go, I know I don't want to do this forever. I've never admitted it out loud to anyone, but now that the question has been asked, and my gut has answered, I can't go on ignoring it.

Actually, I can. I have over eight thousand reasons to ignore it. I can't abandon them.

But maybe I can find happiness outside my career, and what if that happiness came in the form of Nora Cooper? Wouldn't going home to her every night make the rest worth it?

It's been four days since I spoke to her in any meaningful sort of way. I've made a point of leaving the building at times when she's most likely to be at her desk. I have about a fifty percent success rate, meaning I've had a chance to wave and smile at her three times, and once we exchanged a few words, only to be interrupted by that ridiculous Mike the Moose guy, who needed something from her.

This is at least as crazy as me guarding the door, watching for signs of trouble. We barely know each other. I've never seen where she lives or met her parents. We've never gone out on a date, although if somehow we did end up together, I'd lobby hard to have our night at Eden be considered our first date.

My phone pings with a text from her. My pulse races as I scan the words. *Any clandestine meetups in the hall this evening?*

Me: *Nothing yet, but I'm ready to catch them in the act.*

Nora: *I hope not. That would be awkward.*

Me: *Ha! Good one. It's late. Shouldn't you be asleep?*

Nora: *I've been trying, but I can't shut my brain off tonight.*

Me: *What's on your mind?*

Nora: *I decided to check my email before bed. Huge mistake. I was answering emails until after midnight, and now I can't seem to wind down.*

Me: *That happens to me too. I often think people's lives were a lot better before mobile devices, laptops included. When your workday was done, it was done. You could leave it there until the next day. But now...*

Nora: *It's true. Someone should start a revolution.*

Me: *Agreed.*

I stare at our exchange, desperate to keep it going. Desperate to ask if she might want to go out sometime. I chew my lip, then decide maybe there is a way I can test the waters without risking anything.

Me: *Speaking of work, have you ever considered working somewhere else?*

Nora: *Like a different hotel?*

Me: *Sure, or maybe even a job that takes you away from Santa Valentina?*

Nora: *Not really. I've been focused on trying to get ahead where I am.*

Mierda. I'm being too vague, but how does one make it clear without actually making it awkwardly, embarrassingly clear? My heart pounds as I type. *Any chance you want to talk instead of text?*

After a few seconds of waiting with my breath held, the phone rings. When I pick it up, she says, "This might be more efficient."

Hearing her voice does something to me. "That's why I suggested it. I'm nothing if not efficient. Back to your promotion. Assuming you get it, what then?"

"Promise you won't laugh?"

"Yes… unless it's meant to be funny."

"It's not."

"Then I promise." I wander away from the door and plunk down in an armchair.

"I want to buy myself a small cottage on the sea. Something I can fix up a little. I'd like to plant a garden and go out every day to check on it and give it some water, although to be totally honest, my house plants don't fair all that well, so I'm not sure how the garden would do."

"It's worth a try anyway. People can learn to do better than they've done before."

"True," she says.

I smile even though she can't see it. "Tell me more about your cottage, which sounds wonderful by the way."

"Thanks," Nora says. "I want to sit on the deck, listening to the waves lap against the shore while I read great books and on occasion, have a few friends over for dinner for no reason at all, other than the fun of it." She pauses. "That probably sounds stupid to you."

"It sounds amazing." Which it does.

"Are you just saying that to be nice? The life I want would be a massive downgrade for you," she says, sounding slightly self-conscious.

"I'm not. It sounds a lot like freedom to me. That's what life should be about—balance and simplicity." I sigh, all those thoughts of my life bubbling back up to the surface again. "Can I tell you something I've never admitted to anyone?"

"Sure," she says, sounding sleepy and sexy. I imagine she's lying in her bed on her side, and I'm there, facing her.

"Sometimes I'm filled with envy for people who can chart their own course in life," I say, forcing the words out. "I think about my great-great-great-grandfather Alvaro, who started the company. He had a dream and started with one small distillery, then had the pleasure of working hard and watching it grow into something truly amazing. It would feel very different than having it all handed to you. That probably sounds stupid."

"Not at all," Nora says. "I think having to struggle is good for us. Then we know we've earned our success. I think that's a completely different type of satisfaction."

"Exactly." I get up and cross to the balcony. "A sense of true pride in your accomplishments. For the most part, I'm happy with how I've taken care of the company and my family, but I haven't built anything. Even the family I'm looking after is inherited—my brother, my mother—and doesn't need taking care of. But I also have a stepmother who needs help from time to time. It's not the same as if I had my own family, one I'd started with someone I loved." Maybe you. "In another life I would have liked to build my fortune from the ground up, although I'm sure I'd spend that life wishing I'd been handed a fortune."

Nora chuckles softly. "Human nature, right? We always want what we don't have."

"Sad but true."

She yawns, and I realize how late it is. "I should let you go," I tell her. "You need to sleep, and I should get back to my peephole. You know, like a reverse pervert."

Nora lets out a loud laugh. "Gah! You can't be funny at this hour. I'm pretty sure I woke my neighbours with that one."

"Sorry."

"No you're not."

"You're right, I'm not. It was worth it to make you laugh, but give them my apologies tomorrow anyway." I take a deep breath, then say, "Good night, Nora. Sleep fast."

"You too, Theo."

After we hang up, I spend a long time rereading our exchange and thinking about our conversation. She texted me, and it wasn't because of some work-related thing. It was because she wanted to. She must have feelings for me, otherwise why would she send me a late-night message? A flirty, funny one too?

Talking to her is not like talking to anyone else I know. I want to tell her everything, every little thought and secret I've kept hidden away my entire life, because I know she won't laugh at me. She'll listen and understand. We didn't grow up in the same world, but Nora Cooper understands me, and I understand her right back. There is something between us I can't ignore. I don't want to ignore it. I need to find a way to make this work, no matter what.

That's it. Tomorrow I'm going to be brave. I'm going to find her, ask to speak with her alone, and tell her once this competition is over, and we no longer have a working relationship, I'd like to try a personal one. I'll find a better way to put it than that, but I will do it. By tomorrow evening, I'll know if I have a future with Nora Cooper. And I have a good feeling the answer will be yes.

———

Okay, so maybe I was a bit optimistic about the timing of things. It's now after eight p.m., and I didn't get a chance to talk with Nora. I saw her four times, but each time she was dealing with someone from the show. I couldn't very well go back down to the lobby a *fifth* time. Not after the last time, when she narrowed her eyes at the sight of me and told the cameraman, who was in the process of complaining about the lack of variety of sunscreens in the resort's gift shop, to excuse her and then turned to me. "Mr. Rojas, do you need something? You've stopped down here several times."

I shook my head, effectively freeing my brain from any type of logic. "Nope. Nothing. I was just…wondering the same thing about the sunscreen."

The man looked surprised. "Are you a big Banana Boat fan too?"

I nodded. "Yep. Love it. Nothing else works for me."

184

"Same," he said. "You'd think they'd have it here. It has to be one of the most popular brands in the world."

"If not *the* most popular."

Nora stared at me, dumbfounded, then turned back to the man. "If you like, I can arrange for a shuttle to take you into town to buy some."

"Sure," the man said, looking over at me. "You wanna come with? Load up on some Banana Boat?"

"Thanks, but I have some back in my room." I glanced at my watch. "And I've got a thing right now. Good luck though. I hope you find it."

With that, I hurried off, feeling like a complete idiot. *Nice going, Theo. Very smooth.*

So, now I'm sitting on my balcony watching happy couples stroll along holding hands in the gentle evening breeze. I'm restless and bored and keenly aware of how alone I am this evening, which I suppose is what happens when one is most likely in love but hasn't been able to tell the person he's in love with. The thought of an entire evening on my own feels like more than I can handle.

Markos is out with the crew, Nora has probably gone home, and I have *no* desire to find out what Carolina is up to, on account of not wanting to confuse her. It's getting harder and harder to pretend I don't know where she sees things going between us. We're at this awkward moment where I know but she doesn't know that I know for sure, so I can continue acting as though I have no idea. Hopefully this lasts until we return home, so we won't be only one floor away from each other after I let her down.

The best-case scenario would be that something happens between Nora and me *before* Carolina makes her move. That way Carolina can save face, and she and I can go on as we always have, as old family friends.

Okay, that's it. I need to think of some sort of witty text to send Nora. Something irresistible and enticing. Hmm… nothing is coming to mind. I'm totally blank. I type *Any chance you feel like playing cards? I need to win back my reputation.*

Terrible. Delete.

What happened to me? I swear I used to have game.

There's a knock at the door, and my first thought is Nora before I realize it's probably Markos, who seems to have decided he doesn't need to bring a key anymore because his boring big brother stays in his room all the time.

But it could be Nora.

I get up and hurry across the room, checking my breath (pretty good) and putting on a big smile. But when I yank the door open, Carolina is standing in front of me in a bathrobe, holding two champagne flutes and a bottle.

So, not Nora at all. If disappointment could be measured the way earthquakes are, it would register 9.9 on the Richter scale.

She glides past me. "I thought I'd find you here."

Holding the door open, I say, "You were right."

She turns and gives me what I'm sure she thinks is a seductive smile. "I usually am."

"Carolina, I don't think it's a good idea for you to be in my room at this hour. We're trying to set a good example, and you showing up with a bottle of champagne doesn't exactly suggest we're walking the talk."

She sets the glasses on the nightstand next to my bed. "Nobody is here. They're all out at the pool with Markos. He organized some sort of volleyball tournament. Or water polo. Something." Popping the cork, she laughs as the liquid erupts like a volcano onto the tile floor.

Sighing, I go to the en suite to get a towel so I can mop up the mess. In the process, the door slams shut, leaving us in the exact situation I don't want to be in and she does. When I return, her robe is on the bed, and she's stripped down to her bra and panties. The flutes have been filled and are waiting for us, and she has her hands on her hips and a smile on her face. "Leave it. The maid can get it tomorrow."

Averting my eyes, I continue with my mission, tossing the towel on the floor and pushing it around with my foot to soak up the liquid.

"You're not going to leave me standing here like this, are you, Theo?"

Plucking the towel off the floor, I say, "No, I'm not. I'm going to ask you to please put your robe back on and go back to your room."

Carolina blinks. "I don't understand. Why would you want me to do that? No one has to know."

I let out a sigh, then rub the spot between my eyebrows. "Look, Carolina, you're a beautiful woman and a wonderful friend, but—"

"Yes, I am, which is why there shouldn't be a but. Only a yes, let's do this." She steps towards me and puts her hands on my chest. "Think of it, Theo. You and I are the perfect power couple. You want this. I want this. It's going to happen, whether it happens tonight or in the future, so why not tonight?"

I take her hands off me and hold them, stepping back to make space between us. "I'm sorry, but this isn't going to happen. Not tonight, not ever. I don't think of you that way."

Blinking hard, she whispers, "But… why?"

"I think of you as family, and family is off limits."

"Maybe you should start thinking of me as forbidden fruit." She comes towards me again.

Eww. Forbidden fruit. Never say that again. "I'm sorry but no. My heart belongs to someone else."

Anger flashes across her face. "Who?"

"Does it matter?" I ask gently.

"Of course it does. I have to make sure she's good enough for you."

"Believe me, the question should be if I'm good enough for her." I glance at her robe again. "Why don't you get dressed while I get rid of this towel?"

I turn, but her voice stops me.

"It's that little event planner, isn't it?"

I freeze, then turn around, hoping the smile in my heart isn't showing on my face. "Yes."

Scoffing, she says, "You aren't sure if you're good enough for *her*? What a joke! She's so far below you." She shakes her head, then finally bends down to pick up her robe.

187

I take the opportunity to hurry to the bathroom and drop the towel in the tub. When I come back, Carolina is finally a lot less nude but is also wearing an ugly expression. "What did she do? Seduce you when you were out on that island?"

"Nothing happened. In fact, she doesn't even know how I feel. I haven't found a way to tell her."

"You're serious about this? You're not just saying this so I won't feel hurt that you're rejecting me?"

"I'm serious about it. About her."

"But you don't even know her! I've known you your entire life. I know everything about you, and I love you all the more for it." Tears spring into her eyes.

"I don't know what to say, other than my wish is for you to find someone who feels about you the way I do about Nora."

"No," she says, shaking her head. "No. This isn't how it's supposed to go. Not after everything I had to do to get you here."

My head snaps back. "What is that supposed to mean?"

Scowling, she says, "Did you really think Jacardi would pull out after how much money they made last year?"

I stare at her, stunned. "Did you break your contract with them?"

She nods. "As soon as you agreed to come on board. They're threatening to sue the network. My father is furious with me."

"Jesus, Carolina, how could you do something like that? You put your family's company at risk, not to mention screwing over Jacardi like that."

"I did it for you, Theo. Because I love you so much. I always have, and I thought if I could get you out here, and we spent some time together, you'd realize we're meant to be."

Wow, this is some stalker-level stuff. I feel like I don't even know who Carolina is, but I do know she's not someone I want to associate myself with any longer. "I think you should leave."

"No, Theo," she says.

"Go, Carolina. I don't want to be around you right now." I walk past her to the balcony and slide the door behind me.

I cross to the railing and rest my hands on it, trying to process what just happened. After a moment I hear the muffled sound of the door to the hallway closing. First thing in the morning, I'm going to call the head of our legal team to make sure we're not somehow culpable for what Carolina did to Jacardi. One thing's sure: the friendship between our two families is about to crumble to dust at a time when I need all the allies I can get.

25

Missing Booze, Men Who Sell You Out, and Shattered Cottage Dreams

Nora, Twenty Minutes Earlier

I SIT, clicking my fingernails on the top of my desk. I can finally go home for the night, and yet...I'm still here, trying to decide if I should go up to Theo's room to talk to him or not. Obviously he has something to tell me. Or ask. He wouldn't have come down here four times today otherwise. And that last time was just plain weird, with the whole Banana Boat thing? No way he uses Banana Boat. I'm sure he buys some brand I've never even heard of, that costs more per bottle than I spend on a month's groceries.

I should just be bold. March right up to his room and knock. I know he's there, and he was receptive to my text last night. Very receptive. Our conversation was incredible. The way he opened up to me and how he seemed to get me when it comes to my dream. There's something happening between us. I can feel it, and I know he can too. Otherwise, why would he have asked if we could talk? And why would he have come down here four times today?

I'll go.

But first I'll freshen up.

I hurry to the bathroom down the hall with my handbag, take

my emergency toothbrush and paste, and brush my teeth, concentrating extra hard on my tongue. Then I apply some lipstick and check my hair to make sure it's still in the bun. A little messy, but hopefully in that sexy librarian sort of way.

Okay, Nora. This is it. You can do this. Theo is just a man, after all. He puts his pants on one leg at a time. So he's wildly rich, incredibly handsome, well-educated, and highly sought-after. He is just a man.

He's also a man who has given some slightly confusing signals. But still. Signals nonetheless. I'll go up to his room, knock, and tell him I'm about to go home for the day but thought I'd see if he needed anything before I leave.

In the elevator, I press three and wait for the doors to close while my heart thumps madly in my chest. I'm almost to his room when the door opens and Carolina Armas comes out, wearing a bathrobe.

Hide!

There's nowhere to do that though!

She spots me. Her lips curve up in a smile and not a particularly nice one at that. "Nora, what are you doing on this floor at this hour?"

I have no answer for that. "I'm following up on a sunscreen issue."

She lifts an eyebrow. "A sunscreen emergency? At night?"

"Yes," I answer, my voice betraying me with a squeak. "For tomorrow. I told Barry, the cameraman, I'd make sure he had his Banana Boat before morning." I nod a few times, hoping to hypnotize her. "Mission accomplished."

I turn on my heel and go back the way I came, only to have her catch up with me. Damn her long legs. "You're probably wondering what I was doing in Theo's room dressed like this."

"Nope. None of my business." I pick up my pace.

"We've been keeping it a secret, but since you caught me, I guess the cat is out of the bag," Carolina says with a light chuckle. "Please don't tell anyone."

I push the down button at the elevator. "Tell anyone what? I don't know anything."

She presses up, and there's something so smug about the way she does it. It's like she's saying, *I'm going up in life, and you're going down, peasant.* "Tell anyone that Theo and I are going to be married."

My heart feels as though it's been sucked dry and has turned to dust. I stare at her smug, rich face. And boy is it both smug and rich. Not one visible pore. No wonder Theo wants to marry her. My breath has left my body, but somehow I manage to say, "Congratulations."

Come on elevator, where the hell are you? This building only has four floors!

"Not right away, of course. He has far too much on his mind this year to think about a wedding. But when things settle down, he's going straight to Harry Winston."

The up-arrow lights and the doors open. Of course her ride comes first. That's exactly how the rich get richer. Okay, that didn't make sense, but still. Not fair.

Smiling at me, she says, "Well, that's me. Thanks for keeping our secret." She steps on and gives me a wink, putting a finger over her lips.

The second the doors close, I put both middle fingers in the air and aim them at the ceiling, tracking her movement. "Go to hell, bitch," I mutter before feeling silly and putting my fingers away.

A few seconds later, the doors open and I step on, only to be trapped with Carolina's perfume for the ride to the ground floor.

That's it. I'm going home, but first I'm stopping at the gelato place for a large cup of Nutella with whipped cream. And maybe a churro. That would be good too.

———

Text from Mum: *Nora, do you still have Kat at work at this hour? If so, you should really start paying her.*

I stare at her text for a few seconds, trying to figure out how to answer. First off, Kat left over five hours ago. I don't want my mum to panic, but on the other hand, if there's reason for her to panic, she should know about it. Second, *I* should be paying her? As if it's up to me? Grrr....

Instead of answering Mum, I text Kat. *Where are you? Mum's asking if you're still at work, and I don't know what to tell her.*

I wait a couple of minutes and finally see she's typing a reply.

Kat: *I'm out with Gwen and Lola. Just sent her a message to let her know.*

Me: *Okay. See you tomorrow morning at eight!*

Mum: *Don't worry. I just heard from Kat. She's out with her girlfriends. You okay?*

Me: *I'm fine. Filming wraps up in a few days, which will be a huge relief.*

Mum: *Hang in there. Dad and I are praying for you.*

Me: *Thanks, Mum. Hugs to you and Dad.*

I read over our exchange, thinking about what a huge relief it will be when I never have to see Theo again. But not because I hate him. It's because I now want something I can't have. So badly it hurts. But hopefully, that feeling will morph back into hating him again soon.

————

I'm still stinging from last night. My face feels all hot and itchy, and my stomach is churning like there are a couple of pioneer ladies in there with long wooden sticks. I guess I should be grateful I found out before I knocked on his door. Imagine how humiliating it would have been if I'd shown up and did the whole "can I do anything for you before I leave?" thing while Carolina was there?

Urgh! How can he seriously be planning to marry that woman? She's a terrible human being, and he's...so very capable of not being awful at all. Except maybe he's not. He did almost sort-of lead me on, didn't he?

Did he think I'd be one last fling before he settled down? Or maybe he's the type that will cheat on his wife. If that's the case, I definitely dodged a bullet by not getting involved with him. Carolina could be in for a lifetime of misery. She pretty much deserves it, but still, it doesn't exactly make Theo a good guy.

Whatever. I have work to do. I'll have to put Theo Rojas out of my mind for good. My heart too. Evicted. Get out. Done. I don't want any.

I wake up my laptop, which went to sleep while I stewed. Kat finally appears for the day—only twenty minutes late though, so I suppose that's an improvement. She glides across the lobby to her desk without looking up from her phone.

How does she do that without bumping into things? That must be a skill the younger generation has developed, due to having mobile phones attached to their hands at all times. Kat lets out a giggle, then sighs.

"What's that all about?" I ask, trying to sound like a casual, friendly older sister, the type that's cool with whatever's happening, but I'm not and she knows it.

"Nothing. Just a funny meme. You wouldn't get it."

Yeah, right. Likely story. She has something going on with a guy. I'm positive about it. I open my mouth to ask and then shut it, not wanting to know. If she has started up with one of the people involved in the show, I'm better off staying in the dark. They'll all be gone in a matter of days, anyway, and if I don't know anything, I don't have to deal with it.

I have enough on my plate as it is. The flair challenge is today, but even more importantly, the survivor challenge is coming up in two days. The current Eden guests will vacate the island tomorrow at noon, which will bring with it a flurry of activity. Vincent wants me onsite as much as possible. He's been calling me his eyes and ears at Eden since our meeting last week. As great as this will be for my career, I am not looking forward to going back to the island, where I spent one perfect night with one not-so-perfect man who I thought was perfect.

Argh! Stop thinking about him and get back to work.

———

Email from Vincent St. Pierre
To: Nora Cooper
TOP SECRET!!! Flair Challenge Results

Nora,

HUGE UPSET TODAY! HUGE! Paz Castillo, king of the flair pour, went down in flames today. I have a sneaking suspicion he was either incredibly hung over or was still drunk from last night.

Anyway, you know the drill. Paz no longer has access to practice spaces.

Best,
Vincent

———

TO-DO List (Home Version)

Grocery shopping

Buy cacti and snake plants

Vacuum and wash floors (same day so as to actually get on with washing)

Clean out dryer lint holder thingy

———

Two Days Later

I barely slept last night. I'd drift off, only to be woken by stress dreams, most of which ended with Carolina and Theo naked and laughing at me. Not a great start to what will undoubtedly be one of the most stressful days of my career. The Survivor Challenge is filming today. I was out at the island all day yesterday with the crew, helping however I could with the setup. We were there for close to twelve hours and are heading back out in twenty minutes.

Another tropical storm is brewing, and it looks like it will arrive by tomorrow morning. Filming must take place today, or I'll be stuck with all of these terrible people to look after for another several days while we wait for the storm to pass. And by all of these terrible people, I mean Carolina and Theo. Vincent too. Actually, Vincent's not that bad, but he's like the human version of a mosquito, always buzzing around making noise and irritating people. But other than the three of them, the rest of the crew and contestants have been okay. Well, that's not really true either. Several of the crew members are pretty high maintenance, now that I think about it. Case in point: Barry, the Banana Boat fan.

But I could deal with all the Vincents and Barrys in the world for the rest of my life if I can only get what's-his-name and what's-her-face off my island forever so I can forget all about them.

Picking up my coffee mug, I tip it back, only to discover it's empty *à la* Aunt Beth and her martini glass. It's probably for the best. Do I really need to add more caffeine to my already-anxious state?

My desk phone rings, startling me.

"Nora? It's Fidel. We've got a big problem."

I press the receiver closer to my right ear while Fidel tells me that the booze order that was supposed to have arrived yesterday still hasn't shown up. He called the guys at the warehouse to see if maybe it had arrived on the island but hasn't been delivered yet, but it turns out they have no record of an order coming in this week at all.

Shit. Shit. Shit.

"There has to be some mistake. I sent the order last Wednesday." I try to sound calm while I scramble to open my email. "Let me find it."

I consider clicking on the sent items but realize I need to go directly to drafts. And there it is, the email to Jaquell, sitting there, waiting to be sent. Kat added a message to it before forgetting to press send.

Jaquell,
Thanks for this!
Nora

Son of a bitch. Kat didn't send the order.

I let out a hiss of air, like a bicycle tire that's just been slashed. "So, um… yeah, the mistake is on our end," I tell him.

"Are you kidding me?" Fidel asks, sounding as pissed as I would be if the situation were reversed.

"I wish I was," I say, momentarily considering selling Kat down the river. "I am so sorry, Fidel."

"Nora, this is bad. As of this afternoon, I'm out of vodka, whiskey, dark and light rum, and Rojas Breezies. *Breezies*, Nora. Do you have any idea how popular they are?"

"I… I can guess." I rub my forehead with my left hand.

Fidel lets out a long sigh. "You'd better come to the main office right now so we can figure out what to do."

"I'm on my way."

Launching myself out of my chair, I jog out of the building and jump in my golf cart. Throwing it in reverse, I back out, then pop the cart into drive and zip down the path like a bat out of hell. You know, if bats could drive golf carts.

My phone pings and I see a text from Vincent. *What the fuck is this I'm hearing about us having run out of booze?!*

I quickly record a message to him and hit send. *I can fix everything. Don't worry.*

Vincent: *If there's one thing I'm going to do, it's worry.*

I park haphazardly at the main lobby building, then take the steps two at a time. The receptionists must know what's going on because they're whispering to each other. When they see me, they break apart with guilty expressions. I rush through the doors to the main office area and stop short when I see who's here.

Harrison, Libby, Rosy, Fidel, Carolina, Vincent, and oh yeah, Theo, are huddled in a circle. I hear Theo say, "Jaquell would never delete an email without actioning it first."

"So it had to be Nora," Carolina says.

"It must have happened when we were stranded at Eden. She asked Rosy to tell her sister to send the email for her," Theo says, giving Rosy a pointed look.

"Which I did," she tells him. "The second we got off the radio call."

"She didn't send it," I say, cutting into the conversation, my heart pounding. "I just checked my email and it's still sitting in the drafts folder."

All eyes turn to me, including Oakley's. She's been sitting at her desk, intently listening to the entire thing since I got here. *Why does she have to be here for this? Anyone but her.*

Oh God, this is so, so bad. I have never wanted to disappear as badly as I do at this moment. Poof, gone. Transported into some alternate universe where, the minute I got back from Eden, I checked to make sure Kat had sent the bloody email.

"Seriously?" Vincent asks. "And you didn't think to check to make sure it was sent?"

"I am *so* sorry, but I can—"

He holds up a hand. "We're supposed to be on our way to Eden as we speak, but you know what's difficult to set up without booze? A bar!"

Do not cry, Nora. Whatever you do, do not cry. You can still salvage this.

"Honestly, Harrison," Carolina says. "This is beyond incompetent. Theo literally couldn't have made it easier for your team."

"It's a huge mistake, for sure," Harrison says, glancing at me without a hint of his normal happiness. "But I'll take care of it."

"It's going to cost a small fortune to buy everything at retail," Libby says, staring at the order form in her hand.

"Yes, it will," Harrison says. "But we've got no choice. We can't very well allow ourselves to run out of liquor."

"Imagine the reviews," Rosy says, *tsk*ing.

"Forget your reviews," Vincent snaps. "We can't exactly hold the bartending world finals without it either."

"Okay, Vincent, there's no need to get nasty about it," Theo tells him. "Nora screwed up, but we don't need to beat a dead horse."

Oh God, I'm a dead horse, and they probably all *want to beat me right now.*

"A dead horse?" Vincent asks, his voice climbing two octaves. "We're supposed to start filming in two hours!"

Do something, Nora. Anything! "Wait! If you give me the list of what you need at Eden, I'll go to town right now. I'm sure I can get everything out to the island by the time the contestants have collected all the herbs and fruits."

"I think you've done enough," Carolina tells me with a sniff. "We need someone who knows how to complete a simple task."

Do not cry. Not in front of these people. Not while Oakley is here. Do not... Shit, I'm crying. And blinking is not holding back the tears. They're just flowing out of my damn eyes like the world's tiniest rivers. Libby glares at Carolina and wraps an arm around my shoulders.

I manage to squeak out, "I'm okay. It's just lack of sleep. But I'm going to pull myself together and fix this. Everything will be fine, I promise."

Harrison looks at me with pity. "Listen, Nora. You sit this one out, okay? Fidel and I will go source what's needed. Stay here and make sure we've got a boat ready when we get back."

"I wouldn't even trust her with that," Carolina mutters.

I glance at Theo, hoping he'll ask his stupid secret fiancée to go easy on me, but he doesn't. Instead, he says, "I'm sure Nora is more than capable of arranging transportation for some bottles, even if she's clearly not ready to manage staff."

He glances at me, and whatever my face is doing has him scrambling to add, "Granted this event would be a large undertaking for most people."

My head snaps back. Did he just say all that? In front of all three of my bosses? When he knows I've been working my ass off for a promotion to management?

Yes. Yes, he did. And now I have that reason to hate him again.

A few minutes later, I barge through the front doors to Building C, a woman on the war path. I'm going to let Kat have it. Oh boy am I going to let her have it. Except when I get there, her desk is empty. I pull my mobile out to call her, only to see a text from her. *Super bad headache today so I'm staying home. Hopefully I'll be up and around tomorrow.*

I'll give her a headache, all right.

But not right now. Right now, I have to head down to the pier and talk to Justin about having a speedboat on standby.

———

Almost four hours have passed by the time Harrison and Fidel appear on the dock with six boxes of assorted bottles—enough for the three beach bars that will be used by the finalists. I scramble to help them load the first set of boxes into the *Rogue Fun*, my face hot with shame.

Following Harrison back to the golf cart, I say, "I'm so sorry about all of this Harrison. I really am."

"Mistakes happen."

I know it's not the right moment to ask, but I feel I can't go another second not knowing if I've already lost the promotion. "About what Mr. Rojas said, that I'm not ready to manage people. I hope you don't agree with him."

Harrison stops and turns to me, while Justin and Fidel continue loading the boat. "I'm afraid he's right, and it's not just because of this one error. Every time I see Kat, she's on her phone while you've been run off your feet. You're here half the evening to stay on top of everything. A lot of the tasks you've had on your plate are pretty simple. She could have easily taken them on for you."

No, no, no. Please no. "Kat's my sister. You know how hard it is to work with family, especially teenagers. They don't listen to anyone. If I'd had any other intern, I could have made it work."

"A good manager knows how to get their employees to engage. I'm afraid you didn't do that," he says gently. "You're an excellent events coordinator, Nora. You go above and beyond, and Libby,

Rosy, and I value your hard work and talents. We want you to stick around for a long time. I know that eventually you'll be ready to lead a team, but it won't be anytime soon. You just need more experience."

Don't cry. Don't cry. I nod, blinking at lightning speed and try to smile. "Okay. Thanks."

"I'm sorry," he says, glancing at the boat. "You better go. The production crew is waiting."

"Sure." I turn away, my feet heavy.

"Hang in there, Nora," Harrison says. "Today may have been bad, but I promise things will get better."

Please don't say that. You're tempting fate, although how could this day get any worse?

26

Verbally Incontinent Bachelors and the Women Who Hate Them

Theo

It's hard to believe another storm is coming. It's a beautiful, calm day at Eden. The air is filled with hope. I may have struck out two days ago, and I couldn't get any face time with Nora yesterday, but today I'm determined to talk to her. She's on her way to Eden right now with the liquor the crew needs. When she completes her mission, she and I can sit back and relax.

I spoke with our lawyer, Don, yesterday and he said it's doubtful we'd be liable to Jacardi, but the real issue is, if a lawsuit *is* filed, it would likely make the news and our name would get dragged into it. Not fatal but not ideal either. Don figures Armas Productions will settle out of court to keep everything quiet. I hope he's right.

The crazy thing is, I'm only a little worried about it instead of obsessing every second of the day, and that has everything to do with Nora. She's probably upset because of what happened this morning, but when she finds out how well things have been going here, I'm sure she'll feel better about the whole thing. And even if she doesn't, maybe she'll feel better once I tell her how I feel about her. I want to start a life with her. The timing of me confessing my love for her is definitely not ideal, but I have no choice. I'm on a flight out of here first thing tomorrow morning and this is the type of conversation that must happen face to face.

Yes, it'll be fine. I'm sure she feels the same way I do. I'll tell her I'm in love with her and hope that this is the beginning of something wonderful. Obviously, I won't open with that news. You don't just blurt out that you love someone and want to marry them. After all, this is not Regency Era England.

Getting up, I take off the headphones the sound guys loaned to me and set them on my chair. Attempting to look casual, I stroll down to the dock in time to see the *Rogue Fun* arriving.

Damn, that handsome flirt Justin is manning the wheel again. He cuts the engine and jumps off to tie up while Nora sets to work, lugging a large box off the boat. I rush over and take the box from her. "I've got it."

"Thanks," she mutters, letting go, then turning to pick up another one.

That's the only thing she says to me until she, Justin, and I have unloaded the boat. A handful of production crew members appear. One of them is the Banana Boat enthusiast, who gives me a hang ten sign. They take the booze and rush off, presumably to set up the three beach bars they constructed yesterday.

"How's it going here?" Justin asks, peering down the beach past me. "Looks like quite the production."

"Extremely well, thanks to Nora." I smile at her, but she doesn't smile back. "Your scavenger hunt idea was brilliant. It could not be going better." Even Carolina doesn't have anything bad to say, not that I'm talking to her.

She bites her bottom lip and gives me a terse nod, then sidesteps me and walks towards the beach.

Damn. She's upset.

I watch as she makes a beeline for the nearest bar and helps them unload, probably wanting to make sure she got everything they needed. Justin, who is standing next to me, says, "Do you think it'd be okay if I watch from over there?" He points at the set of director's chairs on a wooden platform the crew set up.

"Yes. In fact, take my chair. There's a set of headphones so you can hear what's going on. You can watch on those small screens in front of Vincent. Just stay as quiet as possible."

Justin nods and takes off. I wait for Nora to finish at the bar, my heart in my throat. She seems unsure of where to go, so she stands far off to the side, near the tree line that leads up the mountain.

I go over to her. "Crisis averted."

She freezes for a split second, then says, "Sort of. Harrison managed to get enough to scrape by for tonight, but tomorrow's not looking too good."

"I'm sorry. This must be so stressful for you." When she doesn't answer, I find myself feeling desperate for something to say. "Would you like something to eat or drink? They have a nice spread in the catering tent."

"No, thanks."

After trying to find a good lead-in, I settle on, "It's strange being out here with all these people. Eden sort of feels like it should be our place."

She stiffens, then she runs her tongue over her teeth. I wait for her to respond, but she doesn't, so I decide to dip my toe in the pool to see if the water's really as cold as it seems. Rubbing the back of my neck, I say, "Listen, Nora, you may have guessed that I wanted to talk to you about something, based on what happened a couple of days ago. What happened was me making a fool of myself." I do a bad imitation of my voice. "I love Banana Boat. Huge fan of it."

"I kind of wondered." She gazes into the distance, where Ewan MacClary, a sweaty, exhausted-looking bartender, is running to the botanist with a basket of fruit and herbs for examination. "Don't worry about it. It doesn't matter."

"It matters to me, because I've needed to tell you something, well, for a while, but so far I've been failing badly."

She finally looks at me, and I find myself lost in her beautiful brown eyes. All thoughts other than *kiss her* leave my brain, but that cannot be done at this moment. "I have certain feelings for you that I shouldn't, given my situation and how hard I've worked to prevent anyone else here from having feelings." *Stop talking about having feelings.*

It sounds creepy. "But I'm afraid I can't help it. It's too late. The way I feel is the way I feel."

Her mouth drops open a little, but she doesn't respond. She just blinks at me with absolutely no expression on her face. She could be horrified as easily as she could be delighted. No, that's not true. She definitely doesn't look delighted.

Raking a hand through my hair, I force myself to continue. "I know it's complicated, but you're the first woman I've met in a long time—maybe ever—that I want to get to know better." She shakes her head, and I speak faster to get out the words I need to say before she can stop me.

"You're an amazing woman. You have an excellent work ethic, and you're extremely professional... other than today's issue, that is. That was a pretty big error. But normally, you're quite professional. More than that though, you're a good person. Although you do carry quite the prejudice against wealthy people, but that's understandable, given your experience." *Abort! Everything you're saying is beyond shit.* "I'm rambling, sorry. I can't remember ever being this nervous, to be honest, but I promise to get to the point. I hope this won't sound pathetic, but that night at Eden, playing poker with you, was the best time I've had in years. And the conversations we've had since have meant something to me. I was wondering if maybe, when all of this is over, we could see each other?"

I pause, my heart pounding and my palms sweaty. Nora scowls at me. A full-on scowl. That cannot be a good sign, unless she's squinting because of the bright sunlight. So I do what any sane man would do when he's in love. I keep rambling. "It would be a challenge, given that we don't even live in the same country, but I strongly feel there's something special between us we should explore. Maybe see where it takes us?"

"See where it takes us?" she whisper-yells, her head snapping back. "I don't think so. I know exactly where it would take me. Nowhere fast. I'd be another conquest before you and Carolina form your super rich cyborg union and have highbrow babies together."

What the hell is she talking about? "Carolina? I have no interest in—"

She holds up a hand. "Save it for some other sucker, because I'm not buying what you're selling."

Okay, now she's just being rude. "Honestly, Carolina is nothing more than an old family friend, and that's all she'll ever be." After this show ends, she won't even be that.

Shrugging, she says, "Whatever. It makes no difference either way."

I stare at her, shocked at her response. "Have I done something to upset you?"

"Um, yeah, you have," she says, turning to face me, her face red with anger. "First of all, thanks for having my back this morning. It was lovely of you to tell my bosses how badly I screwed up and that I'm not ready to manage people. It was not only humiliating, but you basically obliterated my shot at the promotion I've been working my ass off for *for years*. Years."

All my hope drains as fast as a bucket with a giant hole in the bottom. "What did you expect me to do? Pretend the mistake was on our end?" I ask. "I'm sorry, but I'm not going to sell out my assistant like that. She's given my family nearly five decades of her life. The least I can give back is loyalty. Besides, the error *was* on your end. You handed an important task to your sister, whom you knew you couldn't trust. You should have checked to make sure she completed it."

"Don't you think I know that?" she grinds out. "Obviously I do. We *all* knew it was my fault, but you didn't have to actually *tell* my bosses I'm not ready to manage staff."

Oh Theo, you really stepped in it this time. "You're right. I'm sorry. I shouldn't have said that. I only meant to get Carolina to back off."

"Yeah well, your clumsy attempt at helping totally backfired, and now I'm back where I started." She waves at me. "But I don't expect you to understand that since you've never had to prove yourself."

"That's not true," I tell her.

"Yes, it is. And here's a fun fact for you: Ninety-nine percent of people in the world don't have billion-dollar corporations handed to them. They have to work really fucking hard to get ahead. You may work to *stay* at the top, but it's a hell of a lot easier when you start out there than to get there in the first place."

"That's not fair," I tell her, righteous indignation replacing my earlier feelings of romance. "I constantly have to prove myself to the board of directors. If I don't perform, they will fire me, as they should."

Scoffing, Nora says, "Oh yeah, I'm sure you live in constant fear of that for a job you don't even want."

My face heats up and I immediately regret telling her my secret. "Of course I don't want to get fired. That would mean I've let down my employees, which is the last thing I'd do. Now, I know you're upset, but you haven't been fired. You still have your job."

Nora rolls her eyes at me. "And thanks to you, I'm going to be stuck where I've been for years. Maybe forever, for all I know."

She lets out a huff and turns to face the set. My attention shifts in that direction, and I see Carolina watching us. As annoyed as I am at her lobbing accusations at me, I force myself to calm down. She may be angry right now, but it's no reason to throw away what we've got. And this is my last chance to salvage things. "You don't have to stay stuck, you know. There are plenty of opportunities for someone like you."

"You don't get it, do you? Everything is so bloody easy for you that you think everyone else can snap their fingers and make their dreams come true. But that's not how it is in the real world."

"I'm not saying it would be easy, but——"

"You know what, Theo? Do us both a favour. You stay in your world, I'll stay in mine, and we'll call it a day."

"Nora, please," I say, in one last ditch effort. "I'm afraid you're letting your disappointment about what happened today get in the way of something that could potentially be really wonderful."

She shakes her head. "No, I'm not. Trust me. I don't know why I allowed things to go... wherever they went. I knew better the moment Paz told me about what happened between the two of you. For some stupid reason, I was willing to give you a second chance, and yes, maybe you displayed some moments of humanity, but that's all they were. Moments. You speak about loyalty as if you know what it means, but you don't." Taking a deep breath, she raises her voice, "Guess what, Theo? I'm not here to make you a better man. That's not some *service* I provide to billionaires who decide to go on a self-improvement journey. So, you know what? Just go *improve* yourself!"

"CUT!" Vincent yells.

Nora and I both start and look up, only to see him staring back at us. Holding the bullhorn to his mouth, Vincent says, "If you two could keep your lovers' quarrel down a little, that would be super helpful. You just wrecked a perfect television moment!"

A deafening silence fills the air. Not even the birds dare to make a peep. All eyes are aimed directly at us. The only person who seems to find the situation remotely amusing is that ridiculous Mike the Moose guy, who is behind the middle bar shaking a cocktail mixer with a wide grin. The other two competitors flanking him, however, are glaring. MacClary, the Ginger Beast, shakes his head while Binna Chu looks like a tiny middle-aged assassin, brandishing a knife in one hand and squeezing a mango so hard with her other one that it leaks all over the bar top.

Wonderful. Not only am I striking out worse than I ever have in my life, I also have an audience to my humiliation.

Nora stage whispers, "Sorry. It won't happen again."

Vincent is both sarcastic and dramatic in his reply. "*Thanks.*"

She stands next to me, pale with anger, whereas I am hot with shame. Nora isn't in love with me. She thinks I'm an entitled jerk. How could I have been so wrong about us? In a low voice, I say, "Please forget I said anything about my feelings. Clearly I mistook your kindness for something more. I apologize for wasting your time. I assure you I won't do it again."

She opens her mouth, but I walk away before she can get in one last shot.

I stop when I'm directly behind the tent where the crew is set up. I shake with emotion as I scramble to figure out what the fuck just happened. I'm not sure I'll ever fully comprehend why she's gone back to hating me again, but one thing she said is true: it makes no difference, because none of it matters. *I* don't matter to her. Nora Cooper and I clearly are not meant to be. I'll have to chalk up my attraction to some sort of early midlife crisis and move on.

But the truth is, it doesn't feel like nothing. It feels like everything that means anything is slipping through my fingers, and there's nothing I can do to stop it.

27

From Bad to So, So, So Much Worse

Nora

"NORA, YOU ARE A STAR," Vincent tells me, hurrying over with a martini glass in each hand. He's absolutely thrilled that the show has wrapped and filming went off without a hitch.

Mike the Moose won, with Binna Chu coming in second. Other than the Ginger Beast (who is pouting under a palm tree), the film crew, and myself, everyone is having a terrific time. Well, I can't say for certain if Theo is having fun because I refuse to look at him. But of the people I *have* looked at, everyone else seems to be in full party mode. The celebrations have been going on for close to an hour while I've been helping the crew dismantle the sets. Not that they need my help, but staying busy is the perfect way to avoid Carolina and Theo, who, let's face it, wouldn't be caught dead lifting a finger.

Vincent hands me a drink, which I wasn't sure he was going to do. I kind of figured they were both for him. "A shining star, in fact. As such, you get to taste the winning cocktail."

He hands me a Mike the Moose Tropical Storm—light rum, fresh squeezed mango and passion fruit juices, 7UP, and jackass bitters. I give him a grateful smile, even though I'm not entirely over what he said about and to me this morning. By that, I mean I'm still pissed at him and fighting the urge to slap that pompadour right off his head.

I sip the cold drink and revel in the sweet yet tangy flavour, knowing I had a hand in its creation. "It's delicious."

"Right?" Vincent tips back his glass and polishes it off. "Listen, I know things didn't go all that well this morning at that meeting, and I feel bad that I took a run at you."

"I hardly noticed," I lie.

"Really? Because I was pretty angry. And rude. I get so freaked out on filming days. The stress of having everything on my shoulders turns me into a monster sometimes. Anyway, I felt bad. And I also want to thank you for everything. You found the perfect spot for the event, and you were right about the scavenger hunt cards." Cupping the side of his mouth, he says, "It literally would've taken weeks for these bozos to find anything if it weren't for you."

"I'm glad I could help."

Or at least I would have been glad if my career path hadn't been swallowed up by a giant sinkhole this morning. I'm as bitter as these jackass bitters, which, it turns out, are really freaking bitter.

He walks away, only to stop and turn. "Oh, and sorry about that thing I said about you and Theo having a lovers' quarrel. I didn't mean to embarrass you."

Sure you did. "Yeah, I was surprised you said that actually. Especially since I was under the impression he and Carolina are a couple."

Yeah, I said it, Carolina. I spilled your secret. What are you going to do about it?

Vincent's eyes light up, and he moves closer, lowering his voice to a near-whisper. "I'd say that's more of a pipe dream than a reality. As in Carolina's dreaming about his pipe."

Shocked, I burst out laughing, and Vincent shushes me. "You cannot ever repeat that. She'd hate me forever if she knew."

"Your secret is safe with me."

"Thanks, sweetie. And sorry again," he says, leaning in and

giving me a kiss on the cheek. "Thank you for putting up with me these past few weeks. I know I can be a lot to handle."

"You're welcome," I tell him, and this time I'm not lying. It takes a big person to admit when he's wrong. Unlike *some* people I better not think about right now, for fear of my stupid eyes leaking again. How could Theo stand there and defend his choice to call me out as not being management material? Seriously, how? Because he's a jerk, that's how.

I finish my drink, wishing there was more coming, then busy myself collecting the used cocktail glasses and boxing them up. The entire time I wish for this day to be over so I can get back home and have a good cry. Or, even better, see if Hadley's free this evening so I can go to her place and have a big cry there. My life is in shambles, and I've got far too much to tell her to hold it all in.

But for now I need to stop thinking about any of it. I refuse to cry in front of Theo and Carolina ever again. I'm going to hold my head high and be the professional I am, knowing they'll both be out of my life forever in a matter of hours.

———

I was on the last boat back to Santa Valentina. The resort used two of the catamarans, as well as the *Rogue Fun*, but with so many crew members, two trips were needed. You know who wasn't on the last trip? The VIPs. It was just like the Titanic—the rich people got off first, because that's how life goes.

Whatever. It's probably for the best, since I didn't have to have an awkward ride back with them. Also, somehow being the last one to leave lets me feel like I did my job well from start to finish, with one giant hiccup that will haunt me for years to come.

The walk from the dock to Building C seems impossible. My entire body is heavy and my feet drag. I'm going to get my handbag and go straight home. I'm too exhausted to cry on Hadley's shoulder. I need to fall into bed and sleep for twelve hours straight.

When I get to my desk, I see the last person I ever thought would be here.

Kat. For once, she's not on her phone. Instead, she's sitting staring off into space with her mouth turned down, her face red and blotchy.

"Kat?" I ask. "What are you doing here?"

She looks up, hope filling her eyes when she sees me. "Oh, Nora, I need your help. I've made a huge mistake." Her voice cracks. "And I don't know how to fix it."

I close my eyes for a second, completely out of patience for her. "You mean about the booze order? Because I already took care of it. Thanks for that, by the way. You cost me my promotion."

Her face goes blank. "What?"

"The email you were supposed to send when I was stranded at Eden overnight?"

"I sent it."

"You didn't."

"Oh, sorry, I was so sure I finished that." She looks taken aback and then her face crumples. "I wish it were something that small."

Smaller than costing me the promotion I've been working my buns off for? I plunk myself into my chair and sigh. "What'd you do?"

She stands. "Come with me. I can't talk about it here."

"But nobody's here."

"Someone might come by."

I force my aching body up and out of the chair and follow her to the ladies' room. When the door is securely closed, Kat sniffles. "It's so awful, I don't think I can even say it." She heaves with huge sobs before launching into the story. "I… well Paz and I… you know Paz, the hot bartender?"

"Yes, I know him."

"We…well he, not me, I didn't know he was doing it…but he made a recording of us having sex."

Every muscle in my body goes limp. "What? He made a tape of you in bed?"

Fresh tears stream down her cheeks. "Technically it wasn't in bed. It was in the ballroom. On top of the bar. You know the one we were using for practices?"

"Oh my God, Kat, what were you thinking?"

"I didn't know he was recording it!" she shrieks.

"But why would you think it was okay to sleep with him in the first place? At my place of work? After it was made clear to you not to do that!"

Narrowing her eyes, she says, "I don't need a lecture. I already told you it was a mistake. I came to you for help, so please don't make me regret it."

"Sorry, but you've just dropped a pretty big bombshell on me," I answer, oozing sarcasm. "It might take a minute for me to catch up with you."

"I haven't even told you the worst part."

"The sex tape isn't the worst part?" My voice rises. "What the hell else did you do?"

"Nothing! But he said if I don't give him fifty thousand dollars, he's going to post the video so he can make money off it."

My stomach lurches, and I clasp one hand over my mouth. "Where does he think you're going to come up with that kind of money?"

"He said I should be able to get it easily, since our parents are pastors."

"I don't think he knows how much pastors get paid," I tell her, not understanding where she's going with this.

"He suggested I steal it from the collection."

I gasp, feeling like I had the wind knocked out of me. "You can't be serious. He wants you to steal from the congregation?"

She nods. "He's giving me until next Monday night to e-transfer him the money, otherwise he's going to post it as Preachers' Daughter Gets Hot and Bothered."

I lean against the bathroom counter to hold myself up. "Oh my God. Oh my God, Kat. This is so much worse than anything I thought you were going to say."

"I know!" she cries. "Please think of something. I don't know what to do. This'll kill Mum and Dad. Especially Dad. I'll never be able to look him in the eye again."

I rub my face with both hands, praying this is all a bad dream, and I'm going to wake up. But it isn't. This will be the scandal that will take my parents down for good. There's no way they'll be able to stand up on Sundays and preach about living the good life after this. Not with the church community thinking their youngest daughter is an amateur porn star.

Rage fills my veins, and I pace the length of the counter. I'm furious at her for being so stupid. I'm furious at Theo for being such an ass. I'm mostly furious with Paz for being such a lowlife, scum-sucking pig of a human being.

When I turn towards her again, she has an awful hope in her eyes, and suddenly she's not my irritating nineteen-year-old sister anymore. She's my five-year-old little sister who just fell off her bike and scraped her knee. She's scared and hurt and counting on me to make everything better again, because that's what I do. "What if we steal it from him?"

"I like that idea," she says, nodding slowly.

I add, "It's probably loaded on the cloud or something, but if we can get his phone, we can probably delete it from wherever it's stored. We'll also need to see if he has a secret USB drive or something. If I were going to blackmail someone, I'd back it up on a USB drive."

Kat wipes the tears off her cheeks. "Oh God, what if we can't get rid of it?"

"No what ifs. They won't help. Do you know where he is?"

She shakes her head. "I went to his room and knocked a bunch of times, but he didn't answer."

"Perfect." I cross to the door and yank it open.

"Why is that perfect?"

"Because it'll be a lot easier to search his room if he's not in it."

When I get to my desk, I call reception. "It's Nora. Has Paz Castillo checked out already? I know some of the contestants left already, but I have something for him." A knee to his groin, but I don't tell the front desk staff that.

"He's still in room 322."

"Excellent. Thank you."

I retrieve my master key, thinking how very fired I'm going to be if I get caught. But I really have no choice. "Come on," I tell her, leading her to the elevators.

My heart pounds wildly, and I'm no longer exhausted. I'm now Super Nora, filled with a righteous anger that will keep me going while I toss the villain's room (or more accurately, gingerly examine everything while being careful to leave no trace I was ever there).

When we get to the third floor, I say, "You're going to hide in the stairwell and keep watch through the window. Call my cell phone if he gets off the elevator."

Her eyebrows knit together. "This could get you fired, couldn't it?"

"Yes."

"I'm so sorry, Nora," she whispers, tearing up again.

"No time for that. We need to get in and out of here." I point to the stairwell door, then tippytoe to room 322. The lock clicks, the light goes green, and I push the door, praying he's not back in here now.

The room is dark and silent, other than the sound of my ragged breath. "Hello?" I call quietly.

When I don't get an answer, I flick the light on, and my stomach drops. The room is empty, as in there are no visible signs that anyone is staying here. I search anyway, briefly hoping he's just a freakishly neat person, but after a few minutes of opening drawers, closet doors, and the bathroom cupboards, I know he's vacated the premises. I'm guessing he did it before he came to Kat with his threats. Of course he would. He'd know we were going to do exactly what I'm doing—or worse—the moment he let her in on his plan.

Panic starts to set in. This is real, and if we can't find him, there's nothing I can do to stop what's about to happen. My stupid sister and our poor parents are about to have their lives ruined forever, and there is literally nothing I can do.

I turn off the light, take a deep breath, and pull the door open.

As soon as I step into the hall, I'm greeted by Theo Rojas. He raises an eyebrow at me. "Good evening, Nora."

Well, shit.

28

Scandals on Scandals

Theo

THE SIGHT of her is a punch to the gut, especially because she is leaving Paz's hotel room. A myriad of emotions rush through me all at once — hurt, jealousy, longing, rage. Then I see the look on her face. Her eyes are wild, and she's red-faced and sweaty. My heart lurches, and I am suddenly filled with concern.

Something bad has happened.

She stares at me for a second, then says, "Good night," and turns quickly towards the stairwell. Her sister is peering through the window, her face flushed and puffy, her crazed expression matching her sister's. Nora shakes her head at Kat, who caves in on herself. Whatever has passed between us becomes irrelevant. I follow Nora to the stairwell, and when she opens the door, I go with her.

Kat looks at me. "Hello, Mr. Rojas."

Nora starts when she realizes I'm standing directly behind her.

"What happened?" I ask.

When neither of them answers me, I say, "I think I can guess, based on whose room you were coming out of." Turning to Kat, I say, "He recorded you, didn't he?"

Kat's jaw drops, tears springing to her eyes as she nods.

"How did you guess that?" Nora asks.

"He did the same thing to my stepmother." Somehow I manage to keep my voice calm, even though I'm shaking with rage.

"Did he use it to blackmail her too?" Nora asks quietly.

I nod. "After my father died, I offered to pay for his tuition and boarding for law school. He asked for the cash instead, and when I refused, hoping he'd change his mind, he made a tape with my stepmother and used it to blackmail her."

"What a bastard," Nora mutters.

"Agreed." I look over at Kat. She's got that same distraught look that Alaina had when he did this to her. I suddenly realize it doesn't make sense for him to have pulled the same trick with a nineteen-year-old intern. "What could he possibly hope to gain from blackmailing you?"

Nora's face screws up. "He knows our parents have access to a lot of money."

My heart drops. "He wants you to steal from their church?"

Nora nods. "How can someone be so cruel? He has to know that either way, he's going to ruin our parents—two innocent people. If Kat were to steal the money, our parents would get blamed and could end up in jail. But if she doesn't..."

I briefly close my eyes, not wanting to think about what could happen. "He doesn't care."

"Why didn't I listen to you? You tried to warn me." Nora lets out a frustrated groan and flops onto one of the steps. "I don't know what to do. I went into his room to try to find anything I could, like a backup drive or something, but he's already packed up and left."

"He would have been prepared to make his escape before he said anything to Kat."

Kat sits next to her sister and lets out a sob. "How could I have been so stupid?"

Nora puts an arm around her and pulls her close. "You thought you could trust him. He does an excellent impression of a good person."

Kat nods and wipes the tears from under her eyes. "He really does. He knows exactly what to say and when to say it."

My mind races to find some way to fix this for them. With everything else on my shoulders, the last thing I need is to find myself tangled up with Paz Castillo again. I could walk away, go home, and take care of the people who want to be part of my life. But I can't very well leave Nora and her family in this situation. They simply don't have the resources to deal with this, and the truth is she may not care about me, but I still care about her.

"Maybe we can still find him," Nora says to me. "What if he's hiding in somebody else's room? We could go to the police. He made the recording without Kat's knowledge, which is a serious crime here."

"It's worth a shot," I say. "But I have to tell you the most likely scenario is that he's already gone."

"I have to try." She takes her arm off Kat and stands. "I'm going to security to see if they have footage of him leaving with his suitcases."

"They'll have it, I'm sure," I tell her. *Last chance to escape without getting involved.* "I don't want to make promises I can't keep, but there might be something I can do."

Nora shakes her head, her cheeks darkening. "This isn't your problem. We can't ask for your help."

Kat turns to her. "Yes, we can, Nora. He might be our only hope."

"Kat, seriously, we can't ask Mr. Rojas to get involved. We'll figure something out. Maybe Uncle Dan and Aunt Beth can help. They have money. They could pay him off."

"Don't pay him off," I tell her. "Then he'll know he can keep coming back every time his bank account is empty."

Knowing I don't have a lot of time, I open the door. "I have to go. I'm sorry this happened to your family, Nora. I really am."

I jog down the hall without looking back—a man on a mission. As soon as I get into my room, I call Jaquell. When she picks up, I say, "I need you to call Jorge immediately. Paz has struck again."

———

I spend the next two hours packing, my gut churning while I wait for our company's head of security, Jorge Martinez, to call me. If Paz got on a flight already, he'll be able to tell me which one and where it's going.

When the phone rings, I lunge to the nightstand and see Nora's name on my screen. "Were you able to find anything?"

"He got in a cab just after one this afternoon, with his luggage. He could be anywhere by now." Her voice is raw with emotion. "I bet you're happy about how things turned out between us, because there's no way you'll want to be tangled up with my family after this. Imagine the scandal if you were with someone whose sister became a porn star."

I sigh, knowing she's abandoned all hope. "The last thing I am is happy, and she's not going to turn into a porn star. She made a big mistake, but it's hardly the same thing."

She starts to say something but her voice cracks, and she lets out a shaky breath. My second line beeps, and I know it's Jorge. "There's a call I have to take. Don't do anything until you hear from me."

29

Nora and the Terrible, Horrible, No Good, Very Bad Week

Nora

It's been three days, and I've heard nothing from Theo. Not one word. If I had to guess, I'd say I'll never hear from him again. I sit, waiting for my phone to ring while I wrestle with the idea of going to Aunt Beth. Kat has begged me not to ask her for help. The poor, naive girl still thinks Theo's going to come through for us, but I know better. Out of sight, out of mind. I'm sure he's back in his office, sitting at his enormous antique desk, counting his billions right about now.

Okay, that's probably not fair. After all, he was very sweet and seemed extremely concerned when he found out what had happened. But I'm having trouble seeing the silver lining in this shit cloud hanging over my family's head right now. I'm also incredibly disappointed with Kat. I'm murderously furious whenever I think of that waste of skin, Paz. I'm still stinging from losing my promotion, and with it, my seaside cottage dream. Someday maybe it'll happen, but it won't be anytime soon—especially not if I take out all my savings to pay off that gaping asshole. It still won't be enough though. I only have $32,000, not fifty. Aunt Beth could probably make up the difference, and I can start over. Anything to protect my parents.

The worst part is I don't have anyone I can talk to about it. Well, that's not the worst part—the sex tape and blackmailing is the worst part, but not being able to talk to Hadley about everything that has happened is killing me. I promised Kat I'd keep her secret, and I intend to, no matter how badly I need my bestie right now. If our situations were reversed, I'd be begging Kat to do the same thing.

So, instead of crying on Hadley's shoulder, and getting her and Heath to help me hatch some sort of plan to make this all go away, I'm just waiting, which is one of the worst things to do in life.

It's Monday morning, and I'm back at the scene of the crime— Building C. I told Kat to call in sick because she hasn't slept in days. As horrible as I feel about what's about to happen, she's devastated. I'm not sure how she's managing to pretend everything's fine around my parents, but I haven't heard from Mum, so I have to assume she's putting up a brave front.

As for me, I'm hoping the humiliation of my screw-up last week will distract me from Kat's massive disaster. I'm currently taking my sweet time cleaning up my desk because as soon as I finish, I'll be back in my stupid office with stupid Oakley Knowles, who, let's face it, is soon to become my stupid boss. And that's going to be the worst thing ever—taking orders from her sneering face, knowing I came *this* close, only to mess it all up and lose everything I worked so hard for.

The irony of it is that Oakley's never had to prove she can manage anyone, whereas when my mum marched in here with Kat, she unwittingly gave my bosses the perfect way to test me. And I failed. Really frigging badly. Harrison's words about how I didn't engage Kat but instead chose to do everything myself have haunted me all weekend. He's right. That's exactly what I did.

I could have done better. I could have been kinder, more enthusiastic. I could have included her in what was happening and made her feel like part of the team. Instead, I was happy to let her sit on her phone, doing nothing. Well, nothing except get into the worst trouble ever with the worst person on the planet.

I realized something about life though. It occurred to me at two o'clock this morning. Poor people can be just as shitty as rich people. It really doesn't matter what neighbourhood you grew up in or how much cash you have lying around. People are people. Some poor people are terrible human beings, and some rich people aren't completely awful.

"Beautiful Nora." Markos Rojas stands in front of me in a rash-guard and swim trunks. In his hand are flippers and a snorkel mask.

"Hi."

He offers me his winning smile. "You were deep in thought just now. I had to call your name a few times before you heard me."

"Sorry, I'm a little distracted," I answer, curving my lips upward in what I hope looks like a grin. "I'm surprised you're still here. I assumed you left with Theo."

"I wanted to stay a few more days to do some scuba diving, now that I'm off duty."

He gives me a wink, and I can't tell if he's joking or not. I decide he must be and force myself to chuckle. "I'm sure it's a huge relief for you to have all that hard work over with."

"Yes, exactly." His eyes narrow. "What about you and my brother? How are we going to make that happen?"

My face burns. "Um, we're not."

"Please don't tell me Theo left without confessing his undying love for you."

"He... made an effort in that direction, but it's not going to work out between us."

"Why not? Was he all awkward about it, rambling and such?" Then nodding, he answers his question. "He was, wasn't he? Listen, I don't think you should let that throw you. He's one of the best people I know. Loyal, caring, honest. They don't make men like him anymore."

Of course he'd say that about his brother. He loves him. He also has no clue I've been waiting for days to hear from Theo, who very likely has abandoned me in my time of need. Looking for the quickest way out of this conversation, I say, "I'm sure he and Carolina will be very happy together."

"Carolina? He has no interest in her."

"Then why did I see her leaving his room in her bathrobe last week?"

"She went there to seduce him, but he turned her down and sent her away."

My stomach flutters a little.

"I heard the whole thing from my room," he says, wincing at the memory. "Trust me, Carolina and my brother will never be a couple. But if you have feelings for him, that would have a totally different outcome. I know Theo better than anyone, and the only person I've seen him come even remotely close to wanting to be with is you."

I swallow hard. "That's nice to hear."

Markos offers me a half-grin. "Yes, it is nice when someone loves you, especially someone like Theo. He would make an exceptional husband, because he always takes care of the people he loves."

Well, maybe you, buddy, but I haven't heard from him in days, so...

"Thanks, Markos, but there's no way we can make things work. It's just not in the cards for us."

"That's too bad, because from the moment I saw you, I thought you'd be perfect together." He taps his knuckles on my desk. "I should let you get back to work. Take care, Nora Cooper."

"You too, Markos," I answer, feeling dizzy as he strolls to the exit.

Oh God, could I have been wrong about Theo? Is it even remotely possible he was serious about a future with me, and I turned him down instead of *locking* him down before this stupid sex tape scandal popped up to ruin everything? I'm going to spend the rest of my life knowing I blew it, and that is *not* going to make for a warm and fuzzy future.

30

Badass Raids and Heart-wrenching Realizations

Theo

It took Jorge three days to track Paz down, which means he's gotten better at hiding since he pulled this crap the first time. He's still a lazy ass though, so instead of disappearing to some foreign country, he's literally a ten-minute drive from my office.

Jorge, Renee (my best IT guy), and I pull up to his grandfather's house to confront Paz. His home is in a nice neighbourhood of wide streets lined with well-cared-for yards. I know his grandfather, and I'm already sorry for the embarrassment he's about to suffer when he finds out what his only grandson has done. The thought makes me sick, and I hope he's not here.

Jorge parks a couple of houses down, cuts the engine, and turns to Renee and me. "I'm going around back. You two give me one minute, then go to the front door."

Renee's eyes bounce back and forth between us. "What if he has a gun? Do you have a gun? Should you be giving me one?"

Jorge says, "No guns. Paz won't be armed. He's a leech, not a gangster."

He gets out and shuts the door, leaving me alone with my

nervous partner. Renee sighs. "I don't know about this. This seems like a bad idea."

"We're not going to hurt him. We're retrieving the files and leaving. That's it."

"Really?" He gives me a skeptical look.

"I'm probably going to threaten him a little." I pause. "Okay, a lot, but that's it."

I open the door and get out, and Renee does the same on his side.

"This is actually kind of exciting, no?" he asks.

It's totally exciting. "It's a job. We get in and get out as quickly as possible, then you get paid handsomely."

I jog up the sidewalk to the house, take the front steps two at a time, and knock loudly on the door. When the door swings open, Paz is standing there in boxer shorts and a T-shirt, a chicken leg in his hand. His eyes widen in surprise when he sees me, and I can almost smell his brain working as he tries to come up with an exit strategy.

"Don't run," I tell him. "Jorge is out back waiting for you. I'm sure you'll remember him from the first time we did this."

"Shit," he mutters and steps aside so we can come in.

I say, "Is your grandfather home?"

"He's gone to the market," Paz says.

"Okay. If you cooperate, he doesn't have to know about any of this. If you don't, we're going to be here for a very long time. So long you're going to have a lot of explaining to do to your entire family."

"I'll cooperate," he says quietly.

"Good decision. This is Renee. He's going to scrub your computer, phone, and any other devices he finds. Jorge is going to come through the back door in a moment. He will search the house for external hard drives or USBs. You're going to hand over everything to Renee, then you and I are going to sit right here while I explain what will happen to you if you try to blackmail Kat Cooper or any other woman again, but here's a preview. You go to jail. Directly to jail. Do not collect two hundred dollars."

Paz takes his phone out of the pocket of his shorts, and hands it to Renee. "It's got my only copy, other than what's stored on the cloud."

I hear the back door open, and Jorge appears. I look at him. "He says he only has the cloud as backup."

Jorge glares at him. "You don't mind if I have a look anyway?"

"No," Paz says, shrinking.

"Sit down," I tell him. When he does, I shake my head. "It would be so much easier to just leave Jorge here and go on with my life, knowing you'll never pop up into it again."

"Why don't you?" Paz asks, head hanging.

"I could never do that to your family, but I wouldn't hesitate to make sure you end up behind bars for a very long time. The first time you did this you were lucky, because The Bahamas didn't have revenge porn laws yet. But we do now, as does the Benavente Islands. Theirs are much stricter. I spoke with an attorney there and you'd be looking at ten to twelve years. Blackmail is another couple of years on top of that. They have extradition agreements in place with nearly every country on the planet, so unless you want to move to North Korea, I suggest you pay attention."

He glances at me, afraid. Gone is the swagger he wears everywhere he goes, and in its place is the shame that should be there. "I'm sorry."

"I don't give a rat's ass if you're sorry, and I'm not going to waste my time trying to get you to think about the people you hurt. I'm not going to ask you what your father would think if he knew the things you've done, because it doesn't matter to me. You don't matter to me enough to try to redeem you. You're a snake that preys on vulnerable women. You're a lazy shit. You're nothing. And you have to live with that." I stop to let the words sink in. I've never said anything so cruel to anyone in my life, but I've also never known anyone more deserving. "I'm going to keep the video, and I'll be keeping an eye on you. You won't know how or by who, but you will be watched."

That's a lie. I have no way of keeping tabs on him, but having him spend the rest of his life worrying is going to be part of his punishment. "If that video ever, *ever* makes its way onto the internet, you're fucked. Do you understand?"

He nods. "I wasn't planning to post it. I swear. I just needed the mon—"

"Save it. I'm not interested."

We sit in silence for over an hour while Jorge and Renee do their jobs. I stare at him the entire time, exuding disgust while he squirms in his chair. When the job is finished, Jorge nods and I stand. "Please don't think that I'm letting you off for your sake. If I had my way, you'd be on your way to prison already. I'm doing this for Kat's family. This would have ruined their lives if it got out."

Paz looks like he could burst into tears at any moment.

"I'm serious, Paz. You ruin them, and I will ruin you."

When we walk out into the sunshine, I'm tempted to high-five the guys for being gangsters, but I won't. I'm a well-respected businessman.

When we get to the car, Renee says, "That felt sort of badass, didn't it?"

"Not really," I say, but I give him a small grin. "Okay, yeah, a little."

Renee breaks into a huge smile. "Totally badass. We crushed that."

Jorge nods, managing to look a lot less impressed than I feel.

———

As soon as I get home, I go directly to my bedroom so no one on my staff will hear. I pull my phone out of my pocket, intending to call Nora immediately, but I stop, finger hovering over her name. I cross to the French doors that lead to my balcony, open one, and walk out and sit, gazing at the sunset over the sea.

I'm not going to call Nora. Not ever again. If I tell her the good news, she'll be so grateful she'll say she didn't mean any of the harsh things she said and that I'm not the person she thought I was. She'll say she wants to give us a try, and I'll agree to it, because I want to be with her so badly, I'd fool myself into believing she's in love with me when she clearly isn't.

We'll wind up wasting a long time—possibly years—with me falling even more in love with her before she realizes she mistook gratitude and obligation for true feelings.

So I won't call her. I'll leave her alone and let her go on with her life, and I'll do the same, even though it's going to hurt like hell.

I dial Kat's number instead.

"Hello?"

"Kat, it's Theo. You don't ever have to worry about Paz again."

After a slight pause, she whispers, "Did you kill him?"

"No, of course not, and if I had, whispering into a phone carries the same risk as talking normally."

"Oh, right. Sorry. But, you really managed to get him to back off?"

"Yes."

"You didn't pay him, did you?"

"No." I give her a brief explanation of what we did and the protection we put in place for her.

When I finish, Kat says, "I can't thank you enough, Mr. Rojas. You've been totally amazing. If there's ever anything I can do for you, please let me know."

"There is one thing."

"Name it."

"Please tell Nora I couldn't help, but you found someone else who could." My heart sinks as soon as the words leave my mouth.

"Why wouldn't you want to take credit for this? She's going to love you when she finds out what you did for our family."

That's the problem. "I can't explain why, but please honour this one request."

"But who do I say helped?"

"Nora mentioned going to one of your aunts for help. Why not tell her you spoke to her, and she fixed everything?"

"I guess I can tell her that." I can hear in her voice she's getting bored of the conversation now that the drama is over.

"Thank you, Kat. I appreciate it."

"I appreciate what you did for me. My parents would call you an angel."

"They'd be wrong. I'm just a regular guy."

A regular guy who is going to spend the rest of his life miserable and alone.

31

Curiosity Killed the Kat's Sister

Nora

"Yes, hello, I'd like to make an appointment with a loan officer." I finally got through to my bank but not before listening to twenty-six minutes of Muzak. I'm pretty sure I'm going to have a jazzy instrumental version of "Born to Be Wild" in my head for weeks.

After not hearing from Theo for another twenty-four hours, I realized I needed to get creative. Instead of going to Aunt Beth, I'm going to see if I can get a loan to pay off Paz. It's a long shot, and it'll set me back about five years on my homeownership dream, but if it saves my parents and Kat, it's worth it. I know Theo might be right that there's a strong chance Paz will come back to the well once I pay off, but maybe he won't, and I couldn't live with myself if I didn't take the chance.

"Can I get your name?" the woman asks.

"Nora Cooper."

"I'm Sara. I see you entered your account information when you called. Your home branch is on Broad Street in San Felipe and you're applying for a loan. Is that correct?"

"Yes."

"Perfect. I'll ask you a few questions, then I can set up your appointment for you. First off, why are you applying for a loan?"

Don't say blackmail payoff. "I need money I don't have at the moment."

"Yes, but what is the reason?"

"Do I have to tell you?"

"Do you want the money?"

"Yes," I say, feeling equally annoyed and embarrassed.

"Then you do have to tell us what it's for. Some lenders won't ask any questions, but we're a respected financial institution, and we need to know."

"That makes sense. Out of curiosity, do people ever say they want a loan for one reason but use it for something else? And follow-up question: what happens if they're caught?"

There's a brief pause, then Sara says, "I don't think we're going to be the right bank to help you out."

Crap. I really should have googled "good reasons to give bank for loans" before I called. *Stupid, Nora. Stupid.* "Thanks anyway. No need to note my file. I'll take your advice and go somewhere else."

"I'm afraid I do have to make notes about today's call."

"Of course you do."

"Is there anything else I can assist you with today?"

"No. That was it."

"Can I connect you to our one-minute survey when we complete our call?"

Say no. "Um... sure." *Dammit!*

"Thank you for choosing Benavente Union Bank. Enjoy the rest of your day."

"You, too."

Shit. I hang up before the survey starts, feeling guilty for lying to Sara and revenge joy (also for lying to Sara).

My door buzzer sounds, and I hurry over to answer it, assuming it's Hadley. I'm going to help her out with some last-minute shopping before the baby arrives. Today's mission is nursing bras. Oddly enough, Heath wasn't as keen to come this time, and to be honest, I'm relieved. I still haven't had a chance to tell her anything that happened after our evening of baby shopping, which was weeks ago. Gah! So. Much. Drama.

Pressing the button, I say, "Who dis?"

"Kat. Let me up. I have great news!"

I press the button to let her into the building, then open the door and stand in the hall, too excited to wait an extra moment to hear that our nightmare is over. At least I hope that's the news, instead of something like, "I got ten thousand followers on TikTok!" Could it be possible I won't have to sell my left ovary to get her out of this mess? Dear God, please say that's the case.

I hear her footsteps on the stairwell, then Kat appears. She squeals and runs over to me. "It's done. Everything has been taken care of!"

"Seriously?" I ask, holding my arms out to give her a big hug.

"Yup!" Kat squeezes me tight.

When we both pull back, I yank her into my flat and shut the door. "But who? How? Are you sure?"

"I can't say who, I don't know how— actually, I think I don't *want* to know how, but I am sure."

"What?" I ask, tilting my head. "If you don't know who or how, I'm a little skeptical you can be sure."

"*I* know who. I just can't tell *you* who fixed things," she says with a big grin. "But based on the who, I know for sure it's done. He's not the type of man to leave any loose ends."

"It's Theo, isn't it?"

"No," she says, but I can tell she's lying. "What would make you think it was him?"

"Because he said he'd try to help."

"Rigghhht, that makes sense," Kat says, nodding. She winces. "Urgh, I promised I'd keep it a secret."

"Why?"

"Because he asked me to."

"No, I mean why would he ask you to keep it a secret?"

She shrugs. "I don't know. He didn't say. But enough about that, because the amazing news is that I'm off the hook! Mum and Dad will never have to know about the *thing*. No one will ever see it. It's over! I'm free!"

She gives me another hug and relief washes through me. If Theo dealt with it, I know it's really, truly over. I don't have to wipe out my savings, grovel to Aunt Beth and Uncle Dan, cover up for her, or find some seedy loan shark. Suddenly my "no promotion" life feels like no big deal.

"I've been thinking," Kat says, parking herself on one of my kitchen chairs. "It's time I grew up. I need to start taking responsibility for my life."

"Praise the Lord," I tell her, raising both hands in the air like the lead singer in a church choir.

Kat grins. "I'm applying for college. I don't know what I want to study yet, but I figure I can start in general arts and go from there. Oh! I also deleted Tinder off my phone. No more wasting my time with stupid hookups. From now on I'm focusing on self-improvement. I'm going to get a job—one that pays—and work as much as I can until school starts."

"Good for you," I tell her, happiness flowing through me.

"Thanks," she says. "And thank you for being such an amazing big sister. You really had my back when everything turned to shit, even though I didn't deserve your help, because I've been a total brat."

"Yeah, you have, but I also could have been a better big sister and a better boss. I should have taken the time to teach you what you needed to know."

"You were swamped. Besides, I wasn't exactly eager to learn."

"True, but I'm thrilled to hear that you are now, because you have a lot of potential."

Kat lets out a contented sigh. "Speaking of potential. I think there's a strong possibility that Theo Rojas might have a thing for you."

My face heats up as soon as she says his name. "What? No, I don't think so." I shake my head a few times, then stop. "But, just out of curiosity, what makes you say that?"

"There was something about his voice when he told me not to

tell you. I can't put my finger on it. Maybe it was the way he said your name? I'm not sure. But if I were you, I'd definitely be making a play for him. Hot, rich, and willing to step up to help a girl out, even when it's for someone he barely knows? I think he might be one of the good ones."

"You might be right," I tell her, chewing my bottom lip.

And if she *is* right, I'm the biggest moron to ever walk the planet.

———

"What about this one?" I ask, holding up the strangest-looking bra I've ever seen. It's got clear plastic where the nipples would go.

Hadley raises one eyebrow. "Why would they give them windows?"

"I have no idea." I put it back on the rack. We giggle quietly so as not to disturb the surly saleswoman who's been hovering around with that "those two look like trouble" expression. We've been in the bra section at Apple Blossoms for nearly forty-five minutes, during which time we've mostly stood around while I told her what happened with Theo rather than doing any browsing. I gave her the rundown of how Theo stuck up for me at the meeting with Carolina and Vincent (good boyfriend material), then sold me out at the meeting with Harrison *et al* (very bad), and how just after I lost the promotion, he decided to confess his feelings for me (horrible timing, which makes us question his emotional intelligence). I told her about seeing Carolina coming out of his hotel room (highly suspicious), but how Markos told me he heard Theo turn her down (decent showing of high moral standards to not take advantage of the situation when he knew he didn't want things to become permanent). This led to a lengthy discussion about Carolina and what type of awful person would pretend they were getting married. In the end we agreed it's because she's so threatened by me. What I don't do is tell her anything about Kat and Paz, even though it kills me to hide something that big from my bestie. I'm keeping my promise to my little sister, and although it's the right thing to do, it feels awful.

I'm half-tempted to use charades as a loophole, so I can share what happened with Hadley without actually having to say it. But I won't because it would take hours to act out each word, and I'm pretty sure I'd be arrested if I pantomimed sex on the bar. At the very least, I might be banned for life from the store.

Hadley plucks another bra off the rack and tests the fabric for stretchiness, then bends over a little and groans. "That didn't feel very nice."

"Was that a contraction?" I ask, already starting to panic.

"I'm sure it's not a real one. I've been getting Braxton Hicks contractions off and on for weeks. That was a bigger one, though. Back to you and Theo. You've told me all the details, except for the most important thing. How do you feel about him?"

That question got my attention. "Confused. He's incredibly attractive. Like, so, so, so hot."

"Obviously."

"He can also be rude and arrogant, and he sometimes thinks he knows more than anyone else about a lot of things."

"Like what?" she asks, unclasping the bra and holding the band to her chest to test the width.

"Like... business-stuff. He thinks he knows everything there is to know about managing staff."

"Uh-huh, well, you did say he has over eight thousand employees, so maybe he does know a thing or two about that."

"True, but did he really need to give Harrison his opinion about me?" A familiar sense of righteous indignation creeps back up.

"Noooo," Hadley moans.

"Exactly," I answer, before I realize she's bent over again, but this time, there's a splash of liquid on the floor underneath her.

"Oh, God, why here?" she asks me, wincing.

My heart starts to pound. "Is that—? Did your water just break?" I whisper.

She nods. "Apparently Apple Blossoms is my go-to place for life's most embarrassing moments."

"And for life's biggest moments," I tell her, tearing up a little.

The saleswoman comes around the corner, then stops in her

tracks when she sees the puddle. Rolling her eyes, she says, "Not again. Why don't you people go bra shopping earlier in your pregnancies?"

"Sorry, I'll clean that up," Hadley tells her.

"No, you won't. Not in your condition," I say. Turning to the woman, I say, "I'll do it."

Hadley has another contraction, adding to the pool on the floor.

"On second thought, maybe we should go," I say.

"Yes, I think that would be for the best," the woman tells us.

The next hour is a flurry of activity and emotions: me rushing Hadley to the hospital, her calling Heath to meet us there, me checking her in at the maternity ward and getting her off to a labour room, where I stayed until Heath arrived. According to the nurse who had a look under Hadley's gown, this baby is coming fast.

So now I'm sitting in the cafeteria alone, sipping green tea and waiting for the big news. My emotions are all over the place, but my main thought is I hope she and the baby will come out of this okay. She's my best friend, and I'm scared for her, though I'm sure there's no reason to be. She's healthy, and all signs point to an equally healthy baby waiting to come out and meet the world.

One thought that keeps popping into my mind is wishing Theo were here. I really, really wish he was. Somehow, I know he'd help keep me from worrying, and we'd have fun passing the time together. He's the man I could do nothing with and still have the best time ever. If that's not a good sign for long-term potential, I don't know what is. And he saved our family. After I bluntly turned him down, he still stepped up and saved us when he had no reason to do so. As far as he was concerned, we were never going to see each other again. Yet he must have gone to a lot of trouble, and likely to some considerable expense, to fix things for us.

My mind wanders back to Hadley asking me how I feel about him. I told her I was confused—and I am—but I'm also in love with him. If things could work out between us, I'd be the happiest woman on earth. I could put up with the odd display of arrogance and his tendency to be overly honest when he doesn't have to be, because there's so much good in him. So, so much good wrapped up in that deliciously hard body.

My phone pings; it's a text from Heath. *Baby's here! Come meet her!*

A girl! I jump up and rush out of the cafeteria, happy tears already flowing.

When I get to her room, I gently push the door open. Hadley is lying in the bed, exhausted, sweaty, and filled with joy. Their tiny baby lies on her, swaddled in a blanket, fast asleep.

Tears fill Hadley's eyes, and mine too, as I cross the room. I look at the baby's tiny, perfect face. She's red and puffy of course, but she has the cutest little nose and a mini-version of Hadley's mouth. "She's absolutely perfect, and I'm so glad you're both okay," I whisper.

"Thanks," Hadley says, beaming. "She really is something, isn't she?"

"Definitely."

"Agreed," Heath adds, bending down to drop a kiss on Hadley's forehead. He takes the baby out of Hadley's arms and offers her to me. "Opal Minerva Robinson, meet your Auntie Nora."

I take her, surprised at how little she weighs in my arms. "Hi, Opal. It's a pleasure to meet you."

I sit in the chair next to the bed and gaze at her little face some more, falling completely in love with her. I blink back tears and think about how much more there is to life than a career. There's a whole universe to explore, filled with experiences just waiting for me. Maybe getting married and having a family will be on that list, maybe it won't. What I do know is I can't sit around waiting for life to happen. I have to go out and get it.

After several solid minutes of the three of us just staring at Opal, Hadley says, "I've been thinking a lot about you and Theo."

"You have?" I ask, surprised she was able to focus on anything other than being in labour.

"Between contractions," she says. "The thing about him selling you out to Harrison shouldn't be a deal breaker. Did he have to say it? No. Was he right? Yes."

Heath stares at his wife, his eyebrows furrowed. "You're going straight to girl talk? Right now?"

"This can't wait," Hadley says. "Nora's at the biggest romantic crossroads of her life. Besides, I want Opal to get a head-start on relationship problem-solving. It's a very important skill in life."

"True," I tell Heath with a smile. "Undeniably vital."

He sighs. "I kind of wanted to keep talking about how perfect my daughter is."

"We'll get back to that," she tells him, then turns to me. "Are you in love with him?"

Finally, I let the truth come out. "Yes. He can drive me nuts, but he also drives me wild."

"Good combo," Hadley says. "Something else occurred to me about an hour ago. He had the courage to tell you he had feelings for you but also the restraint not to allow anything to happen during the competition, and that reveals a lot about who he is. He could have easily taken advantage of the situation—"

"And let's face it, I *totally* would have let him," I say, then glance at Opal. "Sorry, let's pretend I didn't say that."

Hadley grins at the baby. "But he didn't, which means he's not the kind of rich guy who thinks the rules don't apply to him. I'd say that's pretty rare in someone who grew up the way he did."

"Agreed." My heart swells with pride (the good kind, not the bad one), even though he's not mine. Then I remember how I turned him down, and I'm filled with regret.

"I think you should go to him and tell him the truth, that you're probably in love with him and you want another chance to see where things will go between you."

I bite my lip and nod, my stomach doing flips at the thought of doing any of that. "What if it's too late?"

Smiling, she says, "What if it's not?"

32

Wise Younger Brothers in Swim Trunks

Theo

I SHOULD BE HAPPY. I should be relieved. The first episode of the show aired on Thursday night and already our sales are creeping up in the right direction. Our marketing and social media teams are doing a remarkable job of getting the word out about the competition and rebranding us as a young, fun company. I also managed to help Nora's family avoid disaster. That should be enough. I should be sleeping at night, but I'm not.

It's Sunday morning and I'm at home, sitting by the pool, bored out of my mind. I'm also dejected and depressed that the woman I cannot get off my mind will never love me. I keep replaying our time together, wishing I could start over and do everything right this time. But that's just a useless waste of my time. I can't go back. She and I are through.

I'm going to give myself permission to wallow in self-pity today, but tomorrow morning, I'm going back to my regular life. I'll throw myself into work until I'm fine again. Based on how I'm feeling at the moment, I'd say that'll only take six months or so.

Pathetic.

The kitchen door opens, and Markos appears in his trunks. "You look awful."

"Thanks. When did you get back?"

"Around one o'clock this morning." He jumps into the deep end of the pool. When he comes up for air, he swims to the side nearest to me and grips the edge. "So? What's wrong? You should be filled with relief right now. The competition went off without a hitch, no scandals to sully the company name, sales are up, and yet you look like a little boy who dropped his ice cream cone."

"I'm fine." I lie back and close my eyes. "Just a little tired."

"I owe you an 'I told you so,'" he says. "About how sponsoring the contest was a good idea, because nothing even remotely bad happened. I'm not going to say it because I'm above all that, but you could say it."

I'm briefly at war with myself—the temptation to tell him about what Paz did versus my need to protect Nora's family and keep Kat's secret battle it out for a couple of moments. In the end, I go with, "You were right. It was a good idea."

"Thank you." The next sound I hear is a splash as he starts his laps. He'll be at that for at least twenty minutes, which means no talking. Now *there's* a relief.

I spend the entire time allowing the self-pity to really flow, thinking about the life I started to want and how being with Nora cracked open a door to a part of myself I didn't want to meet. The guy who's a dreamer, who wants to start something of his own and watch it grow, instead of being a caretaker for the dreams of my great-great-great-grandfather. I told myself if I could only have Nora, I could handle the rest of my life, but that's not going to happen. And so, I'm doomed to spend the rest of my days unfulfilled and alone.

I hear Markos climb out of the water, his feet slapping against the pool deck, and the sound of him settling onto the chaise next to mine. "What's wrong?"

"I'm filled with envy," I tell him without opening my eyes.

"You could learn to swim like me, Theo. You just have to set aside time to practice."

I can hear the smile in his tone. "Not of you. I envy our great-great-great-grandfather Alvaro. He had a dream, and he went after it. He didn't inherit one."

I expect some sort of ass-y remark, but he says, "So? What's your dream?"

"To start something that's my own."

"Like a family with Nora Cooper?"

Hearing her name out loud is like a kick to the solar plexus. "While we're being unrealistic, why don't I start wishing for a horn to grow out of my forehead so I can stab people who irritate me?"

"All right, no need to get stabby. What is it you want to start on your own?"

"I'd like to open a small distillery. Maybe just bitters or something."

"Bitters would be good. It's an emerging market. It also has a much higher profit margin than liquor."

I glance at him, surprised he'd know that. "Yes, they do."

After a moment of silence, Markos says, "You could do that. Start your little distillery, watch it grow from the ground up. But you won't be happy without Nora."

"*Pfft…* that's crazy talk."

"I don't think it is. You're in love with her, and you're moping because you can't have her."

"That's not true. I barely know her. Even if I was in love with her, it wouldn't matter because she hates me."

"She doesn't hate you."

"Sure she does. I ratted her out about the alcohol order, which she thinks lost her the big promotion. It didn't, but—"

"That was a very bad move on your part, but that's not why she turned you down."

Opening my eyes, I turn to him. "Okay, *hermano*, since you seem to know so much about the inner-workings of Nora Cooper's mind, why did she turn me down?"

"Carolina told her you two were getting married."

I roll my eyes. "Old news. I already set her straight about that. She could never respect a man who was just handed"—I gesture to the house and the estate that surrounds it—"all of this, when she's had to work so hard for everything she's got." Letting out a sigh, I add, "And there's nothing I can do about that."

"Hmph, that is tricky."

"Not just tricky. Impossible. I'm going to forget about her and get back to my regularly scheduled program of being the CEO who works sixteen-hours-a-day until I die alone behind my desk." *Oh boy, now I really sound like a whiny brat.*

"You could do that, or you could quit and start that distillery."

"How could I possibly do that?"

Shrugging, he says, "Turn the company over to me. I've been waiting for my turn."

I scoff at the thought. "You don't know anything about running a corporation."

"I do so. I also have my master's in business."

"That doesn't make you ready to lead a company with over eight thousand employees in one-hundred-sixty countries."

"Ask me anything. I'll prove I know what to do."

"Okay." I give it some thought. "Last year, when the government announced the corporate tax hike, what would you have done to combat the extra losses?"

"First of all, that tax hike was two years ago. Second, it was relatively small, so there wasn't any need for a knee-jerk reaction. I would have gone to our service providers—internet and telecom, etcetera, and renegotiated our rates."

Huh. That's not a bad idea. "How did you know that? About it being two years ago?"

"I do read all my emails, you know."

"You've never once admitted to it."

"That's because you seemed so happy handling everything yourself. I didn't want to get in your way. To be honest, I'm getting a little bored of jet-setting around. I'd like a challenge."

"But taking over the company? There's no way you're ready for that."

"Not yet, but if I had someone to guide me—perhaps an older

brother—I could learn it quickly. Don't forget, I got much better grades than you at university."

"That's because I wasn't trying as hard as I could have."

"Me neither. Most of the time I skipped classes to play poker."

I bark out a laugh. "We may be more alike than I thought, because that's exactly what I did."

He grins. "*That's* how you got so good at it." His smile fades, and he gives me a serious look. "Listen, Theo, if your life is making you miserable, let me help you find one you can love. It would be a tragedy if you stayed on, hating every minute of it."

"I don't know," I tell him, realizing that my little dream had everything to do with Nora, and without her, I don't want it. "It's probably a terrible idea. Majority of startups fail."

"Yours won't."

"We'll never know because I'm not going to do it. It was just a fleeting thought. I'll forget all about it soon and settle back into my routine."

"That's the worst thing you can do," Markos tells me. "Life isn't about routines. It's about living, challenging yourself, getting out there and finding out who you can be."

"You should do ads for Nike."

"Laugh if you want, but deep down you know I'm right." He stands. "I have to shower. I have a date in a few. Think about what I said, Theo. The offer will remain open indefinitely, but don't wait too long to accept. Your life is waiting."

He goes back into the house, giving me a lot to think about.

33

Putting It All on the Line

Nora

WHAT IF IT'S NOT? That question haunted me for days, keeping me up at night and making my gut churn all day. What if it's not too late with Theo, but each second that ticks by, that time grows closer?

So, I'm doing something I never in a million years thought I would. I'm going to get my man. Three days ago, I emailed Theo's assistant, Jaquell, and asked for a meeting with Theo as soon as possible. She booked me in for this morning at seven a.m., telling me that was the only opening in his schedule for the next couple of weeks. Last night, I flew to Nassau and stayed in the cheapest motel I could find. I laid in bed, staring at the water stain on the ceiling all night, my heart pounding at the reality of what I'm doing. I'm about to lay it all on the line—my entire future, my heart, everything. And I have no idea what the outcome will be. It could be the start of a beautiful life we'll build together, or it could be the deepest rejection I'll ever feel. Either way, there's no turning back.

At five-thirty, I got up and took a shower, then spent over an hour doing my hair and makeup, which I've never done before. I'm not sure it's worth it. I look pretty much the same as I did twenty minutes of primping ago. My hair is down, and I've managed to put beachy waves into it, but my makeup looks the same as it always does—good but not "I just spent two hours with Bobbie Brown" good.

I'm dressed in the black silk dress, praying I don't start sweating the moment I get to Theo's office. I wanted to remind him of our first good conversation at the mixer. The first time we actually laughed together. In exactly one minute, the cab is going to pull up and I'll get in, then make the quick trip to the Rojas Rum, Inc. headquarters building, where Jaquell will greet me. And then...

Then I'll find out if it's too late or not.

The four-story building is every bit as grand as I expected. It's British colonial-style, like much of the architecture in The Bahamas. A grand entrance welcomes visitors into the ornate white building, looking less like the international head office of a multinational corporation and more like some romantic hotel from years gone by. When I open the tall wooden door, I'm greeted by an enormous foyer with murals painted on the high ceiling. Potted palm trees line the walls, highlighting the shiny marble floors. I take a moment to look around and am about to go to the reception desk to check in when I hear my name.

"Nora?"

I turn to see a smartly-dressed older woman smiling at me. "Jaquell?"

She nods. "Come this way."

I follow her up a wide staircase that leads to the second floor and a bank of elevators. She pushes the up button, and the doors open immediately. Once we're on, she presses four. "How was your flight?"

"Good."

Giving me a knowing smile, she says, "Did you get any sleep last night?"

"Not a wink."

"Love'll do that to you."

The doors open, and she steps off. I follow her, my cheeks hot as the knowledge that she knows why I'm here sinks in. When we get to the end of the hall, we go through a set of doors that leads to an empty reception area. Of course it's empty. It's not even seven in the morning. This is ridiculous. Who confesses their love for someone this early in the morning?

Jaquell leads me through another set of doors that open to an airy office with a large desk. I immediately assume this is Theo's office, until I notice yet another door behind it. When we go through that one, I know we're finally in the right place. Theo's office is huge, with tall windows overlooking the city and the sea. His desk is enormous and masculine and gives me some ideas about what two people could do at seven a.m. if they happen to be in love. My body heats up at the thought. *Down girl. You don't want to start sweating.*

"Make yourself comfortable," she says with a warm smile. "Theo should be here any minute. He knows he has a meeting, but I haven't told him who's coming. I thought the element of surprise might work in your favour."

I hope she's right. I nod, my heart pounding. When she turns to leave, I'm tempted to grab her hand and ask her not to go, but of course I don't. The door closes behind her, leaving me alone with a few final seconds to prepare for the most important conversation of my life. Oh God, what am I even going to say to him? I had everything so carefully planned out, but now that I'm here, all coherent thoughts have left my brain.

I hear his voice on the other side of the door, and my stomach flips. *This is it. My one shot. Don't fuck this up.*

Suddenly he's standing in the doorway, dressed in his dark grey suit, his gorgeous face cycling through a range of emotions. Surprise, happiness, and anguish are all visible before he settles on his usual neutral, "I'm in control" expression.

"Hi," I say, testing my voice.

"Hi."

Jaquell pushes Theo into the room and shuts the door behind him, which doesn't seem to register because he's just staring at me.

Say something, idiot. "You're probably wondering why I'm here."

"I am."

"In that case, I should tell you."

"I'd say so," he answers without even a hint of a smile.

"I forgot how intimidating you can be."

"I'm not trying to intimidate you. I'm just trying to figure out what you're doing here." He shoves his hands in the front pockets of his slacks.

I fidget with my fingers, utterly terrified. "I needed to tell you something. A lot of things, actually."

"You could have called. You have my phone number." His eyes bore into mine.

"The things I need to say are more of the in-person type than the over-the-phone type."

"Okay."

"I should probably lead with the fact that I don't hate you. There was a time when I… wasn't exactly your biggest fan, but that was *before* I got to know you. Well, and those last couple of days when you were at Paradise Bay, but that wasn't really hatred. It was more of a self-protective pride thing," I say, wanting so badly to move a few steps closer to him so I can smell his aftershave. But I stay rooted to the spot, as does he. "The point is, I'm pretty sure I might be in love with you, but I say that with the caveat that if your feelings about me have changed, that's totally okay. There's absolutely no pressure if you've changed your mind about what you suggested when we were at Eden. About seeing where this thing goes."

I pause and he nods, and I can't tell it's a "yes, I did change my mind" nod, or a "go on, I'm listening" nod. So I go on. "It would be tricky. I know that. Long distance relationships usually are, or so I understand. I've never tried one. Also, we come from completely different worlds, and I haven't exactly been gracious about yours, but since I last saw you, I came to the conclusion that people of any socio-economic background can be horrible, not just rich people. There are some pretty shitty poor people out there. Middle class too. Paz is a case in point."

"That's true," Theo answers, his face still giving nothing away.

"Another reason you may not want to date me is because you'll always know about my sister's sex tape, so maybe that's a deal breaker for you. If so, I totally get it. You may not want to be caught up with a family that could possibly cause some sort of scandal. Although I do have to tell you, Kat has turned a corner as far as bad choices goes, so I think her wild days are behind her. I hope so, anyway." Unable to hold his intense gaze any longer, I glance down at the thick oriental rug under my feet, then I force myself to look back up at him. "You may have changed your mind because I was unforgivably rude to you when you tried to tell me how you felt. That would also be understandable. It wasn't your fault that I'm not getting the promotion. It was mine. I screwed up. You didn't help matters, but the blame is on me."

Okay, your turn. Please say something. Or rush over and swoop me into your arms. Yes, do that.

But he doesn't. He just stands where he is and nods.

"The thing is, I think you were right, and that we could actually be very good together. Well, better than good really. Possibly incredible. That night at Eden was also the most fun I've had maybe ever. And I think we could work really well together at building a wonderful life. We're both hard workers who share a lot of the same values, like loyalty and umm… honesty." *I'm dying here. I should just go. Wrap it up and walk out.* "And so, in conclusion, I'm pretty sure I'm in love with you, because you're all I can seem to think about day and night. I can't eat, and I barely sleep, and I'm miserable about how I left things between us. I'm also relatively certain you're my one shot at true happiness, so I wanted to come here and tell you just in case you still have feelings for me. But having said all that, if the answer is no, I'll go and… leave you alone."

I'll be filled with sorrow every day for the rest of my life, but that might be the price I have to pay for judging people by their bank accounts and assuming the worst all the time. I stand perfectly still, not even daring to breathe as I wait for him to say something. Anything. My heart pounds wildly. My stomach flips when he opens his mouth. *Please say yes. Please say yes.*

"The answer is not no."

"So… it's…"

"It's dependent on you answering one question."

Swallowing hard, I say, "Okay. What's the question?"

"Did you come to the realization you were in love with me before or after your sister told you I'm the one who made the Paz situation go away?" His jaw tightens at the mention of Paz's name.

"What makes you think she told me?"

"Your sister doesn't strike me as the model of discretion. And the fact that you're neither denying it nor surprised by the news confirms you already knew."

"Fair enough."

"Answer the question."

Lie! Otherwise, you'll lose everything!

No, tell him the truth. You can't base your relationship on a lie.

"It was after."

"I see."

Shit. He does not look happy. He's about to reject me. "But that's only because, up to that point, I spent all my time convincing myself I hated you. I also thought you had gone home and totally forgotten about me. The truth is, I just couldn't imagine a world in which someone like you could ever love someone like me. I was looking for every reason I could find to prove it wasn't possible, even if I had to make you a villain to do it. And I'm sorry for that. It's my biggest regret in life, actually. I should have just… let myself believe that this *was* possible, that we could happen. Here, in this world." Tears fill my eyes, but I blink them back and whisper, "It could happen, couldn't it?"

"It could, but not if you're here out of some misguided sense of gratitude or obligation. Those things wear off, and I'm not looking for something that will wear off."

I shake my head. "This isn't gratitude. It's much more lusty than that."

Raising one eyebrow, Theo says, "Really?"

"Yes. Extremely lusty." My cheeks flame hot. "With a side order of deep respect for who you are as a person."

"That could be the basis of something more permanent."

"I'd say so." I dare to take a couple of steps towards him. "Especially if the way you feel about me is at all similar."

He levels me with a smolder to end all smolders. "I'd say my feelings are very much the same. Strong feelings of passion blended with the utmost respect."

"Oh, wow," I whisper. "That's good."

He finally breaks into a smile. It's the sexy smile he gets when something really amuses him. "It will be," he says, taking a few steps until he's directly in front of me. "In fact, it'll be so much better than good." He cups my cheeks with his palms and tilts my face up. Letting his lips hover over mine, he adds, "Incredible, even."

"I can do incredible." I close my eyes and silently beg him to kiss me. I inch toward him until I feel his lips brushing against mine.

"Good," he whispers, pressing his lips to mine, firmly this time.

And finally, after weeks filled with days and nights of longing, he's kissing me. His kiss is both soft and yet somehow commanding at the same time. My knees go weak, my heart spills over with joy, and my lady bits hum with delight. It's every bit as magical as I knew it would be, and all this from a simple kiss. I place my hands on his chest, parting my lips even more to invite him in. Theo accepts the invitation, and soon, our bodies are pressed together, our hands exploring each other over our business attire, and our mouths are moving in perfect unison.

We kiss until I can't tell where I end and he begins, until I'm one-hundred percent positive my future lies with this man, wherever we end up. We kiss until my lips are swollen and red, and my only thoughts are of him sweeping everything off his desk and lifting me onto it. We kiss until his phone buzzes, and Jaquell says, "I'm sorry to disturb you, Mr. Rojas, but your seven-thirty appointment is here."

Pulling back, he says, "Tell her I need another minute."

"Very good," Jaquell says.

Theo rests his forehead against mine as we catch our breath. I lift my face to his and smile. "Your seven-thirty better not be some other woman wanting to declare her love for you."

Chuckling, Theo says, "The chances of that happening are not all that high. I almost never have more than one woman a week coming in for that reason."

I laugh. "Only one per week?"

"Sometimes two, but it's rare." He kisses me again. "And don't worry because after today I'll tell the rest of them they're too late."

"They *are* too late," I say with a happy sigh. "Thank God I'm not."

"You could never have been too late." He brushes his fingertips across my cheek.

"Really?"

"Really. You're the one I've been waiting for my entire life."

I gaze into his beautiful brown eyes, feeling totally weak and completely alive at the same time. "In that case, I'm even more thrilled I got here today."

Grinning at me, he says, "So am I."

———

Mike the Moose TikTok Reel

"I won, bitches!!! Yeah, I did!!!" Mike pans out to show he's in line at a bank with several other customers (all of whom look shocked at his yelling and swearing). "I'm here at the Bank of Montreal to deposit my cheque for $500,000! Whoo!"

A loud shushing sound is heard, then he says, "Sorry. I'm just so freaking excited to be the World Bartending Champion!" He nods at an old lady dressed in a parka and some furry boots. "Me, Michael Gordon. Best bartender in the whole world."

"Congratulations, young man," she says, giving him a thumbs up.

"Thanks!" Turning back to the camera, Mike says, "And thanks to all my Moose Heads who have supported me the whole way. I've got some exciting things coming—I'll be partnering with an up-and-coming bitters company, but I can't talk about that until the papers are signed. But trust me, it's going to be amazing. Oh! It's my turn at the teller next. I'll catch you tomorrow, my Moose Heads! Cheers!"

———

TO-DO List (Home Version) – One Week Countdown Until Theo Arrives for a Visit

Book waxing appointment

Scrub entire apartment – seriously, for real this time

Laundry – sheets, towels, whites, and darks. Fold and put everything away!

Water cacti

Stock up on groceries (including post-coital recovery snacks)

Buy fool-proof fresh-cut flowers day before Theo gets here.

———

"Wow, that was just…" My voice trails off as my brain gets stuck trying to remember words. I flop down onto Theo's naked body, his skin hot to the touch.

"Agreed," he says, lazily.

"I'm so glad you came to visit."

"I bet you are."

I chuckle and lift my head so I can see his gorgeous face. "I want to ask you something."

His smile fades. "Uh-oh, that sounds serious."

"It's of vital importance," I tell him. "I need to know when you first knew you were in love with me. I mean, I know it wasn't love at first sight on account of you describing me as dowdy."

Theo lets out a growl and flips us over so he's on top of me. "Am I never going to live that down?"

"Probably not," I say, offering him a mock-apologetic look. "Now, answer the question. Enquiring minds want to know."

"I can't say for sure the exact moment when I knew I loved you, but I can say the first time I knew I wanted you more than I've ever wanted another woman. Would that do?"

"I suppose it'll have to."

"It was that night at Eden, just after you beat me at poker. You were eating M&Ms and you were just so smug and happy about it, I wanted to pull you onto my lap right there."

I grin at the memory. "Good answer."

"Thanks. And you...when did you know?" he asks, before planting light kisses down the side of my neck.

"Same night, but it was when we were standing in the kitchen after the lights went out. And you told me knowing me was going to make you a better man." My voice is breathy with desire as he gently pulls on my earlobe with his teeth. "I wasn't sure if it was a pick-up line or not, but when you didn't try anything, I decided it wasn't."

"Oh, it was. Believe me, it was," he says, lifting his face long enough to give me a serious look.

Narrowing my eyes, I say, "But you meant it, right?"

He glances up at the ceiling as though trying to decide what to say, then lets me off the hook with a big grin. "Of course I meant it. I also really wanted to get you into bed."

I burst out laughing. "Cad."

"Can you blame me? You're gorgeous."

"I suppose not," I tease. Lifting my head off the pillow, I give him a lingering kiss.

He pulls back, then says, "Wait. So, I could have gotten you into bed that night?"

"Oh yeah. Big time."

"Damn."

"Try not to be too disappointed. You've got me in bed now."

"Excellent point," Theo says. "I should probably make the most of it."

"Yes, you should."

And he spends the rest of the night doing exactly that. We're finally ready to sleep when the sun is starting to make an appearance. I'm exhausted and satisfied and filled with an optimism for my future that I've never known before. I move my head so I'm sharing his pillow and inhale the delicious scent of his skin.

He wraps his arm around me and pulls me closer to him. "I love you, Nora Cooper."

My heart is suddenly so full, it feels like it could burst. Tears fill my eyes as I say, "I love you too."

He lifts his eyelids and offers me a sleepy smile. "There's something you should know about me."

"Really?"

Nodding, he says, "When I love someone, it's forever."

"I think I can handle that."

"Good. Now, I really do need some sleep, so if you could stop being all sex kitten-y for me, I'd appreciate it."

"I'll try, but no promises."

I fall asleep with a smile on my face. My last thought before I drift off is that when Theo loves someone, it's forever. And the person he loves is me.

And They Lived Happily Ever After

Theo – One Year Later

"WELCOME, everyone, and thank you for being here with Nora and me today to celebrate the opening of our little project. As of an hour ago, Jackass Bitters, Inc. switched on our distillery equipment for the very first time, and about a year from now, we will hopefully have created the world's best cocktail bitters. If not, we'll rename the company Jackass Magic Cleaning Solution." I pause to give our small audience a chance to laugh.

Wrapping my arm around Nora's shoulders, I add, "That was my wife's idea, not mine. She's really the brains behind this operation."

"True," Nora says, grinning up at me. "I am."

We exchange a quick kiss, then get back to the business at hand. "I won't bore you with a long speech about the distillation process, which I could talk about all day, but I do want to thank a few people, starting with our staff: Jonas, Bethany, and Lovell, all consummate professionals who are going to help Nora and me take this company straight to the top. Your dedication to Jackass over the past year has been incredible, so thank you from the bottom of my heart. We're so lucky to have you on our team."

"*As* our team," Nora says, beaming at them.

"And to my brother, Markos, who took over the reins at Rojas so I could up and move to Santa Valentina to start my real life. Markos is doing an amazing job running the company, and I couldn't be more proud of him. Turns out he's a total genius, who was just waiting for his chance." I lift my champagne flute towards my brother. "Gracias, *hermano*. Your wise advice and willingness to take over for me have made my dreams come true."

He grins. "*De nada.*"

Turning to Jaquell, I say, "And to Jaquell Morales, the new COO at Rojas Rum, and the person making Markos look like a genius, just as she did for me and our father. Without your support and expertise, there is no way Markos would be able to keep his head above water, so thank you."

Jaquell winks and mouths, *You're welcome.*

Looking around the room, I spot Nora's family, including her Aunt Beth, who, by my estimate, is going to drink half our operating budget for this quarter if we don't end the party soon. Nora's mum is next to her, smiling. She and my father-in-law don't necessarily approve of our venture, but they do approve of me, which is all that really matters. "Thank you to my wonderful, welcoming in-laws, Gary and Lori, and my terrific sister-in-law, Kat, for making me part of the family and having us over for dinner several nights a week while we've been too busy to think about food. You truly are the best a son-in-law could ask for."

I hold up my glass to them, and they smile back. "It's our pleasure," Gary says. "We couldn't have picked a better husband for our Nora."

"And speaking of Nora," I say, pulling her close and dropping a kiss on her forehead. "Without you, I would still be an empty shell of a man. My life truly started the moment you finally admitted you were in love with me, even though I knew it from the second you first laid eyes on me."

Nora laughs and swats me on the chest.

"But seriously, thank you for being my best friend and partner, and for making me a better man. Every day I wake up knowing how lucky I am to have you and recommitting myself to being the man you deserve."

Some "Awwws" are heard around the room.

Tears fill Nora's eyes and she whispers, "You're already so much more than I deserve."

Leaning down I whisper in her ear, "Not true. You deserve the world." Then, glancing around the room again, I say, "Anyway, everyone please enjoy the food and the drinks and being together as we celebrate this fresh start."

Applause fills the space, and Nora and I grin at each other, then give each other a big kiss, not caring that we're surrounded by people.

"We did it," she says.

"We sure did."

The next couple of hours are filled with laughter and stories, good food and even better wine, music and friendship. I make sure to take it all in. This must have been what my great-great-great-grandfather felt like all those years ago. Exactly like this. Young, in love, and filled with the excitement only potential can bring.

Nora slides an arm around my waist and smiles up at me. "What do you think, Mr. Rojas? Are you glad you decided to forge your own path?"

I grin down at her. "Glad doesn't even begin to describe it. I'm thrilled, content, and in love. What about you? Any regrets on leaving the resort and becoming an entrepreneur?"

"Hmm...tricky. On the one hand, I *do* get to spend my days working with a highly intelligent, super sexy man..."

"Would it be presumptuous of me to assume you mean me?"

"A little, but I'll allow it," she says, lifting her face to mine and planting a kiss on my lips.

"Thank you," I say, catching her for another kiss. "But on the other hand?"

Tapping her cheek as if trying to decide, she says, "Well, if I'd stayed, I'd have job security, and the pleasure of working under Oakley Knowles."

"Right, so I'll put you down as undecided on the topic of whether this was a good career move."

Nora laughs a little and leans her head on my chest. "Exactly, but I promise I'll let you know once I've decided."

"Perfect."

In a little while I'll be at home with my wife, who got her dream seaside home, even though it's not the tiny cottage she had in mind. Instead, we bought an oceanfront villa two doors down from Pierce Davenport and Emma Banks. It's small enough to feel homey for her and big enough for me to feel comfortable. She has a veranda to sit and read on while the tides come and go, and I sit next to her and read too, or I stroll out to the water and cast a line to see if I can catch us supper.

We've promised each other and our staff that we're only going to work from nine to four, Monday to Friday, because you're supposed to work so you can live and not the other way around. We also don't allow any work-related texts or emails after hours. Nothing we're doing is so urgent we need to interrupt someone's home life.

We're starting out, not with nothing like my great-great-great-grandfather, but with the same risks as any new company. No matter how much money we pour into it, if it's not a good product, it won't sell. But I know it'll be good, deep in my bones, just like I knew Nora was the one for me. Just like I know Nora and I are going to live happily ever after.

THE BEGINNING...

YOU'RE INVITED TO CELEBRATE
THE WEDDING OF

Nora Cooper
& Theo Rojas

SATURDAY, 20th MAY
AT 5 PM

PARADISE BAY RESORT
BEACHSIDE CEREMONY SO PLEASE WEAR
FLAT SHOES

RECEPTION TO FOLLOW

PLEASE JOIN US TO CELEBRATE THE OFFICIAL
LAUNCH OF

Jackass
Bitters Inc.

HORS D'OEUVRES & COCKTAILS
Nov 14 • 7:00 PM
5 OCEANVIEW DRIVE, SAN FELIPE

Coming Soon: Beach, Please
A PARADISE BAY ROMANTIC COMEDY

COMING SOON.... the compelling, witty, and oh, so tempting description of book 6 of the fabulously fun Paradise Bay Series!

But for now, these flattering reviews...

"*Resting Beach Face* by Melanie Summers was a riveting tale of love, loss, and mega humor. The plot, storyline, character development, dialogues, and writing style were crafted to perfection. I also laughed so much, which enhanced the feel-good vibe given off by the book. My favorite character was Minerva! She was a force to be reckoned with, and I couldn't get enough. As humorous as the book was, it had depth. Melanie wrote such a beautiful story that I wanted to read more at the end of every chapter... Good job, Melanie."

  ~Jennifer Ibiam for Readers' Favorite Awards

ABSOLUTELY LOVED IT! *The Honeymooner* is a must read...I didn't want this book to end. Get it today and start laughing.

  ~Jilleen, SeasideBooknook.com

A must-read! More than 5 stars! Melanie Summers could write a menu and I'd read it... I love her stories, they are all heart and soul. All I can say is I want to move to Paradise Bay!

~*Lori Zenobia, Goodreads Reviewer*

"My favorite voice in the romantic comedy genre—clever, modern, and laugh-out-loud funny."

~*New York Times Bestselling Author Lauren Layne*

Pre-order today!

About the Author

Melanie Summers lives on Vancouver Island in Canada, with her husband, three kiddos, and two cuddly dogs. When she's not writing, she loves reading (obviously), snuggling up on the couch with her family for movie night (which would not be complete without lots of popcorn and milkshakes), and long walks on the beach near her house. Melanie also spends a lot more time thinking about doing yoga than actually doing yoga, which is why most of her photos are taken 'from above.' She also loves shutting down restaurants with her girlfriends. Well, not literally shutting them down, like calling the health inspector or something. More like just staying until they turn the lights off.

She's written over twenty novels and has won one silver and two bronze medals in the Reader's Favourite Awards.

If you'd like to find out about her upcoming releases, sign up for her newsletter on www.melaniesummersbooks.com.

Made in the USA
Las Vegas, NV
17 September 2022

55495584R00164